TALES FROM THE CLOUD WALKING COUNTRY

illustrated by

CLARE LEIGHTON

Tales
from the
Cloud Walking
Country

by

MARIE CAMPBELL

GREENWOOD PRESS, PUBLISHERS
WESTPORT, CONNECTICUT

Library of Congress Cataloging in Publication Data

Campbell, Marie, 1907-
  Tales from the cloud walking country.

  Reprint of the 1958 ed. published by Indiana
University Press, Bloomington.
  Bibliography: p.
  1. Tales, American--Kentucky. I. Title.
GR110.K4C3 1976   398.2'09769   76-14944
ISBN 0-8371-8607-2

Originally published in 1958 by Indiana University Press,
Bloomington

Reprinted with the permission of Indiana University Press

Reprinted in 1976 by Greenwood Press,
a division of Williamhouse-Regency Inc.

Library of Congress Catalog Card Number 76-14944

ISBN 0-8371-8607-2

Printed in the United States of America

To Stith Thompson

Contents

Introduction

THESE seventy-eight tales, recorded from the oral tradition of eastern Kentucky mountain areas where I have lived and worked, are all "from across the ocean waters" brought to Kentucky "by our foreparents way back in time." Most of the tales are what folklorists call *Märchen*, a German word for what the ordinary reader or storyteller calls a "fairy tale," though the great majority of such tales have no fairies. A few of the tales are Irish hero stories from the Finn and Cuchulain Cycles. This book of tales, making up somewhat less than half of the total group of *Märchen* which I collected in Kentucky, were all told me by six "right main tale-tellers" who not only had "a fine sleight at tale-telling" but who also had "a bigger store of olden tales for the telling."

My recording of Kentucky folklore began in the summer of 1926, when I was teaching at the mountain settlement school on Caney Creek in Knott County. That year I had read John C. Campbell's *The Southern Highlander and His Homeland*, and what he said of the Appalachian region and its peo-

9

ple led me to accept the position at Caney Creek for the summer. I wanted to see for myself what this region and its people were like. The school at Caney seemed indeed remote in those days. From outside it could be reached through Hindman or through Wayland by jolt wagon, on horseback, or on foot. The fourteen miles from Wayland to Caney, on a road which followed right up the creek bed most of the way, was "for sure and certain a far piece to travel."

At Caney I was fortunate enough to live with Miss Mignon Couser, a native Irish woman who was teaching at Caney. Our two-room cottage called The Crow's Nest was near the top of the mountain overlooking the school buildings on the slopes along Caney Creek. This association with Miss Couser was the beginning of my interest in folklore. She sang for me old Gaelic lullabies and other Irish songs which she had learned from her Gaelic grandmother in rural Ireland. While I cooked our meals and did our sewing, she read to me from contemporary Irish writers—Yeats, Synge, Lady Gregory, and others —who make use of Irish folklore as subject matter.

With her I went to visit Aunt Susan, an old mountain woman who lived down the creek and who sold us eggs, apples, and other foodstuffs. During my first visit, Miss Couser said that Aunt Susan reminded her of her grandmother in Ireland. Aunt Susan rejected the comparison with anybody Irish. She was Scotch and sang "The Bonnets of Bonnie Dundee" to prove it. "My pap, iffen he weren't dead, could track that song-ballet clean back across the ocean waters," she told us. Also on my first visit, Aunt Susan sang "The Silver Dagger" to give point to her statement that my family was being very careless to let a nineteen-year-old girl go "by her lone self such a far piece from home." During that summer, she sang other ballads for us and told some horrific ghost stories of Caney Creek.

At the end of the summer, when Miss Couser was returning to Ireland, I had a chance to go for the school year to a new school in Letcher County "seventeen miles—maybe twenty" across the mountains from Caney. The people in this Letcher County Community, which was then named Gander (yes, there are legends about the origin of the name) had built their own school and had sent to the school on Caney to ask about getting two teachers from outside the mountains. Teachers from "the level country" they thought would have more to offer their children than local teachers.

Miss Virginia Bryson was chosen as the "main" teacher and I was asked to be her assistant. The seventeen mile trip to Gander (now Carcassonne) meant a day-long journey on a jolt wagon loaded with books for the new school, a journey across mountains and along creeks with folk names: Troublesome, Betty's Troublesome, Defeated, and others equally picturesque.

In the Gander Community the mountain slopes were steep, the valleys scarcely wider than the creek beds. Farming was entirely a matter of subsistence. To earn "a little cash money to piece out their living" some men walked or rode the family nag to work in coal mines several miles away. The people were poor but self-reliant and independent. Even when they asked the teachers for nothing more than old magazines and newspapers to "line" their houses, they insisted on giving something in exchange, "not wanting to beg-take nothing."

Only one man in the Community, Big Nelt, had a two-horse wagon in 1926–1927. Almost every family had a family nag, most often a mule because a mule is more sure-footed and it eats less than a horse. Hitched to a homemade, wooden "ground slide" the nag did the short distance hauling, such as corn from the steep cornfields or of coal. The nag also was (and still is) used to tend the steep hillside fields, to ride to the store a few miles away "to do trading," or to ride to "meeting" on the weekends. Frequently the nag carried two or even three riders, a woman riding behind her husband, a courting couple on one nag, or two children riding with their mother.

By 1933–1934 the roads had been improved to the extent

that cars could go all the way up the mountain to the school. Yet with all the improvement of roads and transportation, there are still places in the mountain region accessible only by jolt wagon, on horseback, or on foot. During the summers of World War II, when I was making home visits with Miss Vera P'pool of the Kentucky Crippled Children Commission, some days we had to walk a few miles to homes which could not be reached by car. One day in the Mossy Bottom Creek area when we were hopeful of driving to a home at the head of the creek valley, we asked a mountain man if he thought we could make it. He said, "Maybe you could get up there in your automobile, but you shorely to God couldn't get back." On a trip to the same area in the summer of 1954, I had to ride a horse to reach an old man who had promised to tell me some tales. It was too far to walk and not even a jolt wagon could have reached his home.

When the school was opened at Gander, the people of the community were dependent on their own resources for entertainment and leisure time enjoyment. There were singings and play-parties at any time of the year. Occasionally a wedding "brought on a frolic." In the late summer and early fall, a "working" was often turned into a festival such as a bean-stringing, an apple-peeling, or a corn-shucking (*not* husking). These work occasions often ended with a singing, a play-party, or a square-dance. Then there was the regular, monthly Saturday and Sunday church meeting, no less a social occasion than a religious one. The same was true of the funeral meetings (memorial services) held in summer after crops were laid by and creeks ran low, making travel easier in a land where roads often followed the creek beds much of the way.

The improved roads made other places more accessible. "We ain't so hemmed in with these here mountains since we got better roads to travel on," was the comment of the community folk, "and we get mail six days a week now, instead of just three days like always before and more folks uses up more time a-reading in them papers and things." "And the school,"

Nelt added, "it takes up time a-reading and a-studying to learn a heap of knowledge. And with basketball and other school occasions for gatherings of the scholars and growed folks too, they ain't such a needcessity for the old time gatherings, or old time ways of pleasuring yourself at home, neither."

In 1930 one of the teachers had the first radio in the community, and by 1934 Nelt had a small radio in his own home. A few years later the University of Kentucky established the Carcassonne Community Listening Center at the school. These changes did not eliminate the old folk ways of entertainment and leisure time enjoyment, but did make them less necessary to the community and less popular, less often used. At least through 1933–1934, the last year I taught at Gander, the traditional ballads and other types of folk song remained closely woven into the lives of this community and others served by the school. Unwritten and unrecorded except in the memories of generations of mountain people, the "song-ballads" had been known everywhere through isolated mountain communities and had been a part of the daily life and social interests of the people.

"In a few years' time," said a mountain woman, at the opening of the school at Gander, "learning will be all wove into the pattern us mountain folks lives by. But the old time ways will keep on making the main figure of the pattern." Through the years of my teaching at Gander, her statement remained, in a measure, true. As Tom Fields jogged down the creek on his old mule with the mail, he sang the old songs "Mammy and Aunt Cindy sang afore me." As Jessie Whitaker went skelping over the rocks and mountain sides in evening cowhunting, she sang "It's Lamp Lighting Time in the Valley." As Lissie Adams set tables in the school dining hall, she sang of the tragedy of "Liddy Margaret." Families might gather by the fire in winter, on the porch in summer, and sing between supper and bedtime. One evening, when a mountain child was showing me the way to a neighbor's house, we passed a house where the family was singing on the porch after an early supper. After we had passed, the mountain child said to me, "All them Amburgeys are good singers, but can't nary one of them pack a tune."

The old tales were far less a part of mountain life. Each of the six narrators whose tales appear in this book said again and again, "Tale-telling is nigh about faded out in the mountain country." At play-parties or workings older people often gathered to tell tales, usually ghost tales or tales of haunted houses and other local legends. The traditional European tales that constitute this volume usually were told to me as the sole audience. The usual attitude of older people was that the folk tale or ballad "belonged to be told or sung, not put down in writing."

"But," Aunt Lizbeth Fields said, "iffen you don't trust your recollection, then I reckon you're a-bound to write things down. And I'll be more'n glad to tell or sing to oblige you and to pleasure myself." Others agreed with her that it would be well for me to get "things took down in writing to keep." So I continued to collect with at first no definite plan in mind other than the preservation of traditions that are fading from the lives of the people to whom they have for generations belonged.

Except for publication of three tales in the *Southern Literary Messenger* in the 1940's, I had done nothing with my folk tale material until I went to Indiana University in the fall of 1953. Acting on the advice of Dr. Stith Thompson, I set out to transcribe my notes in order to see what kinds of folktale material I had and how much. The transcription amounted to nearly fifteen hundred pages of folk tales which have been organized with Dr. Thompson's help and advice, for publication in five volumes. *Tales from the Cloud Walking Country*, the first of the two volumes of *Märchen*, is a collection of tales by six master tale-tellers, who "took a sight of pleasurement in tale-telling." In the second volume of *Märchen*, there are more narrators and none has more than three or four tales;

for the most part these tales, although as interesting in themselves, are not so well told as those in volume one.

Classical Greek and Latin Myths preserved in oral tradition through several illiterate generations make up another volume. These I found with only a few tale-tellers. One man said these tales that he knew came from his granny's pap who was an "educated man from Virginia and knew a fine lot of tales in a book." With Aunt Lizbeth Fields the story of Pluto's kidnapping of Persephone becomes "A Girl That Picked Flower Blooms A Far Piece from Home." With another teller of tales the story of Pyramis and Thisbe becomes "Just a Fool Mistake."

There is one volume of local legends, tales of ghosts and of haunted houses, and "all manner of scarey things." Uncle Blessing tells of "My Favoritest Ghost Spirit" that comes down through the high weeds to the side of the road and talks to him when he goes by the old Dixon graveyard. Uncle Tom and Aunt Liz Witt tell of all sorts of "queer things on Defeated" to explain why no one lives along a certain lengthy stretch of the creek.

A fifth volume is made up of stories of the Little People (Irish fairies, usually). Some are benevolent, such as the little man who helps a boy learn to play the bagpipes. Others are malevolent, and steal babies, substituting changelings, play fairy music to entice people into fairy knolls where they keep them for years, or play other mean tricks on mankind.

My recording has been done in writing and in my own style of shorthand. Tale-telling is a leisurely matter, and with a keen ear and quick hand, it was not too difficult a matter to record the narrator's comments as well as the tale. Some tales which I first heard without opportunity to write them down were later retold for recording. The tales are here presented as they were told to me, with the narrators' comments as they wove them into the telling of the tales.

The tales in this first volume, *Tales from the Cloud Walk-*

ing Country, all come from Letcher County, though not all from the Gander Community. Two of the narrators lived elsewhere in the county. All the tales told by Aunt Lizbeth Fields, Uncle Tom Dixon, and Doc Roark were given me within the period of spring 1927 to spring 1934, most of them during 1930–1931 and 1933–1934. All of Sam Caudill's tales were recorded before 1933. To those of Big Nelt and Uncle Blessing I have added more recently, especially in the summer of 1941.

Sometimes the narrator comments on the source of the tale, sometimes not. If there is no comment, that means it is a tale "I always just knowed," "it was just born in the generation," "our foreparents used to tell it around the fireplace of evenings," or some other vague indication that the source was a matter of folk inheritance.

There is more than one version of a given tale only when the narrators do not recognize variants as the same tale, and there is a certain matter of ethics in the reluctance to tell a tale that is felt to belong to some other person's repertoire. For example, Uncle Tom Dixon liked "tales where things go in threes," but some of those tales he considered as "belonging to be told" by others whose skill in telling had given them first rights. The same was true of Aunt Lizbeth Fields and her preference for "tales with all manner of things golden." She knew "The King's Golden Apple Tree," but it was Big Nelt's favorite, and it would not be ethical for her to give it to me.

The four versions given here of Type 480 were considered different tales. "The Golden Rain," "Ash Cakes and Water," and "The Shining, Beautiful Lady" certainly are sufficiently unlike that only the folklorist would recognize that all three are examples of Type 480, "The Spinning-Women by the Spring." Another and different version of Type 480 is added to Aunt Lizbeth's version of the Snow White story which she calls "The Stepchild That Was Treated Mighty Bad." The two stories flow together smoothly and make one for Aunt

Lizbeth and for any one other than the folktale specialist. Of all these versions, only "The Golden Rain" has the spinning-women by the spring which give the tale its type name.

There are also presented here four versions of Type 510B, "The Dress of Gold, of Silver, and of Stars," sufficiently different that the narrators did not think of them as the same tale.

As to organization of this volume of European folk tales, the material is arranged in six chapters, a chapter for the tales of each narrator. The chapter titles are taken from comments of the narrators. The first tale in each chapter carries the comment which provides the chapter titles, though this is not the order in which the tales were told. The titles of the tales are those given by the narrators at the time of recording.

Where mountain speech is a matter of a turn of phrase or of special vocabulary such as *mort* (a large number, a great quantity) or *sleight* (skill), I have kept that dialectal flavor. I have not attempted to indicate dialectal pronunciation. It seems to me that to use distorted spelling for that purpose loses more than it gains for the reader. Phonetic spelling would have meaning only for the student of linguistics. Therefore I have used a standard spelling in recording and in transcription.

Tale type numbers and other notes on the tales in this volume are given a section at the end of the book. Tale types are based on the Aarne-Thompson, *The Types of the Folktale*. Dr. Stith Thompson's *The Folktale* has also been useful for further clarification of some tales. The Grimm collection and the Bolte-Polívka *Anmerkungen zu den Kinder- und Hausmärchen der Brüder Grimm* have been helpful with tales that have Grimm parallels, chiefly as a finding guide in efforts to identify tales. The Warren E. Roberts' *Aarne-Thompson Type 480, A Comparative Folktale Study* was used; also Ernest W. Baughman's *A Comparative Study of the Folktales of England and North America*. The Baughman study did not cover certain tales which are American variants of Irish and

Scotch Gaelic tales. Apparently such tales have been rarely collected in America. For identification of such tales in my collection, it was necessary to turn to O'Suilleabhain's *A Handbook of Irish Folklore*, to Cross's *Motif-Index of Early Irish Literature*, and to Irish collections by Curtin, Kennedy, Jacobs, and others. The Scotch collections of Campbell, Mac-Dougall, and Macgregor were among those used to "track down" Scotch tales difficult to identify. Leonard Roberts' *South from Hell-fer-Sartin*, a recent collection of Kentucky mountain tales, was another useful reference, particularly since the tales were collected in countries of the eastern Kentucky region, similar to the areas from which my collection comes.

In a way, the book belongs not to me but to the narrators and the generations of their kin who kept the tales alive in their memories. When my *Folks Do Get Born* was coming out, I saw an old Negro woman who had given me two chapters and who had sat for one of Clare Leighton's drawings. In answer to her question, "When's our book going to be out?" I said, "The first Monday in May."

"The first Monday in May?" said Aunt Viny. "And this is just February. That's a long time for me to wait."

"How about me? I have to wait too," I reminded her.

"Oh, well," she said, "you only but *wrote* this here book."

That certainly is true of *Tales from the Cloud Walking Country*. I only but put these tales down in writing because, as Aunt Lizbeth Fields said, I didn't "trust my recollection." And, if Aunt Lizbeth could see the book, I'm sure she would say as she did about a book treasured by a great-grandparent, a book which she dimly remembered from early childhood— "a fine lot of tales in a book." Primarily it is the intent of this book to make these tales from the oral tradition of eastern Kentucky available for folklorists "to study on," and for folk-lorist and general reader as well "to take a sight of pleasure-ment in, iffen he's of a notion for a fine mort of olden tales a-telling."

ONE | TOLD BY *Aunt Lizbeth Fields*

TALES WITH ALL MANNER
OF THINGS GOLDEN

Aunt Lizbeth Fields

Aunt Lizbeth Fields

AUNT Lizbeth Fields had the richest and most varied offerings of all the people who have given me tales or other folklore. She looked as if she herself might have come straight from a fairy story or some other kind of folk tale. She was little and old—"upwards of eighty," she said in 1931. She was bent and walked with a stick, walked incredible distances for a woman her age—sometimes the whole six miles from her home to my cabin at the school. Always, even at church, she wore a big white apron, fresh and clean, crackling with starch, and reaching almost to the hem of her dark dress.

Aunt Lizbeth claimed certain privileges because she was aged. Though she condemned young girls for smoking, she herself smoked a little clay pipe, scarcely larger than a thimble. Smoking was begun as a remedy to relieve toothache, and, by the time she had no teeth, she could not think of giving up her pipe. One summer at a big funeral meeting held in the graveyard, Aunt Lizbeth slipped out of the group of relatives of the man being funeralized and joined me on the edge of the crowd. There were six preachers, each taking his turn; and, after two hours of their preaching, Aunt Lizbeth needed to smoke. "I know it ain't noways proper for me to leave from amongst Sam's kin when the preachers are still bragging him up to heaven. But I had to smoke me a pipeful. I ain't sure I'd be plumb happy up in heaven without my pipe. It gives me a sight of pleasurement here on earth."

On another occasion I slowly starved while Aunt Lizbeth sat in front of me in church eating apples and cookies during a four hour session of preaching, communion, and foot washing. "I'm old," she said to me afterward, "and folks knows I got a weak stomach and hadn't ought to go hungry." Everybody loved Aunt Lizbeth and never seemed to grudge the privileges she claimed for herself.

My first glimpse of Aunt Lizbeth was on the first day of school at Gander. She was riding a horse borrowed from a neighbor and carrying with her on the horse two small children of another neighbor, one on the saddle in front of her, the other clinging on behind. She introduced herself to me. "Howdy," she said, "I reckon you're the Little Teacher I heard about. I'm Aunt Lizbeth Fields, and I'm proud to make your acquaintance. Now would you reach this baby down offen the nag for me and let it run to its mammy? No, I don't need no help. I can still get offen a nag by myself. The little boy can, too. You're come a far piece, ain't you, now, to teach school in these here mountains?"

Aunt Lizbeth alighted from her sidesaddle and tied her horse to a small tree at the edge of the school yard. She took from her saddlebags a fresh, starched, white apron, shook out the folds, and tied it on. "Now I reckon I'm ready for the gathering," she said, and moved on into the first-day-of-school crowd.

Only a few weeks after that first meeting, Aunt Lizbeth gave me the first of her many offerings in folklore, a version of "Barbary Allen." She heard a girl at the school singing it about her work. "Tain't the way I always heard it," Aunt

Lizbeth said, and proceeded to sing it her way. Later she sang it again for me to write down, though she had never before heard tell of such a thing. "A song-ballet belongs to be sung and listened to and remembered and sung again. But if you don't trust your recollection, I'd be more'n glad to accommodate you so you can put it down in writing."

Through the years that I knew her, she gave other traditional ballads, some of them Child ballads. She also sang a few old folk lyrics such as "The Moon Walks High." "I just love the evening time; that's why I'm singing about the moon," she explained. From her I have what she called "Play-party tunes and fritter-minded song-ballets." One sentimental song of the 1890's, "After the Ball," she said she learned from a "traveler passing through this mountain country." Folk hymns she sang, and also what she termed "funeral ballets," meaning hymns customarily sung only on funeral occasions. She sang for me those "funeral ballets" which she had selected for her own funeral meeting.

What she called "The Marrying Ballet" was not a ballad at all but a survival of song drama. It is similar to an Elizabethan jig with the title "A country new Jigge between Simon and Susan, to be sung in Merry pastime by Bachelors and Mayden," the text of which is given in Baskervill's *The Elizabethan Jig and Related Song Drama*. Aunt Lizbeth knew nothing of Elizabethan jigs. She sang "The Marrying Ballad" for the purpose of expressing the old saying that a woman who "died a maid was doomed to lead apes in hell."

Aunt Lizbeth had a "heap of knowledge" of the medicinal qualities of roots, barks, herbs, and other folk remedies. She had practiced midwifery for years and was full of lore concerning pregnancy, childbirth, and child care. She knew many folk superstitions, beliefs, and practices for almost every phase of living. Several months after I had first met Aunt Lizbeth, and from some one else, I learned that she knew "a sight how many olden tales."

One spring morning, as I walked across the Mountain with

Nancy Jane Jones, she picked a red flower, kissed it, and stuck it in her hair. Then she explained why, as she gave me a flower and told me to do as she had done with hers.

"It's a flower of dew," she said, "and I learned about it from an olden tale Aunt Lizbeth Fields told when she tended my mammy at a birthing. Mammy told it to me, though she didn't recollect any of the details and particulars that made it a long tale and a sight how pretty. Aunt Lizbeth don't never tell black-guard tales at a birthing like some granny-women. She always tells pretty tales, and Aunt Lizbeth knows a sight how many olden tales. This here tale she called 'The Flower of Dew,' and it's about a flower bloom that broke a witch's spell. A flower of dew is any kind of a wild red flower bloom with a drop of dew in the middle early of a morning. It ain't easy to find nor plentiful like it sounds. Folks that knows that tale always kiss a flower of dew when they find one in the woods or fields and put it in their hair to keep off witch's spells. I'll send Aunt Lizbeth word you'd love to hear her tell that pretty tale about a flower bloom that was magic."

"The Flower of Dew" comes first in the group of Aunt Lizbeth's tales and was the first she told me, though her preference was for the "tales with all manner of things golden," which she told later. "You don't need to coax me to tell olden tales," Aunt Lizbeth said when she found out I was an eager audience. "Nobody much wants to hear me tell tales any more, which I dearly love to do," she added. "And I am likely to forget the tales I always knowed iffen I don't have no practice a-telling."

Though I met Aunt Lizbeth here and there around her section of the mountains, she told me all her tales while visiting me at the school. Nothing delighted both of us more than for Aunt Lizbeth to be rocking in my chair, telling some olden tale in her own leisurely fashion, commenting on the tale when it suited her to do so.

She found many occasions to visit at the school—errands of her own or for her neighbors, school occasions to which people in the community came, or as she sometimes said, "Just purely to have me a visit and tell olden tales to you in private, and pleasure ourselves and not be plagued with my kinfolks thinking I hadn't ought to go here nor go there nor do this nor do that." Twice when I was at the school alone because the other teachers and the students were away on vacation, Aunt Lizbeth slipped in on foot, once to spend a week, the other time three days.

One of these times, Christmas 1930, she spent one whole evening telling only tales "with all manner of things golden." I had given her a gift that she had said she had always wanted— "a pair of gold beads." The last time I saw Aunt Lizbeth she told me she always wore the gold beads inside her dress, "not to seem prideful with wearing golden jewels."

"And now," she said, "I been rummaging around in my mind, and I've got some more olden tales for you to listen to. It ain't modest for me to say so, but I do take pride in all the olden tales you got set down in writing from my telling. It's a prideful thing to say, but you won't never meet up with nobody that loves tale-telling better than me nor that's got a bigger store of olden tales for the telling."

THE FLOWER OF DEW

LIKE Nancy Jane Jones told you, a flower of dew is any kind of red flower with a drop of dew in the middle early of a morning. It ain't easy to find nor plentiful, like it sounds. "The Flower of Dew" is my favoritest olden tale, after the tales about all manner of things golden—them I love the best of all the olden tales. Now and again, whenever I come to see you, I'll tell some of the olden tales with all manner of things golden for you to hear. Nancy Jane said, though, you were hankering to hear me tell "The Flower of Dew," after she showed you a flower of dew in the woods one day last week.

So's I'll go according to your rathers and tell first the olden tale you're hankering to hear me tell. An old woman that could speak in foreign tongues told it to my granny.

Maybe a thousand years ago, an old witch lived in a high castle in a big woods. When young girls came near her castle, she changed them into birds and put them in cages. She had a million cages, all different kinds of birds, and all used to be pretty young girls.

A pair of young lovers used to walk in the edge of the witch's big woods. The girl's name was Melinda, and she was a sight how pretty. I never did hear what her lover was named. They were promised to marry, and it was untelling how much they loved each other.

They had been cautioned to walk along the edge of the woods, for fear of the old witch that had her high castle deep in the woods. But the old witch had made her woods the prettiest in the whole country, with laurel blooms and lacy ferns and dogwood trees and sourwood and all kinds of pretties. It was so pretty it enticed the lovers to walk on and on till they got lost in the witch's deep woods.

They got so deep in the woods they could hear a million birds a-singing. Then they told each other they had come too far. But it was too late to turn back. That very minute the old witch turned the pretty girl into a bird. Her lover just stood there with no power to move. The old witch came and caught the bird and put it in a cage. She let the girl's lover go, for she took her spite out on just pretty, young girls.

Melinda's lover went away, grieving over what happened to her. He walked a thousand miles, trying to find some way to get her back or somebody that could help. Then one night in a far country he had a dream. He dreamed about a red flower with a pearl in the middle. He dreamed he picked the red flower with the pearl in the middle and used it to make things free from witches' spells.

He woke up thinking about it, and he figured the pearl could be a drop of dew in a real flower in the woods. Maybe his dream was the help he had been looking for to turn Melinda back to a girl. Anyhow, he aimed to try. He set out to find a red flower with a drop of dew in the middle, early of a morning. It weren't no way plentiful nor easy to find.

He searched nine years before he found a flower of dew. Then he walked the long miles to the witch's castle—not all the way to the castle, just to the bird cage with Melinda in it. He held the flower of dew up to her cage, and the bird that was Melinda kissed it with her bill and changed back to a pretty girl. They ran away through the woods, and all the other birds kept still, so the old witch wouldn't wake up.

Melinda and her lover hunted nine more years for enough blooms of flower of dew to change all the other girls in the old witch's cages back to young girls. Melinda had sharp eyes to find scarce flower blooms in the woods. When they had a-plenty blooms of flower of dew, they went back to the old witch's woods and changed all the birds in the cages back to young girls. The witch got in such a frenzy she died, and that left her woods safe for lovers to walk in.

Folks that knows that tale, when they find a flower of dew, kisses it and puts it in their hair, playing like they might get changed to a bird.

THE SPINDLE, THE SHUTTLE, AND THE NEEDLE—ALL GOLDEN

Do you recollect when I promised to tell you some olden tales with all manner of things golden? Well, while I rest here in your rocking chair, I aim to tell you a tale of that nature, that I loved to hear Granny tell.

A girl's granny took her to raise when all her other folks died. Her granny was good to her and raised her to have nice manners and be modest and not brash and bold. From her granny she learned how to spin and weave better than any woman in the whole country.

The girl was about sixteen years old—you might say a woman grown—when her granny was about to die. Her granny brought out from some hiding place three keepsakes a fairy gave her one time when she was young: a spindle, a shuttle, and a needle—all golden. Granny never had used the golden things; she used just her common everyday spindle, shuttle, and needle, and saved the golden ones for keepsakes. She had always thought they might be magic, but she never had tried them out to see for sure. Now she gave them to the girl and told her to use them and earn her living with pretty goods she could spin and weave. Then Granny laid back and died.

After her granny died, the girl lived by herself and wove such pretty goods that she made a nice living. She was modest and shy and never did show her golden things she worked with, not wanting to seem proud. She never had no lovers yet, but she never worried none about that. I reckon she figured lovers would come when they would come.

One day a king's son was out a-traveling, a-looking for a bride. He said his wife had to be the poorest and the richest. It sounded like a riddle, but what it meant was plain to his mind. He was sure and certain he would know the right girl to suit his wishes when he found her.

He came riding past this girl's house and saw through the window and the door that was open to the springtime air that she was spinning thread. She blushed and looked away from the window till he rode off. She was just that modest and shy not to stare at a stranger with bold looks. As he rode off, she looked out of the window till he was plumb out of sight. Then she said to her golden spindle some words she had learned from her granny:

"Spindle, haste away,
  Bring my lover here today."

Her words worked magic, and the golden spindle left her hands, spinning a golden thread as it went. The golden spindle caught up with the king's son, and he followed the golden thread back to the girl's house. He could see that she was weaving cloth now. She blushed and looked away from the window till he rode off again.

Then she said to her golden shuttle some more words she learned from her granny:

"Shuttle, weave for me today,
  Show my lover along his way."

These words worked magic too. The golden shuttle jumped out of her hands; and, without no loom to weave on, it started weaving a golden carpet with silver flower blooms on it. The golden shuttle wove the golden carpet all the way till it caught up with the king's son. He followed the golden carpet back to the girl's house and looked in at her door and window. He could see her stitching some kind of goods. She blushed and looked away from the window till he rode off again.

Then she said to her golden needle some words she learned from her granny:

"Needle that stitches all so fine,
  Get my house ready for lover mine."

These words worked magic like the other words, and the golden needle started to work stitching new curtains for the window, new coverlets to spread on the beds, new tablecloths, and other housekeeping things—all golden. The girl put on her floor the golden carpet that her golden shuttle wove. The golden carpet had rolled itself up behind the king's son till it got back to the girl's door. When the girl had her house all fixed fine enough for a queen, she sat down to work again and wait for her lover.

That time the king's son didn't need golden things to lead him back to the girl's house. He just got to thinking about her, and his thoughts led him right back to her door. He looked in and saw her sitting in her house all fixed fine with golden curtains and golden coverlets and all things golden. It looked to him fine enough for a queen. But the girl was wearing her old clothes and working away to earn her living. She suited pine-blank what he was looking for, "the poorest and the richest." He loved her with all his heart and mind, and he asked her would she be his bride and live in the king's castle with him.

She said she would, and so they had a big wedding, and she went to live in the king's castle with him. She took with her the golden spindle, shuttle, and needle her granny gave her, not just for keepsakes, though. She used them to spin and weave and sew, not to earn her living any more, but just for the pleasurement in working with things all golden.

THE QUEEN WITH GOLDEN HAIR

SOME folks makes foolish promises and then think they've got to keep their promises, no matter what. They was a king like that one time. He had a queen with hair all golden, but she took down sick and died. The king loved her so good he made promise not to marry again excepting to a woman with hair all golden, thinking he never would find another woman like that.

He musta not paid much attention to his onliest child, for she was a woman grown before he ever noticed that her hair was all golden like his dead queen's hair. He knowed it was a wicked shame to marry his own born daughter, but he said he had to keep his promise. So he told the girl he aimed to marry her.

She was scared and shamed and put her mind to thinking up ways to get out of doing any such a wicked thing. She said she wouldn't marry him lessen he could get her a cloak made out of the fur of all the animal creatures in the whole wide world, thinking he never could do it. But he got her the cloak made out of all kinds of fur in the whole wide world— musta looked a heap like a crazy quilt pattern all patched together, only it was fur and not goods wove on a loom.

After he got the cloak for her, the king kept pressing her to marry him. No way out of it, fur as she could see, but to run off from home. She put on the fur cloak and hid her golden spinning wheel under it—musta been a play toy, not a working sized golden spinning wheel—and she ran off and lost herself deep in the big woods.

Some hunters found her and hired her out to work. They put her to work in the cook room of a king's castle and made her do all the nasty work and pure drudgery. One day she slipped and watched the king at a big feast, and she wished she could be there, for she was raised to be at a king's feast, not to be washing up nasty pots in the cook room.

One day after that, she was cracking some nuts, and one had inside instead of a kernel a silver dress thin as skim ice and all over set with little golden stars. She tried it on and it was a true fit.

The next time the king had a feast, she washed herself good and put on her silver dress with the little golden stars, and she went to the feast. The king thought she was the prettiest thing, far and away, that he ever laid eyes on. He wanted to talk to her, but she ran off back to the cook room and put on her old raggedy clothes.

The king took down sick and the girl with the golden hair made him some soup and put one of her golden hairs in it. The king got mad when he found a hair in his soup, and he sent for the cook to come and see him about such a nasty trick.

But the girl with the golden hair never went till she made him some more soup. She put her little play toy golden spinning wheel into that soup. And she put on her fur cloak that covered her up all over, and she took the soup to the king. He liked the soup, and he wanted to talk to her, but she ran off.

She washed herself and put on her silver dress with the little golden stars. Then she went to see the king. He knowed she was the strange lady that came to his feast, and he loved her and married her for his queen.

THE GOLDEN RAIN

In all the years I was a granny midwife I never tended but one woman that birthed twin babies, and them as like as two peas. It was different with the twins in an olden tale I aim to tell you while I wait for Dicie to get her business tended to.

The twin girls in the olden tale weren't no ways like each other. One of them was ugly as homemade sin and lazy and idlesome. Tother was pretty as a picture and helpsome and work brittle. Their mammy favored the ugly, idlesome girl and made a pet of her. The pretty, helpsome girl they made do all the work around the place. She had to spin and weave and pack water from the spring. They never let her rest or have a minute's peace.

One day they got so mad at her that they drove her off out of the house and made her sit by the spring and spin yarn. Maybe she liked better to be out away from the house where she couldn't hear them quarrel at her. She spun so fast she stuck her finger with the spindle and made the blood come. She stooped down to wash off the blood with spring water, and she fell into the spring.

She fell down and down through the water and on down past the water. When she came to herself and looked about, she was in a fine meadow, all over green and pretty with flower blooms and with birds a-singing. Falling straight down for such a far piece had made her feel scatter-wit. She sat there till she gathered up her wits, and then she got up and set out walking across the meadow.

First she came to a little house with some bread baking in the oven. The bread said to her, "Please take me out of this here hot oven or I'll burn up. Hurry, for I'm already a-scorching." She took the bread out of the hot oven and set it to cool. The bread said to her, "Thank you, mam, and put a piece of good fresh bread in your pocket to eat on while you are a-traveling."

Next she came to some walnut trees, all bending down clear to the ground with a heavy load of nuts. The walnut trees said to her, "Please to shake our limbs and make some of the nuts fall off so we won't break down with such a heavy load." She shook off nuts till the walnut trees' limbs raised up some. The walnut trees said, "Thank you, mam, and take some nuts for your journey."

Last she came to a little house where a little old woman was a-working. "Please," the old woman said, "come in the house and cook me some supper; I'm all tired and wore out and I can't cook me a bite to eat."

She fixed the old woman and herself a good supper. She washed up the dishes and cook pots and shook up the old woman's feather bed so she would rest easy. Weeks and months passed by and she went on living at the old woman's house, doing all the house work and spinning, and weaving goods to make the old woman some new wearing clothes. She hoed out the garden and tater patch and sang song ballads while she was a-working.

After a time she got homesick and wanted to go back for a visit. Seems like she was lonesome for her kin, no matter how bad they had treated her. The old woman asked her how much wages were owing, and the girl said, "You don't owe me nary penny."

To show her thanks the old woman made a shower of gold around the girl. The golden rain fell on her till she was all over covered with gold. She went back home like that, and they mirated over how she was all over covered with gold. She let them pick off her gold and hide it away to spend for things, and she told them where she had been and what took pl•ce.

The ugly, idlesome girl wanted to have a shower of gold fall on her. So she set a spinning wheel by the spring and stayed there a while. She never got no blood on her finger, for she never spun no yarn. She just stood up (after a time) and jumped into the spring.

It happened the same way with her, only she wouldn't help the things that begged her to. She walked right on and let the bread burn black as a cinder, and she let the walnut trees break down with such a heavy load of nuts. At the old woman's house she said she wouldn't do a lick of work lessen she got high wages. The old woman agreed to that. The girl turned out lazy and hateful and just sat around and collected her wages. After she stayed long as she figured she had to for the gold to rain down on her, she left the old woman's house to go back home. No shower of gold for her, though. It rained down sticky, black tar all over her, and she never could wash it off. Though she scrubbed and scoured till she wore the skin off of herself, she never could clean herself up; and she had to live that way, all black and sticky, to the end of her days.

THREE SHIRTS AND A GOLDEN FINGER RING

THIS here tale starts off with a queen a-dying, though this here queen had three sons and a daughter, not just an onliest child like most of the queens that died in olden tales. Before she died she gave her golden finger ring to her daughter for a keepsake.

After a time the king married again, and he was afraid his new queen would be mean to the first queen's orphans. So he raised them a house yon side of the big woods, where they could see everything but couldn't nobody see them. Whenever he went hunting, he would pay them a visit.

He had an ugly daughter by his new queen, but everybody despised her, for she was so hateful. An old witch told the new queen about the king's other children and plotted how to kill them. She told the queen to pretend she was a-dying and nothing would cure her but to see the king's children by his other queen. The king took pity on her and sent for them to come. Soon as she laid eyes on them, she got up out of the bed and said she was cured—though she had been well the whole enduring time.

With the old witch a-telling her what to do, she sent the king's children to get a fine comb. Musta been a dog they went to, for it said to them, "Sons of the father and mother I loved, and many a time I licked their dishes. Come under the bench with me." The king's sons got down to pet the dog under the bench, and they turned into hound-dogs. What seemed like a dog was an old witch. The girl never turned into a hound-dog, for she had on the queen's golden finger ring. She tore the old witch's arm off, and then she went to hunt her brothers that had run off like fox hounds into the big woods.

She walked a long time till she came to a little house and met up with an old woman in a green kirtle. No, I don't know what a kirtle might be, some kind of wearing clothes, I reckon. The old woman let the girl stay all night at her house and in the morning she gave her a shoe that would keep her on the right road. Looks like she woulda give her two shoes, but that's not the way the tale goes.

She found where her brothers in the shape of hound-dogs lived. She fixed a good supper for them and dropped the queen's golden finger ring into a cup of wine. That way her brothers knowed who she was. They told her she could lift the spell on them if she would spin and weave and sew them a shirt apiece, not saying one single word till the whole job of work was done.

Pretty soon after that, a king married her, long about the time she had spun as much thread as she needed to weave cloth to make three shirts. After she married the king she set to work weaving and not speaking one single word. She birthed the king a pretty boy baby, but a hand snatched it away while the granny midwife was asleep.

The granny midwife was scared of her life, and she smeared blood on the queen's mouth while she was still asleep and told the king that the queen ate up her boy baby. The queen never dared tell how it was. The king loved her so good he forgave her. But when it happened three times, he said the queen would be hung the next day.

Still not saying a single word, the queen sat up all night stitching on the last shirt that would lift the spell on her brothers. Just before it was time for the hanging, she made the last stitch and spread the three shirts out smooth on her bed. That minute her three brothers came in their own shape, and they had her three little boy babies with them, all safe and well. The three brothers tried on their new shirts, and the king stopped the hanging of his queen and hung the mean stepmother queen and the old witch that had one arm gone. Then everybody could live happy.

THE GOLDEN CHILDREN

You know how folks makes fun of them that are different from them—making fun of their betters a heap of times, but causing hurt feelings, anyhow. That's how it happened in this here tale.

A fisherman one time caught a talking fish. It scared him mighty bad at first, but then the talking fish started to bargain with him to put it back in the water and not tell nobody. He put the talking fish back in the water and promised not to tell.

Then he went along home, thinking how would he manage for supper and not no fish for his wife to cook. But when he got to where his little old house had been, he saw a big fine house and everything in it brand new and shining. A wide table was spread with a white tablecloth and chicken and cake and all kinds of fine victuals in silver dishes. It was a big surprise to his wife, and she begged him to tell her how come all this fine house plunder and good things to eat. He wouldn't tell and he wouldn't tell.

But all night long and every night his wife never gave him no peace till he couldn't stand it no longer, and he told her about the talking fish. While they still lay there in the bed, all the fine new house and everything new and fine melted away. And it was their little old house again and the old house plunder and nary a thing to cook for breakfast.

He got up after daybreak and went fishing, though he didn't favor fish for breakfast. Same as the other time, he caught that same talking fish and made the same kind of bargain. It took a longer spell of talking for his wife to wear him down with his secret this time, but she made him tell in the end. Same as before, everything melted away, and he had to go back to fishing.

The last time he caught the talking fish it just gave up and let him take it home with him. His wife cooked it for supper, not thinking it was different from any other fish she had put in her skillet through the years she'd been keeping house. The man wouldn't eat none; seemed like he would be same as eating a person, and it made him puke to think about eating the least bit of the talking fish. His wife ate it all up, unbeknownst that it was a magic fish that could talk.

Seemed like it done her nary bit of harm, but she had two golden boys, and her man blamed it on the talking fish, though he never did name it to her. And he was right proud of his golden boys and would a heap rather to believe he occasioned their birthing his ownself.

But the golden boys naturally looked different from other folks, and people made fun of them till they couldn't stand it no more. One golden boy hid away in the loft at home and wouldn't show himself at all, no matter how much he was coaxed.

Tother one ran away from home into the big woods to hide. He lay down in the big woods and covered himself over with leaves till not a speck of gold showed any place at all. While he was a-laying there with his golden self hid from sight of anybody that might chance to be in the woods, a pretty girl chanced to be walking through the woods.

She saw the golden boy all covered up with leaves and got

scared mighty bad, for it looked to her like a wild bear. Then the golden boy had to crawl out of the leaves and show her that he weren't no wild bear. She was so pretty and good that he wanted to marry her. And so she married him and she let on like she never saw that he was all golden. He loved her more than ever for having such fine manners and not shaming him for being different from other folks.

That night they were a-laying there talking pillow talk, and the girl told him she had a secret to tell him. In the bed she was all golden, and so they had found their true mates and they lived happy together.

He got lonesome, after a time, wishing he could see his golden brother. He went hunting to wear off his lonesome, and he found his brother hiding amongst some golden lilies. He took him home to his own golden wife that never made fun of golden people, and his golden twin brother lived with him after that. And he dug up the golden lilies and planted them in the garden.

THE GOLDEN PRINCESS

Now Susie's been telling you how she got a pair of beads from a pack peddler one time—blue and silver beads—and spent all her fifty cents she had saved up to buy store calico for a Sunday dress. I used to know a tale with a pack peddler in it—not true facts like Susie just told you, but just a tale for idle telling. I'll see if I can recollect the olden tale with the pack peddler.

Well, a king lay a-dying and he wanted to talk to old Faithful John. When old Faithful John knelt down by the side of the king's bed, the king said he wanted old Faithful John to make him a solemn promise. When he was dead he wanted old Faithful John to promise to show the king's son all the land and the castle and other things he fell heir to and to make a binding promise not to let the king's son see into one certain room.

In that room a picture of a golden princess hung on the wall, and it was dangerous for the boy to see. Old Faithful John promised what the king wanted him to and the king turned over and the breath left him.

Old Faithful John waited till after the burying, and then he took the king's son—a young man grown, as best I can make out—and showed him all the lands he fell heir to. Then he showed the king's son the fifty rooms in the castle, all but one. He just passed by that door and went on to show the boy money and other things he fell heir to. But the king's son wouldn't be fooled. He made old Faithful John open up that door. Soon as he looked at the picture of the golden princess hanging on the wall, he fainted dead away.

Old Faithful John brought him to, and he said he purely had to see the girl in the picture. He had to travel to the far-off country where he could find her at. Old Faithful John tried to talk him out of going but he wouldn't listen. Then old Faithful John told him to take the golden princess some presents so he would find favor with her.

So the king's son got a ship and loaded it up with golden cook pots, and golden birds and golden jewels and all manner of things golden. And old Faithful John went along with him, a-sailing across the ocean waters—him and the king's son dressed up like pack peddlers.

Old Faithful John went on land in the golden princess's country with a peddler's pack full of golden things. He saw a girl drawing up water from a well in a golden bucket. She took him to the golden princess, and she wanted to buy the whole peddler's pack full of golden things.

But he said, no, she would have to go on the ship and see what a heap of things all golden. Them in the peddler's pack were just for a sample. She went with old Faithful John on the ship, and it took her a mighty long time to look at all the golden things. While she was looking, the king's son sailed the ship back towards his own country.

When she found out she was out on the ocean waters, she made a big fuss and tried to make them sail back to her country. They wouldn't. The king's son told her who he was and he wanted to marry her. She said it would be a big risk for the king's son.

Well, they got back to his country and their bad luck set in. Right along in this part of the tale I don't remember so good how things went. But, anyhow, the king's son nearly got killed somehow and old Faithful John saved his life. Old Faithful John was put under a spell not to talk or he would be turned into solid rock. The golden princess nearly got killed on her wedding day, and old Faithful John saved her, though it looked like he had tried to kill her. Some time after that old Faithful John was about to be hung, though what for has slipped my mind—something he never done, though. On the gallows he made a speech to tell how he never done it, and the spell was still on him, and he turned to solid rock.

The king's son and the golden princess took the rock that was old Faithful John to their castle and kept it. And after some years it came alive again, though I can't recollect how it come about.

THE GOLDEN COMB

I'M much obliged for you bringing my poke of meal into the house when it set in to rain. By rights I oughta taken my turn of corn to the grist mill closer to where I live at, but I wanted some excuse to come by the school and talk to you. So I just rode my old nag with my turn of corn in this direction, going to the mill down the creek first and then up here on the mountain. And now I'm a-setting here in your house. Would it pleasure you to hear a tale about a miller way back in olden times acrost the ocean waters?

Well, they was a miller that had bad luck and things got worser and worser. Then one day, long about sunup, he was a-walking across his mill dam; and he saw a pretty woman there on the edge of the mill pond and her not wearing no clothes, but covered over with her long, thick head of hair—maybe golden hair, I don't know.

Granny told me this here tale; and, when I asked her how could any woman cover up her shame with her head of long hair, Granny said, "Don't be so bodaciously modest! This ain't nothing but a tale for idle telling. And besides, I heard tell of a natural woman one time that had hair that hung down below her waist. Now just you be satisfied to hear me tell however the tale goes."

I never raised no more objections, and Granny went on to tell how this here woman dressed up in her hair called the miller by name and promised him good luck if he would promise her whatever came out of the next birthing at his house. He thought it would be pups from his bitch dog. His wife was up in years for birthing and never had no babies in all their married life. So he promised and went on to his mill to grind a turn of corn.

And after that his luck turned, and he started to prosper. But, strange to say, in spite of her years, his wife birthed a fine boy baby. When the miller never seemed to be one mite happy over the boy baby, his wife wanted to know what ailed him. And he had to tell her what he promised the nixie by the mill pond—I forgot to say back there at the start of the tale that the woman bare naked and hid with her long hair was a nixie—

The miller and his wife had a heap of worry raising their boy. They watched him close and wouldn't let him go anyways near the water. Somebody trained him to be a hunter. And one day, when he was in the woods a-hunting, he met up with a pretty girl and he fell in love with her.

He raised a little house on the edge of the woods, and he married the pretty girl he met in the woods. One day he killed a fine deer. He skinned it and dressed the meat. A-doing so he got his hands all bloody, and he stooped down by the mill pond to wash his hands. The nixie in the mill pond had been watching for her chance, and she pulled him down under the water with her.

The miller's boy's wife went to hunt for him when he never came home at sundown. She found the deer meat and the deer hide, and she found his hunting gear by the side of the mill pond, but she couldn't find him. The miller and his wife musta been dead and gone by that time, for the tale don't say no more about them.

The girl was wore out with hunting for her man and spent with grieving for him. She went to sleep and woke up in the morning way over across a meadow, a-talking to an old woman. The old woman told her to sit by the mill pond of an evening time and comb her hair with a golden comb. The old woman gave her a golden comb. She done like the old woman said, and in the full moon she saw her man's head rise up out of the water and then sink down.

The next time the old woman gave her a golden harp to sit by the mill pond and play music on. When the moon came up, she saw her man rise out of the water to his waist and then sink down.

After that the old woman told her to sit by the mill pond and spin on a golden spinning wheel, and the old woman gave her a golden spinning wheel. The girl done like she was told; and, when it was full moon again, all of her man rose up out of the water and stood there. And while she sat there a-looking at him, the mill pond turned into a big tide and flooded the whole country. Granny said the way the tale was told to her it said all the people turned into frogs after the flood. But Granny didn't favor that end to the tale, so she always stopped telling when the flood waters spread over the country.

A SILVER TREE WITH GOLDEN APPLES

No telling what stirs my recollection of a tale about a family of folks that had queer ideas on how many eyes it was proper for a human person to have. Seems like it keeps a-running through my mind, and I aim to tell it to you while I'm rocking in your chair and resting my old bones.

They was a man with one big eye in the middle of his forehead; and he married a woman with three eyes, two eyes where a body's eyes belong to be and an extra eye where his onliest one eye was. They had one girl with three eyes like her, and one girl with one eye like him, and another girl with two eyes like human people belong to have. All the family called the girls One Eye, Two Eyes, and Three Eyes instead of giving them pretty names for girls.

The whole family of folks hated little Two Eyes because she was different from them. They treated her mean and made her sleep on a pallet with the dog, and fed her scraps from their table like they would treat a dog. One day they drove her off from home. She walked and she walked till she got so tired and hungry she couldn't go no further.

An old woman came along and gave her a little tablecloth big enough for one person to eat off of. She told little Two Eyes, "Whenever you get hungry, just say, 'Little tablecloth, spread yourself out.'"

Little Two Eyes tried it out, and a fine feast was on the little tablecloth in no time at all. Everything she liked best to eat: chicken livers, and biscuits with butter and sorghum molasses, and sugar cookies. I don't know what all. She had much as she wanted, though she offered the old woman some first. When they were done eating, the old woman said, "Little tablecloth, fold yourself up." It folded itself up no bigger than a woman's pocket handkerchief.

Little Two Eyes took her magic little tablecloth and went back home. She didn't eat the scraps they gave her, but let the dog have them. She nevermore would eat the scraps, and they spied on her to see how she kept from starving.

Little One Eye watched first, but she went to sleep and never found out nothing. The next night little Three Eyes watched. She let two of her eyes go to sleep, but she stayed wide awake with her one big eye in the middle of her forehead. She saw little Two Eyes' magic tablecloth spread itself out with fine things to eat that made little Three Eyes' mouth water. She ran back home and told on little Two Eyes.

They took little Two Eyes' Magic tablecloth away from her; but, before they could try it out, the pet goat swallowed it. They killed the pet goat and cut it open to get the magic tablecloth. No sign of a tablecloth of any description in the goat's insides. They cooked the goat for dinner and wouldn't let little Two Eyes have a bite.

Little Two Eyes took the goat's stomach and guts and other insides—they had cooked the liver and lights—and buried them. That night a silver tree with golden apples grew out of the ground where little Two Eyes had buried the goat's entrails. One Eye and Three Eyes tried to pick some golden apples, but they couldn't. Then little Two Eyes picked a whole basket full. They snatched some out of her basket, but the golden apples melted away to nothing in their hands.

Then a king's son came riding along and they made little Two Eyes go and hide in a darksome place under the stairs. The king's son asked would they give him a limb from off the silver tree with golden apples. They tried to break a limb, and they couldn't do it.

About that time, little Two Eyes rolled two apples out of her hiding place. The king's son picked up the golden apples and put them in his pocket, and he asked did they have another sister. They lied and said they never had, but the king's son hunted her up in the darksome place under the stairs. And she broke a limb from off the silver tree with golden apples and handed it to him. Then he took her up behind him on his horse and rode off and left One Eye and Three Eyes looking after. He married little Two Eyes and he planted her silver tree by her castle window where she could reach out and pick the golden apples.

THE GOLDEN BRACELET

SEEMS like the queens in olden times were mighty weak and puny, for mostly they would have an onliest child and then up and die and leave an orphan behind. Mostly they made their king promise he wouldn't marry and bring a stepmother over their onliest child.

Maybe the queen that I aim to tell about now knowed it ain't according to a man's nature to live single; anyhow, she never made the king promise not to marry. She musta been warned she would die. Anyhow, she lived a long enough time to make a present for her daughter that would be a protection to her. The queen wove a bracelet out of gold thread and her own golden hair. Musta been a sight how pretty. I knowed a woman that had a breast pin wove of her man's hair, though it weren't golden but just a common brown color. Right pretty, though, it was.

The queen had the strength left to put the bracelet on her child's arm and told her not never to take it off and nothing nor nobody could do her any bad harm. Then she died.

The king married again—though I reckon he waited a decent time. His new queen already had an ugly daughter that was mean-natured and spiteful. The king's daughter was pretty and sweet as laurel blooms in the spring and gentle and kind-natured like the first queen had been.

Behind the king's back, the stepmother took all the best things for her daughter. She wouldn't let the king's daughter go to play-parties or any kind of frolic in the neighborhood. But the king's daughter weren't no sneaping tattletale. She took pride in her golden bracelet and loved it so good that she never hankered after other fine things. She stayed off to herself and

sewed with silk thread, making flower blooms and other pretties on the goods she sewed. Instead of play-parties and frolics
that she weren't let go to nohow, she walked about in the fields
and woods with her little dog.

Seems like the little dog had been the first queen's pet,
maybe. The tale don't tell, but I just figured it musta been.
Anyhow the first queen's daughter had it by her side all the
time and talked to it like it was a human person.

One day she was sitting out under the front yard trees sewing on a piece of white goods, when a strange man rode past
and asked what was she making and who was it for.

Just for a joke, she said, "I'm making a fine pocket handkerchief for the King of Spain."

He said—and it weren't no joke—"I am the King of Spain,
and you can give it to me, if you please."

She said it would take a week's time to finish it up—musta
been mighty fine, with a lot of pictures stitched into the goods,
to take a week to make a handkerchief—

Well, he waited a week, and then he said he wanted to
marry her. She said she'd have to study about it a while. The
stepsister done some studying too. He was the King of Spain
and handsome and rich besides. So she wanted to marry him,
though he hadn't asked her to.

The King of Spain sent back for his girl that stitched him
a fine present, and the stepsister went back to Spain with her,
saying she went along because it weren't proper for a pretty
young girl to go a-traveling without another woman went
along.

Somehow or other the stepmother had found out she
couldn't do the girl no harm on account of the golden bracelet.
So she told her daughter to make a chance to steal the golden
bracelet. The person that told me about it couldn't name the
manner of doing it, but the stepsister got hold of the golden
bracelet before they got to the King of Spain's castle.

The stepsister put the golden bracelet on her arm and made
the first queen's daughter promise not to tell no human person.

Then the stepsister changed to look pretty, and the other girl got ugly to look at. Their dispositions stayed the same, though. The golden bracelet never worked no magic on the stepsister's black, ugly insides.

When they got to Spain, the King never knowed what to think of the way his lover had changed; even her voice was ugly, he thought, not knowing the stepsister had turned herself into his false bride. He didn't love her no more; but he married her anyhow, for he felt obliged to keep his promise. Everybody in his castle hated her like poison, she was so hateful and mean.

They loved the ugly looking girl that was the true bride. The old king loved her like she was his own born daughter. But the false queen of the young king still had the golden bracelet on her arm, and she had the power to make the true bride go back home and be out of her way.

The true bride had let her little dog follow her to Spain, and it was a heap of comfort to her to talk to it every night and tell how she lost the golden bracelet that was her protection from harm. She held to her promise not to tell it to no human person. But the old king's serving woman heard, and she told the old king.

The old king made the stepsister give back the bracelet, and he told the young King of Spain how they had been fooled. The true bride was the prettiest she had ever been in her whole life, as soon as her golden bracelet was on her arm again. And it's untelling how the King of Spain loved her. Mighty quick he got rid of the wicked girl that fooled him and married his true bride.

THE GIRL WITH THE GOLDEN FINGER

A wood chopper had a pretty little girl, but he was too poor to feed her. One day he went out in the deep woods way off from home, thinking maybe he would just leave his little girl there to starve. But he couldn't find it in his heart to do such a thing.

All of a sudden he saw a shining lady standing there in front of him in the deep woods. She told him she was the Virgin Mary, and she wanted his little girl. He gave her and gladly to the Virgin Mary and watched like a dream while the Virgin Mary flew up to heaven with her. Then he went on back home, I reckon. The tale don't make no more mention of him after that.

Up in heaven the Virgin Mary gave the wood chopper's little girl all kinds of pretty and good things to make her happy, golden clothes to wear and sugar cookies to eat every day. And she had little angels to play with.

When the wood chopper's girl was fourteen years old and of an age to know right from wrong and do according, the Virgin Mary had to go on a journey down to the earth. She told the wood chopper's girl goodbye and gave her the keys to the thirteen doors of heaven. The Virgin Mary said she could open all the doors of heaven but the last one and to not even put the key in the lock of that door.

The wood chopper's girl opened one door every day till she had opened twelve doors. Then she kept fooling with the lock on the last door. The little angels begged her not to open that door; they said it would be a sin. She opened the door anyhow and looked into the room. There was the Holy Trinity sitting in golden splendor on a shining throne, and it nearly put out the wood chopper's girl's eyes to even take one look at such a shining holy thing. She shut up the door quick and snatched the key out of the lock and made like she hadn't been anyways near that last door. But her little finger on her right hand had turned gold, and the gold wouldn't wash off.

The Virgin Mary came back up to heaven from her journey down to the earth and asked the wood chopper's girl to give back her keys to the thirteen doors of heaven. She gave them to the Virgin Mary with her left hand and kept the right hand with the golden finger in her jacket. The Virgin Mary asked her how many doors she opened and she said, "Twelve." And she wouldn't say anything different, though she knowed she told a lie—and up in heaven, too, where it went against the rules to tell a lie.

The Virgin Mary coaxed her to own up and tell the truth, but she wouldn't do it. Then the Virgin Mary took away all her golden wearing clothes and sent her out of heaven and back down to the earth in a big woods, but not the woods where the wood chopper went. She had to live in a hollow tree and eat just whatever she could lay her hand to. Her long hair was the onliest clothes she had to cover her nakedness, and she was shamed and hid in her hollow tree.

But one day a king's son found her, and he took her home with him to the castle. She had been by herself in a hollow tree till she was shy like a woods creature. And she couldn't talk; that was a punishment from the Virgin Mary, who had told her that as soon as she owned up to the mean thing she done in heaven, she could talk again. And she still had the golden finger. The king's son mirated over the golden finger, and he wanted to marry her, and the king was willing.

When the wood chopper's girl had birthed a boy baby for the king's son, the Virgin Mary came and stood by her bed and asked her would she own up now that she opened the last door of heaven. She shook her head, no, and the Virgin Mary flew back up to heaven with the boy baby.

Three times it happened the same way till the Virgin Mary had three boy babies of the wood chopper's girl up in heaven. The girl couldn't talk to tell the king and the king's son how things happened. So they thought she had killed her babies, and they made a law to burn her. Then she sent for the Virgin Mary and told her the God's truth and said she was sorry for her sins up in heaven. And the Virgin Mary flew up to heaven and brought back all three of the boy babies and let her have them to keep and raise for the king's son.

But her little finger on her right hand stayed golden all the days of her life to make her not tell lies any more. Times when

I hear somebody tell a big lie, I look to see if their little finger on their right hand has turned golden. It might happen that way some day, just for a token of warning to tell the truth all times, up in heaven or down on the earth.

GOLDEN APPLE

THIS here tale is different from my other tales about golden things, for Golden Apple ain't nothing but a name. I'll tell it to you, though, for it's been a-laying on my mind today, and me a-wondering how it turned out in the end.

They was a king had an onliest child, a boy. And the queen she took sick, and she knowed she was too plumb bad off to get well. So she called the king to come to the side of her bed, and she told him she had to die and leave him and their boy. And she wanted him to promise her not to marry till their boy was a man grown. Seems like women a-laying on their death bed always has mean stepmothers on their minds and are fearful for their orphans left behind. And, times like that, a man always promises not to marry, though mostly they don't hold to their promise no long time.

This here king was different. He went on living in his castle with just his boy. And he didn't marry and he didn't marry. And folks made a big fuss about it and said he oughta marry and bring a woman there to keep house in his castle and fix things so he could have company to come and eat dinner and live sociable.

The king got mad with folks butting into his business like that. He got so mad he said he would marry the first woman he laid eyes on. Then he thought about his promise, and he took his boy way off to some other country to live till he was a man grown. I hadn't said so yet, had I? but the king's son was named Golden Apple, though he was just a human boy.

Coming back from taking Golden Apple to another country

to live, the king met up with an ugly old hag of a woman. She said bold as you please that she wanted to marry him. He said he wouldn't, and she told him she heard him say he would marry the first woman he laid eyes on. He argued and swore and vowed he wouldn't do no such a thing. But she wore down his arguments till, after a few days time, he married her and shut her up in a dark room upstairs in his castle.

One day when he was passing by underneath the room where she was shut up, he looked up at the window. She leaned out of the window to talk to him, and she had turned into a mighty pretty woman. He went back into the castle and opened the door of her old dark room and brought her out to be his wife and keep house in his castle.

She turned pretty on the outside, but she was still a wicked old hag of a woman on her inside. First thing, she started plotting harm to do to Golden Apple. But first she had to coax the king to let him come back from the other country. She acted loving and gentle, though she was poison mean in her heart. And she fooled the king till he sent for Golden Apple to come home.

She played checkers with Golden Apple and she beat him. She took that for an excuse to put a spell on him to bring her the head of an eight-legged dog. But Golden Apple had learned some charms too, so he put under a spell to stand on the top of the castle till he got back from hunting the eight-legged dog.

And that's as far as I can tell. I never did hear about Golden Apple but one time. It was when I was a girl and went a-visiting in another settlement. After I went back home, I never thought about Golden Apple for a time. Then, whenever I did think back and try to tell this here tale, I couldn't go no further than the pretty hag of a stepmother standing on top of the castle till Golden Apple got back with what she sent him after. The rest is clean gone from all remembrance.

Ever since that time I tell stories over to myself so's I won't forget how they turn out in the end. And I reckon it's a heap like reading in books is for you, maybe, a-going back over the pages.

STOCKINGS OF BUTTERMILK

THE place where I heard this here tale was at a wedding frolic, and I never did hear it any other time. A man told it at the wedding frolic to poke fun, saying folks that went to weddings by rights ought to have the presents, not the bride. He never had no sleight at tale-telling, and he left out the details and particulars, skipping over most things that took place so he could get to the foolishness at the end.

The man at the wedding said that one time a king had a notion to go a-walking, just for the pleasurement in it. Then he changed his notion and got in a boat to sail on the ocean waters. He aimed to drift along close to the banks and not get out where it was deep waters. But a magic wind came up and pushed his boat a far piece out on the ocean waters.

He thought to himself, "Now I come this far, might as well go further." And he sailed on to visit the King of Ireland. They got to be good friends, and they fixed it up for the King of Ireland's son to marry tother king's daughter named Flower Bloom of Youth. She weren't old enough to marry yet, so the King of Ireland's son had to wait.

The man telling the tale said the King of Ireland's son had a heap of things happen to him while he was waiting to marry, but he skipped over the telling. When Flower Bloom of Youth was old enough to marry, the King of Ireland's son started across the ocean waters to the castle where she lived. When he got there, an old man with a white beard had stole Flower Bloom of Youth, and he would have to get her back if he aimed to marry her.

An old woman showed him old White Beard's castle. He had to fight a thousand champions to get Flower Bloom of

Youth away from old White Beard. They rode a man back to her castle. They had a big wedding feast with a thousand people sitting down to the table at one time, besides the ones that had to wait. And all the folks that went to the wedding got fine presents: shoes of paper and stockings of buttermilk.

I had a heap rather heard about Flower Bloom of Youth and her wedding clothes and her presents and things than to leave them out and just end up with a piece of foolishness. This here tale don't belong to be treated like a joke, and the tale-teller was just a fritter-minded person.

A STEPCHILD THAT WAS TREATED
MIGHTY BAD

Hearing some women talking about a man over at Vest marrying again and pondering with them on how his new woman will treat her stepchild, his pretty, little girl, put me in mind of an olden tale about a stepchild that was treated mighty bad. Set down and rest yourself a little minute while I tell.

They was a man and a woman, not nobody you ever heard tell of, but way back in time. Everybody has done forgot their names. A king and a queen they are said to have been, anyhow that's what I always heard tell. They had an onliest child, a girl it was, and pretty as a picture; good too, I reckon. Named her Snow White and Rose Red on account of her skin was white as snow in wintertime and her cheeks were red like blooms on the rosebushes in the summertime.

The way some folks tell the tale, the mother died when she birthed little Snow White. Some tells that she had a fever. I don't know; anyhow, she died and left her man and the baby. On her deathbed she made her man promise not to marry again and bring no stepmother to be mean to Snow White. He made promise, and I don't misdoubt he aimed at the time to do like he promised. But he had to hire somebody to do the

needful things for his child that it takes a woman to do anyways right.

Well, the nurse-woman was a clever person, not bad-look-
ing, neither. She made little Snow White like her and acted real
motherly and nice. The man took notice how good she tended
Snow White. Then he started to notice she weren't bad-
looking. First thing you know, he was a-courting her—just
what she had in her mind from the first minute she hired herself out to take care of Snow White for him. Pretty soon he
named marrying, the promise he made to his dead wife gone
clean out of his mind. The nurse-woman jumped at the chance,
and so they got married and she moved her house plunder to
his house and rented out her place for cash money.

When Snow White got to be of an age to be noticed for
being pretty in a way to make womenfolks jealous of her, her
stepmother turned poison mean. She wanted to be the best-
looking woman in the neighborhood, and she treated pretty
girls like poison, more especially her stepchild that was far
and away the prettiest girl that ever lived in the neighborhood.

The stepmother had a looking glass hung up on her wall
and she loved to look at herself in it and think how pretty.
It made her so mad to see how her stepchild was better favored
in looks than she was her ownself that she couldn't hardly
stand it. She would stand there and sass her looking glass for
not making her look pretty all the time. Some tells how the
looking glass sassed her back and always told her Snow White
was far and away the prettiest. I don't never tell it that-a-way,
for I ain't got no faith in a looking glass that talks.

This mean-hearted woman thought up ways to get rid of
Snow White. She said one day to a strange man going by with
a gun and a hound-dog like he was a going to hunt in the
wood, "I'll give you six bits, maybe a dollar, if you will toll
this girl off in the woods a far piece and leave her there to
perish. I purely can't stand the sight of her any longer." He
wouldn't promise till she gave him ten dollars and six bits, all

the cash money she had. Then he tolled the girl off, telling her he could show her fine places to pick flower blooms in the woods.

Once he got her way back in the deep woods, a far piece from home, he slipped off and left her picking wild flower blooms. But his hound-dog stayed with her, close by to be a protection. So the man had ten dollars and six bits in his pockets for doing a mean-hearted thing; but he lost a good hunting dog, though I don't know how much it woulda been worth.

Come night, the hound-dog led her to a little house he had found, and it had beds and things in it. The dog went off somewhere, and Snow White flew busy and cooked up a good supper. She waited for somebody to come and eat up what she cooked; but, when they never came, she had much as she wanted for supper and put the rest of the supper in the cupboard in the cook room.

Seven rocking chairs she found in the house, and she rocked much as she wanted to till she felt rested. Then she found seven beds, all made up smooth and nice but one. It was all rumpled up, and she smoothed out the covers and fixed it nice. Then she laid down and went to sleep.

Seven little men came home from the day's work chopping trees in the woods. Rummaging in the cupboard, they found what Snow White cooked; and they washed their hands and had a good supper. They rocked a while to rest from the hard day's work, and then they got sleepy. They went upstairs to the room with their beds all in a row, and they found Snow White. They tipped around, being quiet, and didn't wake her up at all. One of the little men slept on a pallet bed on the floor so Snow White could sleep on his good soft bed.

Come morning, they made their manners to Snow White, and they asked her to be a sister to them and keep their house tidy and cook and sew, and they would make her a good living, and they would dearly love to have her for their sister. The hound-dog came back and stayed with her in the daytime to be a protection while the little men chopped in the woods. Of nights the dog would go off somewheres.

After a time the mean-hearted stepmother found out that Snow White was still living and getting prettier every day of her life. So the stepmother fixed herself up so Snow White wouldn't know her and went to the little house in the woods where Snow White lived with the little men. And the hound-dog barked and raised his bristles, but she looked like an old woman peddling things around the country. And Snow White made the hound-dog hush up and lay down.

The stepmother had a golden comb that she gave to Snow White. When she put it in Snow White's hair, she fell down like dead, for the comb had poison in it. Then the old woman went off.

The dog went and fetched the little men to come see about Snow White. They pulled the poison comb out of her hair and she got right up and cooked supper. They told her not to let no strangers come in the house when they went off to their job of work.

Another time the mean-hearted stepmother found out Snow White had come alive. She had to think up a new way to get shut of her. She put some poison on a finger ring and sent it to Snow White. I don't know how, maybe by a neighbor passing through. Anyhow, the finger ring made Snow White fall down like dead. The hound-dog went and fetched the little men from their job of work, and they pulled off the finger ring, and Snow White got up and cooked supper.

The last time it was some fine apples the mean-hearted stepmother sent to Snow White. The finest red apple had poison in it, and Snow White had scarce swallowed ary bite till she fell down like dead with a piece of apple in her mouth. That time the hound went and fetched the little men, but they didn't see nothing to pull off of her to make her come to. So they had to give her up for dead. They laid her out in a coffin with glass so they could look at her. They fixed flower blossoms fresh around the coffin every day after they put it in a church up on a mountain. The hound-dog stayed by it to guard it from harm.

One day a fine man, maybe a king, came along and looked through the glass coffin at Snow White. The hound-dog liked the man and let him look. The man loved Snow White and wanted to have her with him. When the little men came home from work, he talked and coaxed till they let him carry Snow White in her glass coffin home with him to his big fine house. Going down the mountain, he dropped the coffin, though he didn't aim to. Being dropped jarred the piece of apple out of Snow White's mouth and she came alive again. They went back to the little house and told the little men about it, and they let Snow White marry him and go to live in his big fine house.

At his house she didn't have to cook and keep house, so she took the hound-dog for protection and went a-walking about the place. Some old apple trees were all bowed down and about to break. They begged her to shake their limbs and make some of the apples fall off so they wouldn't break. And she was glad to do it. Then some cows asked her would she milk out their bags so they wouldn't get all sore. And she was glad to do it. Then she came to an old woman with a heavy basket. And she was more than glad to carry the old woman's basket, not even waiting to get asked. I reckon the old woman went home with her and stayed all night. Anyhow, in the morning the old woman said to her, "You can keep that old basket to pay back for your trouble."

When the old woman had gone off, Snow White opened up the lid of the basket and it was full of all kinds of fine clothes made of gold and jewels besides a heap of other pretties more than just clothes to wear.

Snow White dressed up fine and her man thought she was mighty pretty. Then they went to visit her daddy, and they took the old woman's basket full of things, for the more Snow White took fine things out, the more the basket got full of things again. And she filled her daddy's pockets up full of gold money and made him a present of some more golden things. And she even made a present to her mean-hearted step-mother.

And the mean-hearted stepmother tried to steal the basket away from Snow White. But when she took hold of it, the basket got so heavy she couldn't lift it or even budge it one bit, and she couldn't take nothing out of it neither.

So after Snow White went back home, with her man a-carrying her fine basket, the mean-hearted stepmother took it in her head to do just like Snow White and get her a fine basket of golden money and things to wear and jewels and other pretties.

She walked through the woods to the house where the seven little men lived. They were off at work, but she never turned her hand to do a thing about the place. She just sat down and rocked all day till she broke down all the rocking chairs and left the pieces piled up in a heap. Then she laid down to sleep and rumpled up all the beds. The little men ran her off and wouldn't put up with her at all.

She walked around in the woods hunting a place to stay all night, and I don't know if she found any place or how she made out. I reckon I just forgot that part.

Anyhow, come morning, she met up with the apple trees that had too many apples again, for what Snow White left on the trees had got bigger and heavier. The orchard trees asked the mean-hearted stepmother would she shake their limbs and make some of the apples fall off so they wouldn't break and she said she never aimed to do no hard work, and she walked on.

The cows asked her would she milk out their bags so they wouldn't get all sore. But she wouldn't do that neither.

She kept on walking and looking for the old woman with the basket full of fine things. After a time, she found the old woman setting down to rest. The mean-hearted old stepmother never even said, "Howdy." She just grabbed up the basket and ran off fast as she could. Whenever she got home, she opened up the basket quick as she could and made a grab. She nearly fell down dead in a fright when she saw what she grabbed—handful of snakes and toad-frogs. She flung them away in the weeds and tried to empty out the basket. But it stayed full to the brim with toad-frogs and snakes, full of poison and mean as could be.

When her man saw what she fetched home that he couldn't get rid of, he left her and went to live with Snow White and her man in his big fine house.

The mean-hearted stepmother got killed to be rid of her meanness but I don't know how she got killed. And it don't make me no difference.

THE LITTLE OLD RUSTY COOK STOVE IN THE WOODS

An old woman my granny knowed told me about the first cook stove she ever saw back here in the mountain country. She said she was used to eating things cooked on a fireplace hearth, and stove victuals riled her stomach—and I've heard other folks say that too. Then this here old woman told me a tale about a little old rusty cook stove in the woods; and, cook stoves being a new thing to me when I was a girl, it pleasured me a heap to hear such a tale.

A king's daughter wandered off in the woods like she had been told not to, and she got lost. She was scared mighty bad, and she hollered loud as she could. Then she heard somebody else holler. Whoever it was kept on hollering, and she tried to find out where the hollering came from. After a time she stumbled over a little old rusty cook stove in the woods. Seemed like the hollering came from inside the little old rusty cook stove.

While she listened to hear again, a low voice came from inside the little old rusty cook stove and it was a king's son witched into being shut up inside the little old rusty cook stove. It said it would help her find her way back to the castle where she lived if she would get him out of the fix he was in and then marry him. She said she would.

He said for her to bring some kind of tool and poke a hole in the stove and let him out. She said she would. Then he found somebody to show her the way back to her castle—how he could I don't know and him shut up in that little old rusty cook stove. Anyhow, she got back to her castle, and she told the king what happened in the woods and how she had to go back and poke a hole in the little old rusty cook stove and let the king's son come out, and that she had promised to marry him.

The king said his daughter wouldn't do any such a thing; it was too big a risk. So he sent the miller's daughter to the woods to do what the king's daughter had promised. The miller's daughter poked and poked at the little old rusty cook stove in the woods but she couldn't even scrape off any of the rust. The king's son inside the little old rusty cook stove made her say things that gave away who she was, and he sent her back home.

Then the king sent a fisherman's daughter. Same thing. Then the king could see that he would have to let his daughter keep her promise. She went back to the woods and poked at the little old rusty cook stove. In a few minutes time she had made a peep hole. She peeped in and she saw a good-looking young man. She went back to work poking harder and pretty soon made a hole big enough for him to crawl out of.

He let her go back to her castle to tell the king goodbye, providing she wouldn't say no more than three words. She got to talking and said a heap more than three words. When she went back to the woods, the little old rusty cook stove and the good-looking king's son weren't there no more. She looked and looked till it got dark in the woods. She was scared witless, and she climbed up a high tree to be safe.

Up in the tree, she could see a light a far piece off through the woods. She climbed down out of the tree and ran fast as

she could to where the light was. It was a little old house full
of toad-frogs having a play-party.

She knocked on the door and the biggest toad-frog of all
opened it. He listened to her tell, and then he stopped the
play-party and asked the other toad-frogs what to do to help
her out. They thought about the matter, and they agreed the
best way to help her out would be to give her two needles
and a plow wheel and three nuts—what kind of nuts it don't
tell. She thanked them kindly, and they gave her instructions
how to travel and what direction to take. They said she would
have to use the needles to help her climb a glass mountain. I
never did hear tell if they told her what she would use the
plow wheel and the three nuts for. Anyhow, she got across
the glass mountain and came to the castle where the stove
man lived.

She hired herself out to be a cook. After supper she cracked
one of the nuts in her pocket, aiming to pick out the kernel
and eat it. The nut kernel was a pretty blue dress all soft and
silky. The girl that was the bride of the stove man wanted the
dress, and the king's daughter said she could have it if she
would let her sleep that night in the room with the stove man.
The bride promised, but she put magic herbs in some wine,
and he slept so sound it was no satisfaction for the king's
daughter to be there in the room with him.

The next night another fine dress, white as milk and soft
as fur, came out of another nut kernel. The bride made the
same trade for that dress, but she made the stove man drink
wine with magic herbs again, and he never did know who
stayed in the room with him all night.

Another night a golden dress came out of the nut kernel.
The bride wanted it the worst of all. She made the same bargain, but that night the stove man wouldn't drink no wine.
He said it made his head ache and gave him a misery in his
stomach the next morning after. That night he didn't sleep
sound, and he heard the king's daughter taling to herself about
how she helped him out of the little old rusty cook stove in

the woods. He got wide awake and he loved her to her satisfaction, and he got rid of the girl that had fooled him. He married the king's daughter. And I always wondered what they done with that little old rusty cook stove. When I was a little girl, I used to wish I could have it to play with in my playhouse in the edge of the woods by a big old hollow tree.

TWO | TOLD BY *Big Nelt*

A FINE MORT OF OLDEN TALES

Big Nolt

Big Nelt

"He's the ballad-singingest man in the mountain country, and the tale-tellingest, too, I reckon." This was the first I ever heard of Big Nelt.

On the initial trip by jolt wagon from Caney Creek to Gander, Tandy Gent, the driver, told us something about various people in the community where we would be teaching. Tandy went on to say of Big Nelt, "He got that name from being so big and stout-like, and can't nobody beat him a-working and a-heaving. He's got more land and more cash money than ary other man in the neighborhood. Folks 'low that he's mighty queer-turned and droll-natured, but a right accommodating man and a plumb sight to humor his woman."

In answer to my question as to how I would know Big Nelt, Tandy answered, "Iffen you meet up with him, you can know Big Nelt on account of him being so big and high and not wearing no shoes but in chilling weather. Growed men don't foller going barefooted in this here settlement—just women and younguns. But Big Nelt he don't wear no shoes but when

65

it comes on cold, for he 'lows the old time ways give him a heap of comfort. So he don't wear no shoes of a summer time. It ain't needing cash money makes him do it, for he has got nine hundred acres of land in these here mountains and cash money buried about his homeplace. You can get back on the wagon now (we had been walking up a mountain to "spell" the horses) and we'll mosey on down to Hendrix Caudill's where you air to take the night."

At Hendrix Caudill's the bed-ridden old grandmother entertained us with talking about people in the community. When we asked her about Big Nelt, she told us, "He air from over on The Mountain, sorter rough-natured but better than most. And a plumb sight he air to humor his woman. He air kinder queer-turned but plenty work brittle, and can't nobody beat him a-picking the banjo and a-singing song-ballets or a-telling old time tales, neither. Hit's been give out that he goes a-gin the law a-stilling, but a heap of folks does that; and, anyways, hit ain't never been proved on him nohow."

Nelt sounded like the most interesting person in the community, and we hoped to see him among the crowd on the first day of school. But we did not see him. His wife told us later that he had already seen us by climbing a tree by the road and watching as Tandy drove the jolt wagon up The Mountain. He was also present on the school grounds the day school opened. The following account of his whereabouts on that day came from his family and was woven into one of the chapters in my book *Cloud Walking:*

Nelt kept his binding word to Sary when she went to tend a sick neighbor that he would fetch their boys to school diked out in their meeting clothes, and he gave counsel to them to use their best manners they learned from their Mammy. All scunnered with fright, they followed Nelt up the narrow trace through the mist of the early morning. As they came along through the woods Squire brushed the spider cradles off as they caught on his clothes and dodged the mist drops that fell from the bushes as they passed through. Nelt and the other boys weren't so proud. It never crossed their minds to keep tidy in the woods. They traipsed along and no words till they come close where they could see the school house and the folks gathered about. Then Nelt spoke up and gave out to the boys what to do.

"I ain't natured for things like this. I ain't bold like some folks and I ain't fixed for a gathering. I fail of knowing how to act and do so's not to shame my ownself and my younguns. It would be more helpsome for you to go along with your ownselves. And, iffen you don't walk right up and take learning, I aim to tear off your leg and beat you with it."

They made promise they would go right straight. Nelt watched till they got with the crowd and then he took a path slaunchways around the mountain where he could hide in the laurels and watch.

All day till school was out Nelt stayed down in the laurels. While folks were in the school and he couldn't tell what curious things were going on, he went off down the mountain side and picked blackberries. He figured to eat some, that being the only victuals he could lay hand to. A hatful he aimed to carry to the teacher women to show he favored learning. After school let out, he studied he ought to go up and speak to the teacher women and offer his free gift. He felt shamed he had no better vessel than his old hat to carry the blackberries in, and he stood still not a far piece from the teacher women's house and figured how he would make his manners.

It chanced while he stood there studying, Nelt took notice of the Little Teacher sitting on the stile to the school house fence. She looked like it were a lonesome time to her.

The old fire ball was going down behind the mountain and before long it would be getting dusky dark. Things sounded lonesome too. From down in the hollers the cowbells made a sad-like tune when the cows moved their heads slow licking their new calves. Boys and girls were cow-hunting for cow-critters that didn't have new calves to come home to at milking time. As the younguns climbed up and down the mountain sides, they took up sing song ballads about death and doom.

Nelt could hear these lonesome tunes quavering up from the mountain sides around him. He figured the Little Teacher could too, for she looked to Nelt like she were nigh about to lonesome to death for her kin and neighbors back in the level country.

Whenever somebody started up singing "Lamp Lighting Time in the Valley," she looked like she purely couldn't stand it, so Nelt got brash to step up and speak to a lady from the level country. "Now I wouldn't go for to lonesome to death, Little Un," Nelt said then to Little Teacher.

"You're Big Nelt," she named to him.

"I shore air," Nelt answered her back. And then the other teacher woman come out of their house and she would be for Nelt to set on their gallery and talk a spell. But Nelt hated to shame the ladies talking to them when he looked such a sorry sight. He just gave the hatful of blackberries to them, made his manners, and went off down the mountain.

As for being the "ballad-singingest man in the mountain country," Big Nelt not only knew more ballads and other folk songs but he also knew more kinds than anybody else. At first he was so shy that, when asked to sing, he would go into another room to pick his guitar or banjo and sing while I listened and copied the song. After a while Nelt overcame that shyness, and then it was never hard to get him to sing ballads, to tell tales from Grandpap's time, or to share his opinions on whatever subject. As he said, "I learned to spend my opinions before the teacher women and not be shamed."

Of my collection of several hundred ballads and folk songs, Nelt contributed more than any other singer and a greater variety. Not only was he "the ballad-singingest man" but it was literally true that he was also "the tale-tellingest *man*," though he could not rival Aunt Lizbeth Fields for either number of tales or variety. Unlike her, he had no special type of tale that was his favorite, though one individual tale that had been often told him by his mother was his all-time favorite. He took a shy sort of pride in knowing "a fine mort of olden tales."

Most of Nelt's tales he traced back to his mother, his granny or his grandpap. It appears that his grandparents' tales often reached him through his mother's telling. He said his granny and grandpap or "granny's granny" could "track them olden tales from across the ocean waters clear back to the old country." He was not sure what the "old country" was. He thought it might be Ireland or Scotland; he couldn't tell "which from tother."

The other main source of his tales was an Irishman who stayed with Nelt's family several weeks when Nelt was a boy. He did not know, or at least did not remember, the Irishman's name. "We just called him 'The Irishman' amongst ourselves or to other people. To his face we called him 'Irish.'" The Irishman was "not to say old, not to say young. Where he came from it's untelling and where he went to it's the same. He was a clever man and a sight of company to me, a lad of a boy."

What Nelt remembers best of the Irishman are the tales he told, even the occasion for telling some of them, such as telling about "The King of Spain's Magic Cow" to tease Nelt about bragging too much about his heifer. (Perhaps the rarest of the Irishman's contributions are tales from the Finn Cycle of Irish hero tales.) Nelt had no idea where the man got his tales, but he was certain that the Irishman could not read.

Nelt himself learned to sign his name but he could not read for enjoyment. He said he sometimes told tales to himself "for company, not saying the words but going over the tale in my mind from the start to the end, maybe when I'm riding along by myself, maybe sitting by the fire, or other kinda lonesome times, or maybe not lonesome but just wanting to pleasure myself with tale-telling and nobody wanting to hear." Nelt said his boys were no longer interested in telling or hearing tales. They wanted to play basketball and do "other things up with the times."

He did not know exactly how old he was. His birth date was not set down in writing anywhere. Nothing was made of birthdays when he was a boy, so the date had "slipped everybody's mind that ever knowed it." In 1933 he told me that he was "a little this side or yon side of sixty." He wasn't sure which.

Nelt liked to remember that many of his tales were told to him by his mother while he helped her work at jobs not too noisy: apple peeling, winding yarn to knit or weave, washing clothes down by the spring—not weaving, for the clack and thump of the loom would drown out the telling. Sometimes the tale matched the occasion—"The King's Golden Apple Tree" told while peeling apples—but by no means always. In his own tale-telling some occasion or bit of conversation sometimes reminded Nelt of a tale to tell.

The first time I ever saw him, Nelt had found me sitting on the stile crying with homesickness. Afterward he remembered this time and told me an olden tale to suit the homesick occasion. The last time I saw Nelt we rode his two nags to catch a bus at the mouth of Defeated Creek. As we jogged along its whole length, six miles or more, he told supernatural legends of Defeated Creek and tales of the Irish "Little People" and their kindly or malicious acts toward humankind. I was reminded of the mountain tale-teller's characteristic attitudes toward the two kinds of tales. The local legend is always the "God's truth." The tale-teller claims it as personal, actual experience, or else he knows someone to whom it really happened. He takes great pains to establish the authenticity of his story. But the "olden tale from across the ocean waters" is told without concern for whether it be truth or fiction. If a listener questions the veracity of any detail, he is reminded that this is "a tale for idle telling and not a-bound to tell the true facts."

At the mouth of Defeated Creek the journey and the tales came to an end: "You might say, for a fact, I got a fine mort of olden tales to tell."

THE KING'S GOLDEN APPLE TREE

SITTING here peeling apples to make sulphured apples for winter time is like one time when I was helping my mammy peel apples to dry. That day she told me a tale about a king's golden apple tree. From that day till now it has always been my favoritest olden tale. I coaxed her to tell it over again every time we would peel apples. That's the reason why I know it so good, I reckon. I told it to the Irishman one time to pay him back my thanks for him telling me tales. Other times I told him some more tales; and he said to me, "You do know a fine mort of olden tales, I swear you do." I'll just tell "The King's Golden Apple Tree" while I peel, and you can set down the words iffen you're a-mind to. Anyhow, it will give you something to think on any time after this whenever you sit down to peel apples.

One time a king was getting old and wore out, but he stayed healthy from eating a golden apple every day. I don't see how a body could eat a golden apple; but this is just a tale for idle listening, and such a tale don't have to tell the true facts. Anyhow, the king had a tree outside of the window of his castle, and every day in the year it bore one golden apple— never but one. And the king would reach out of his window soon as he waked up of a morning and pick the golden apple. He had it for his breakfast, and it kept him healthy and spry, though he was way up in years.

One morning, just as the king reached out of the window to pick his golden apple, something flashed in his eyes and made him blind for a minute. When he could see again, there was a golden bird flying off with his golden apple. So he had just common victuals for his breakfast, and he started to feel weak and puny.

He sent for his three boys to come, and he told them what happened to his golden apple. "It will purely kill me," he said to his boys, "not to have a golden apple to eat for my breakfast. So's you got to kill that golden bird and save my golden apples for me. My hand is old and not steady to aim and shoot straight, so's you'll have to do it for me. The one that saves my apples for me, I'll give him the kingdom and the prettiest girl in the world to marry and more besides."

The oldest boy said, "Me first! I'd love to shoot me a golden bird."

The king agreed for him to try first and give him a new bow and arrow to shoot with. He told the oldest boy to stay awake enduring the night and be ready to shoot when the bird flew into the tree, come daybreak.

But the oldest boy was lazy and trifling. He sat down under the apple tree and leaned his back against it and went to sleep. He never woke up till the next morning when the king was hollering and making a big fuss because the golden bird had stole another golden apple.

The king was mad at the oldest boy and sent the middle boy a new bow and arrow and cautioned him to stay awake. But the middle boy never done no better, and the golden bird stole another apple.

Then it was the youngest boy's turn. The king said to him, "I'm feeling mighty weak and puny from not having my golden apple two days now. You better shoot that bird, or you boys will be orphans before long. I can't keep up my strength or even keep on living without my golden apples."

"I'll do my best, Pap," the youngest boy said. And, come dark, he set himself down under the apple tree to keep watch. Just when day was breaking, he dozed off. He woke with a flash of light in his eyes as the golden bird flew and lit in the apple tree over his head. He took aim in a hurry and let the arrow fly. The golden bird was quicker than he was, and it flew away in a hurry with the golden apple in its bill. The arrow barely grazed the bird a little as it flew, and one golden feather dropped to the ground.

The youngest boy picked up the golden feather and took it to the king, who was too weak to holler and make a fuss, since he had nothing but common victuals for three days. The youngest boy made his manners to the king and said, "I'm sorry I dozed off and missed that golden bird. Seems like I'd better go a-hunting and follow to wherever that bird stays and kill it there."

But the oldest boy said, "No, I aim to go a-hunting for the golden bird. I'm the oldest, and I stand on my rights."

The oldest boy tied up a little budget of bread and meat for the journey and started off. When he sat down in the woods to eat along about noon, a red fox came up to him and said, "I don't like to beg-take what I eat, but I'm perishing and nary thing to eat in this whole woods. Could you please spare me a few bites?"

The oldest boy took big, greedy bites and said with his mouth full, "Ain't got hardly enough for myself, and I won't give none away to nobody."

The red fox sat down on a mossy bank and leaned against a big oak tree. "I aim to give you some good advice," he said. "After sundown you will be thinking about some place to stay all night and you will come to a little town. On one side of the road you will see a big house with bright lights a-shining and loud music a-playing. On tother side will be a little bitty house with no more light than a glimmer of a candle and no more music but an old woman a-singing some old time song-ballad while she cooks supper. The modest choice is the best. That's all I can tell you." And the fox went loping off through the woods.

It happened like the red fox said. The oldest boy looked at the two houses and he thought to himself, "That old woman in that little bitty house won't have much to eat, and I don't care nothing about her old time song-ballads. Tother place has fine band music to dance by, and I don't misdoubt they got honey cakes to eat and good liquor to drink. I aim to try my luck there."

His choice turned out bad. The big house with loud music was full of robbers all drunk and mean as poison. They robbed the king's oldest boy and stole his fine clothes and turned him out half naked to beg-take whatever he could get to keep from starving to death.

It happened the same way with the king's middle boy. And I won't tell all the details and particulars over again. I want to get to the part about the youngest boy and what chanced to him on the same journey.

Well, the youngest boy left the king feeling mighty bad, for every morning early the golden bird flew off with a golden apple and no telling where it went to. The youngest boy was well-hoped that he could find the golden bird, though, and save the king's apples so the king wouldn't perish away and die.

Like the other boys, the youngest one took along a snack of bread and meat. He used better manners than they did, though. When the red fox asked him to please give him a few bites, the youngest boy said, "Share and welcome," and gave the red fox the biggest part of his snack of bread and meat. They sat there together under a big oak tree while they snacked, and they talked right neighborly together. The youngest boy told the red fox the reason why he was a-traveling, and the red fox said, "I aim to give you a piece of advice." Then he told the youngest boy about the two houses and said, "The modest choice is the best; and, whenever you need me, I'll come, only don't call on me lessen you have to, for I got business of my own to tend to." Then the red fox went off through the woods after the youngest boy thanked him kindly.

After the sundown, the youngest boy came to the two houses on the edge of town. The old woman was singing "Lamp Lighting Time in the Valley" and it sounded mighty good to the youngest boy, for he loved old time song-ballads, and his mammy used to sing to him when he was little, before she died and left him. So's he said to himself, "This here house is where I aim to stay if this old woman will let me."

The old woman was tickled to have company, and she fixed the best supper she could. Then they sat by the fire after supper and she sang song-ballads that the youngest boy named to her till it was past bedtime. She fixed him a good clean bed up in her loft, and her pet dog followed him up the ladder and slept on the foot of his bed all night. It's a good sign whenever a pet dog takes a fancy to a stranger traveling through.

The next morning the youngest boy milked the cow and chopped up a pile of stove wood, the dog following after him every step, while the old woman cooked breakfast. Then she fixed him a snack of bread and butter—she was too poor to have meat—and gave him a heap of good counsel for his journey. He thanked her kindly, and her dog went with him a piece of the way till he come to a big woods before it turned back.

On the other side of the big woods that he was two days going through, he came to the castle that belonged to the King of Spain. By the fence around the castle he met up with the red fox again. It waved its tail and put all the guards and watchmen to sleep so they couldn't object to the youngest boy going in the castle. Then the red fox waited outside. The King of Spain was wide awake and listening to a bird singing to him. It was a golden bird in a golden cage. And in the cage with the golden bird lay as many golden apples as the number of days gone by since the golden bird first stole a golden apple off of the king's apple tree—I lost count of how many days.

The youngest boy told the King of Spain what he wanted. And the King of Spain said, "You can take the golden bird home with you, cage and all, if you will bring me a fine black horse that belongs to the King of Greece."

The red fox went part way with the youngest boy and told him not to put the fine gold bridle on the horse when he led it out of the stables, or things would turn out bad. And the youngest boy kept that in mind.

The King of Greece said he didn't like to ride a prancy horse, anyhow; and he would give him the fine black horse, golden bridle and all, if he would bring him the prettiest girl in the world for a wife. The youngest boy was willing to try.

He found the prettiest girl in the world, and he loved her the minute he laid eyes on her and couldn't bear to think about her marrying the King of Greece. She loved him too, and said maybe they could figure out a way for her not to marry the King of Greece. She kissed her pap goodbye and promised she would come back on a visit. Then she went off with the youngest boy.

When they were too wore out with walking to put one foot before the other, the red fox came out of a big woods and said, "Sit on my tail and ride." He stuck his tail out straight behind, and they sat down on it, with the girl in front so she wouldn't fall off. And they flew like the wind to the King of Greece's castle. The fox slowed down to stop, but the girl said, "Keep a-going. The King of Greece has got his fine black horse with a golden bridle that he aims to swap for a chance to marry with me. But I don't love him, so let him keep his fine black horse and the golden bridle. And would you, please, Mr. Red Fox, to carry us a mite further?"

"Glad to and welcome," the red fox said, and he flew along so fast the youngest boy nearly fell off behind.

The red fox stopped by the gate of the King of Spain's castle and the guards and watchmen had not woke up yet. So he left the youngest boy and the prettiest girl to sit in the shade of a big oak tree and he went back and got the fine black horse, though with an old leather bridle, and I don't have no idea what kind of trade he made with the King of Greece. The red fox handed the bridle to the youngest boy and told him to go make the trade with the King of Spain, but for the prettiest girl to wait outside, lest the King of Spain take a fancy to her and keep her for his wife.

The King of Spain got right on his fine black horse and rode off out of sight, hollering back to the youngest boy, "Take the golden bird and welcome."

The youngest boy started to take the golden cage and the golden apples that the golden bird had saved up. Then the words of the red fox came to his mind, "The modest choice is the best." So he caught the golden bird and put it in the old wooden cage and went back to where the prettiest girl and the red fox were waiting for him.

They got on the red fox's tail, and in no time at all they were standing under the king's apple tree. It was night time, and the king hadn't woke up yet, being weak and sick like he was from doing without his golden apples.

"Now you are safe home," the red fox said, "and I want you to do me a favor. Let the prettiest girl hold the golden bird, and you take your sharp knife and cut off my head."

That didn't look like doing a favor, but the youngest boy was compelled to do it. With his head cut off, the red fox turned into the prettiest girl's brother that had been witched into a red fox. And it turned out that he had in his pocket the golden apples that the golden bird stole from the king's apple tree.

They woke up the king and made him eat all the golden apples in one day to make him well in a hurry. The king loved the prettiest girl and her brother and made them welcome in his castle. He wanted to have the wedding for his youngest boy and the prettiest girl the next day, but the youngest boy raised objections. "I aim to go and find my brothers," he said. So he set out to look for them, and the prettiest girl's brother went along. The two brothers of the youngest boy had turned to robbers, and they had lots of gold money, and they liked being robbers and would not think about going back to live in the king's castle.

"Well, you done what you could," the king said when the youngest boy got back to the castle. "Now we can have a big wedding and a frolic."

So the youngest boy and the prettiest girl got married and all the neighbors came to the frolic. The king asked the prettiest girl's brother to live in his castle, but he wanted to go back home. The king sent two wagons full of money and fine things with him and even sent one of his golden apples to the prettiest girl's pap, though he had to go without for his own breakfast that day.

THE BIRD OF THE GOLDEN LAND

RECKON I take after Grandpap loving birds like I do. Mammy
said Grandpap was rough-natured some ways, but he was
gentle with birds and little animal creatures. He could mock
birds till they would be fooled and come to him, thinking
what they heard was their own kind. He got a lot of pleasurement out of hearing birds sing; and, the best I can recollect, he
told mammy "The Bird of the Golden Land" one time, maybe
when they listened to a bird a-singing. I don't know for sure.

Golden Land was just the name of a place where a bird
came from. Nothing else golden in the whole tale about the
King of Erin that got the most of his pleasurement out of a
bird that flew from the Golden Land every day and sang in
his window.

The King of Erin had three sons, and one day they said
they wished he would find them each one a wife. The oldest
one asked him in the morning, the middle one at noon, and the
youngest one in the evening. The King of Erin said he would
think about it.

The king thought to himself, "Now I'm not rich, though
I am a king. I don't have much to give my boys when they
marry." He thought how he could give half of his land to the
oldest boy and half to the middle boy. Then he could give
his crown to the youngest boy. "No, that won't do," he said
to himself. "They would all three want my crown."

The King of Erin had a dream that night, and the next
morning he done according to his dream. He sent his sons to
find the Bird of the Golden Land. Maybe they would meet
girls to marry in some place where they traveled.

The first night the king's sons stayed with an old woman
who knowed who they were and made them welcome. The
next morning the old woman gave them presents. She gave
the oldest boy a big sledge hammer, she gave the second boy
a cradle, and to the youngest boy she gave a stout rope. They

thanked the old woman kindly and went along till they came
to a big rock. The oldest boy hit the big rock with his sledge
hammer, and the ground opened up a big hole.

This here hole was the way to the Golden Land. They
had to go down this hole in the cradle tied to the stout rope.
The oldest boy went down till he got scared, and they had to
draw him up again. Same way with the middle boy. The
youngest boy went all of the way down. He got out of the
cradle and walked around till he met an old woman at a castle.

She offered him a horse out of her stable, and he chose to
take a shaggy, little, old mare. He cleaned her and combed
her and put the bridle on her. The old woman said he had the
right horse, and he would have good luck. She told him the
mare could talk and keep him on the right road.

They came to a wide sea and they got across. And another
sea and they got across. They came to the widest sea of all, but
the mare told him they could get across the widest sea. She
said there were three islands scattered about in the widest sea,
and she could rest on the islands. The mare would swim a
while and then rest on an island and swim some more. That
way they got across the widest sea.

Then they rode up to a shining castle. The mare told the
youngest boy to get off at the stable that was thirteen, and
look after his own horse. While he was tending the talking
mare, the king came out of his castle and said he knowed why
the youngest boy came to the Golden Land. The king said he
would hide, and the youngest boy would have to find him,
come morning.

That night the youngest boy slept in the stable with the talking mare. Come morning, she woke him up and told him to walk
in the garden. The talking mare said to pick a red apple from
off a tree in the garden and cut the apple in two. She said the
King of the Golden Land would be hiding where the apple
core belonged to be.

The youngest boy saw pretty girls a-walking in the garden,
but he tended to his business. He picked a red apple and cut

it in two. The king came out of the red apple with one cut on his head.

The youngest boy had to find the king the next day. He slept with the talking mare, and she woke him up and gave him instructions. She told him to go to the cook room and pay no mind to anybody at all, but do what she said do. He went to the cook room, and the cook gave him some soup but no spoon to eat with. He tried to eat soup with his knife, and the king rose up out of the soup with two cuts on his head.

One more day the youngest boy had to find the king. The talking mare gave him instructions, and he done according. He took a few grains of corn and went to the duck pond. He fed the duck some corn and it came to land. He caught the duck and held it till it laid an egg. The king was in the duck egg; and, when he came out, he had three cuts on his head.

Then the King of the Golden Land had to hunt the youngest boy. The talking mare made him into a flea, and the king couldn't find him. Then the talking mare made him into a honey bee, and the king couldn't find him. One more time the king tried. The talking mare turned the youngest boy into a hair, and the king gave up and went to the castle and lay down to sleep.

The talking mare said, "Now is your best chance. The King of the Golden Land goes to sleep once every seven years. This is the time for him to sleep. Grab the bird's cage and run back here to me." The boy took the advice the talking mare gave him. Then he jumped on the mare's back and they went across three seas to the place where the old woman gave him the talking mare.

The old woman was right proud to see them. She told the youngest boy that the bird in the cage was a queen with three crowns, and the talking mare was a queen with two crowns. The old woman was a queen with one crown. Excusing the queen with three crowns, they had no power to change back to their natural selves. She said the oldest boy could have the queen with one crown and the middle boy the queen with two crowns. The queen with three crowns would belong to the youngest boy.

The bird in the cage turned into a queen with three crowns, and she touched the old woman and the talking mare. They turned into a queen with one crown and a queen with two crowns. They all went to the hole where the youngest boy came down to the Golden Land.

The queen with one crown went up in the cradle and the oldest brother took her. The queen with two crowns went up in the cradle, and the middle brother took her. Then the queen with three crowns put a big rock in the cradle instead of herself. The brothers drawed it up a little ways and then cut the rope and let it fall to the bottom.

The two brothers and their queens started back home. They met the old woman that gave them the presents. She asked how come they were going back home without any bird. Then she changed the queens into two birds.

They got back to the King of Erin's castle, and he asked about the youngest boy. They lied to him, but I don't know what they said. The oldest boy hung up his bird in a cage, but it wouldn't sing. The middle boy hung up his bird in a cage, but it wouldn't sing.

Back at the hole down to the Golden Land, the queen with three crowns changed herself into a bird. She flew up through the hole, and then she changed to a stout woman and drawed the youngest boy up in the cradle. I reckon she spliced the rope that was cut. Then she changed back to the Bird from the Golden Land. They went to the King of Erin's castle. The youngest boy hung up his bird in a cage, and it sang a sweet song. The King of Erin knowed it for the Bird from the Golden Land.

It changed back to the queen with three crowns and changed the other birds back to queens. The King of Erin said he would forgive his oldest and his middle boy, so they could all live happy together.

The tale don't say no more about the king worrying his

mind over how to divide up his things when his boys married. I would love to know who got what.

LITTLE CAT SKIN

MY mammy used to tell me this here olden tale when I helped her work. Her granny told it to her whenever she was little. The tale starts with a man that had a woman and three girls. The woman died, and he put her wedding dress away real careful, saying he wouldn't never marry till he could find a woman as pretty as her.

The oldest girls growed off to be hateful and got fine clothes and traipsed about the country. The youngest one they treated bad, and her wearing clothes got so plumb wore out she patched them up with cat hide. That was how she came to be named Little Cat Skin.

One day, whenever her sisters had traipsed off, and her pap was working in the corn patches, Little Cat Skin dressed up in her mammy's wedding dress and went by where her pap was hoeing corn. He begged her to tell him who she were, and she said she would iffen he got her a dress the color of all the clouds that went by. He done it, and then she said she wouldn't never tell lessen he got her a dress the color of all the flowers that bloom. He done it, and she said, "It's me, Little Cat Skin."

That made her pap ramping mad, and he ran her off from home. She tied up her pretty dresses in a budget and went to hire out to the queen. The queen put her to work amongst the niggers, but she flew to work and redded up the place and cooked so good the queen liked her right off.

In a month's time after she hired Little Cat Skin, the queen had a play-party. She told Little Cat Skin she could go, and she gave her one of her old dresses to wear. It was right pretty, but Little Cat Skin had prettier dresses in her budget.

She got out the dress the color of all the clouds that go by; and, whenever she decked out in it, she looked mighty pretty.

The queen's oldest boy ran all the sets with her till she slipped off and left him and went back to the cook room amongst the niggers.

She done that for two more play-parties at different times. The last time she wore the dress the color of all the flowers that bloom. She was so pretty that the queen's oldest boy loved her so good he couldn't hardly hold hisself. He gave her a finger ring and wanted mighty bad to see her home. But she ran off like always.

The boy was so bad in love of her that he couldn't be satisfied. He took down sick and couldn't no doctor make him well. His mammy, the queen, tried every way to get him cured.

One day Little Cat Skin said to the queen, "Let me cook him up some good victuals."

The queen misdoubted he would eat it, but she gave in to try. Little Cat Skin baked a fine little honey cake and put in the bottom the finger ring the queen's oldest boy gave her at the last play-party she went to.

Whenever she took the little honey cake to him, she just put her head inside the door. But the queen's boy said, "Little Cat Skin, you look pine-blank like the pretty girl at the play-party." But Little Cat Skin ran back to the cook room.

Eating along on the honey cake, the queen's boy ran into the little finger ring. Then he knowed pine-blank that Little Cat Skin had fooled him. He got cured right that minute and ran down to the cook room quick as he could put on his britches. He loved Little Cat Skin and named marrying to her. She loved him back and they got wed to each other.

ASH CAKES AND WATER

TALKING about stingy neighbors 'minds me to tell you the olden tale about the stingy old woman that was outed in the end. Mammy told it to me from her granny's telling.

Talking about folks being stingy with their cash money and other things—they was once an old woman named Gally Mandy that was too stingy to eat decent victuals but lived on ash cakes and water. Her cash money she tied up in a piece of cow hide and stuck it in a crack up inside the chimney.

Whenever her boy got to be of an age to wed, she sent him acrost the ocean waters to get a woman so's she wouldn't know about the cash money saved up. One day after he was wed, old Gally Mandy set out to trade and left her boy's woman to mind the house. Gally Mandy said to her, "Now mind you don't look up the chimney."

Soon as Gally Mandy was gone the girl looked up the chimney and poked with a stick till the budget of cash money fell amongst the ashes. Then she put on her bonnet and set out to go back home acrost the ocean waters.

First she came to a pieded cow with a sore bag. It said to her, "Come milk out my bag, so's it will quit being sore."

But the girl went on like she never heard nary word till she came to a nag with a sore back. It said, "Come wash my back so's it won't keep sore."

But she wouldn't do it. Nor she never paid no heed to a peach tree saying, "Come pick some blooms so's I won't break down whenever too many peaches comes on me."

But she wouldn't do it. And all the time, the old woman, Gally Mandy, was about to catch up with her. Whenever Gally Mandy asked the cow and different things about the girl, they said, "She's but a little way ahead."

And the old woman made haste to catch up with her and flung her into the ocean waters.

It happened the same way with her boy's next woman. And it was like that with his last woman—three women he married, though one at a time and all from across the ocean waters. It was like that with his last woman up to where the critters asked her to be neighborly. She was more helpsome and she milked the cow and washed the nag's back and picked the peach tree blooms. Then, whenever they answered Gally

Mandy about the girl, they said, "She's a far piece ahead and you won't never catch up with her."

And the old woman lost heart and went back home. And the girl carried her cash money across the ocean waters and used it up for good things.

THE WEAVER'S BOY

WHENEVER I would help my mammy wind yarn to knit or weave and help thread up her loom, I would beg her to tell me "The Weaver's Boy." She would say I was a weaver's boy myself.

But the weaver in the tale was a man that lived next to a big woods. I never did know a man that did weaving to earn his living, but that's what it says in the tale. My mammy said her granny said her granny's foreparents could track the olden tale about a man weaver back to the old country. Times were different then, and maybe men tromped the treadles and flung the shuttles and wove cloth same as women. Anyhow, the weaver in this here tale was a man.

He musta been working at his loom mighty steady, for he ran out of wood to burn in the fireplace, and he went out into the big woods to chop down a tree to burn. He took one of his girls along, him not having no boys.

On the way back home, sledding a big load of wood, they met a stranger on a fine bay horse. They "Howdied," and then the stranger said, "Give me that pretty girl."

And the weaver said, "No, I won't. Who ever heard tell of such a thing?"

The stranger said, "She's a sight how pretty, and I'll give you her weight in gold." He got down off his horse and took gold money out of his saddle pockets and piled it on the ground. "That's how much I'll give for your pretty girl," he said to the weaver.

The weaver kissed his girl and gave her to the stranger for the pile of gold. He was ashamed and afraid to tell his wife, so he buried the gold in a deep hole in the garden. He told how he sent the girl to the neighbors on some errand. Night came on and no girl. She never did come back, and the weaver's wife worried and cried for many a day.

The next time they needed wood to burn, the weaver took the middle girl with him. Another stranger gave him a pile of silver for her, and he buried the money in a deep hole in the garden and told his wife the same tale. That girl never came home no more, and her mammy worried and cried for many a day.

The next time they needed wood to burn, he took their last girl with him. Another stranger gave him a pile of copper for her—I reckon she weren't as pretty as the ones he got gold and silver for. Anyhow, he buried the copper in a deep hole in the garden and told his wife the same old tale.

"I don't believe nary word you're a-saying," she told him. And so the weaver had to tell her the truth, and he dug up the gold and the silver and the copper out of deep holes in the garden to prove it to her. She wouldn't spend the money though; she said it wouldn't seem right to do that. She just put it away to keep.

After a time, they had a boy baby and weren't as lonesome as they had been. Their boy was a great big fellow before he ever heard tell of his sisters. One day he saw his mammy a-grieving and a-crying, and he asked her what was the matter. She told him, and she showed him three piles of three kinds of money stored away in the loft.

He studied about his sisters for a year and a day. Then he said, "I aim to go a-traveling till I find my sisters, and I don't aim to sleep two nights in one house till I find where they are at."

His folks grieved over him a-going, but they wove him a warm coat and baked two fresh loaves of bread for his journey, and cried in their hands whenever he left home.

He traveled on till sundown along the big road. Then he sat down on a mossy bank to eat. A little red-haired man came along and asked for some, and they ate the first loaf of bread down to the last crumb. Before they parted, the little red-haired man gave the weaver's boy three things to be a help to him on his journey: a sword of sharpness that would cut anything, a cloth of plenty that would spread a meal's victuals whenever it was asked to, and a cloak of darkness that would hide a person till nobody would know he was there at all. The little red-haired man showed the weaver's boy how to fold up all three things till they would fit in a walnut hull in his pocket. The weaver's boy said, "Thank you kindly," and the little red-haired man traveled on and left him.

It set in to rain and the weaver's boy stopped under an oak tree to take shelter. The earth just opened up and he fell down the big hole till he came to another country. In front of him was a high castle with nine fences around it and nine gates. A girl came to the outside gate and cautioned him to stay away from there. But he knowed somehow that his sister that was traded for a pile of gold money lived in that castle. So he sent word to her and she came to the outside gate and opened up all the gates and let him come in.

She told him her man was witched, and she didn't see him only of a night time, after he come home late in the evening. It turned out the way she said. Whenever the sun went down, her man came rushing home in the shape of a big white ram with curly horns. The ram that was a man asked about the company, and the weaver's boy's sister explained it all to him. He talked and acted right neighborly. As he was leaving the next morning, he asked the weaver's boy to stay and pay his sister a visit. But the weaver's boy said he had to find his other sisters, and he couldn't stay. The ram pulled out some of his wool and handed it to the weaver's boy. "Whenever you are in trouble," he said, "call on all the rams."

Being in a strange country, the weaver's boy put on the cloak of darkness so nobody would see him a-traveling by.

Times when he got hungry, he just spread out his cloth of plenty and ate his fill.

Before sundown, he came to another castle with nine fences and nine gates. His sister that was traded for a pile of silver money lived there. Things happened the same as before except that her husband was a man witched into a salmon. When he left in the morning, the salmon gave the weaver's boy a fin and said, "Whenever you are in trouble, call on all the salmon."

At the castle where the sister traded for copper lived it was the same, only her husband was a man witched into an eagle. He gave the weaver's boy one of his feathers and said he could call on all the eagles in time of trouble.

Now the weaver's boy had found all his sisters, and he could stay there and visit a while. Looking around to see the sights, he saw a big castle a far piece off. His sister told him a wicked giant lived there that had carried off a pretty girl. The weaver's boy got mad at the giant and wanted to kill him. His sister tried to argue him out of the notion, but he wouldn't listen.

He put on his cloak of darkness and took the road to the giant's castle. After he got there, he took off his cloak to talk to the pretty girl the giant had carried off. Then he put it back on again and sat down to wait till the giant come home.

The giant could smell him and made a big fuss about it. The boy kept his cloak of darkness on and fought the giant with the sword of sharpness. He hurt the giant bad and then rested till the next day. The giant got well in the night, and the next day they fought till noon. The giant made the girl tie up the places where the sword of sharpness cut him. He said to her, "That man can't see that he won't never kill me, for my heart is in a duck egg and the egg is in a duck swimming on the wide, deep pond."

The weaver's boy heard what the giant said, and he called on all the salmons. They swam around and caught the duck and locked it up in a big chest. The weaver's boy couldn't open the chest, so he called on all the rams. They butted the chest and opened it up. The duck flew out, but the eagles caught it and ate it, egg and all and the giant's heart in the egg. Then the giant couldn't help but die.

The weaver's boy took the pretty girl at the giant's castle for his wife. They helped themselves to all the giant's gold they wanted. They visited nine days with each one of the weaver's boy's sisters, and they gave back the ram's wool, and the salmon's fin, and the eagle's feather. And the witched men all turned back into men.

Then they met the little red-haired man and gave him back his presents and some gold besides. After that the weaver's boy and the pretty girl went and lived with his folks and paid visits back and forth with his sisters that lived in the castles with nine fences and nine gates.

THE TERRIBLE VALLEY

Some raggedy-poor folks are good and kind and treat folks of high degree gentle. Some raggedy-poor folks are mean-hearted and jealous and hate anybody better off than they are. In particular they hate kings and queens with fine clothes and high castles.

This here tale starts with a poor, raggedy man that was jealous and mean-hearted. One day he went to the fair; and the King of Erin was there too, walking about, looking at the fair and being sociable with the people. He was a-talking to a farmer about his crops when this here raggedy, mean-hearted man stepped up behind the king and knocked him down and stomped on him and then ran off in the woods and hid.

The farmer picked the king up and carried him back to his castle and laid him on his golden bed with silk quilts spread over him. The farmer called for doctors to come look after the king and see how bad he was hurt. The king was all bruised up, and he had lost three teeth. The doctors stayed right by his bed with all kinds of remedies, but the king stayed sick and sorrowful and couldn't get up out of his bed.

The king's three sons had gone off from home a-traveling. One was named Arthur and the youngest one was named Larry and the other one's name has slipped my mind. The king's three sons stood around his bed, and he asked them each in his turn what they would do about the raggedy, mean-hearted man that knocked him down and stomped on him.

Arthur and the one I can't name bragged and boasted what they would do to the man that would dare to treat the king so bad. Larry, the youngest boy, had no bragging words to say. He just said he would try to find the man and give him his just deserts.

The king was feeling sick and sorrowful, and it sounded to him like Larry was talking too humble for a king's son, and it made the king mad. He disowned Larry and said he didn't want to even see him about the castle no more. The other boys he gave cash money and instructions how to travel and find the raggedy, mean-hearted man wherever he went to hide.

Arthur felt sorry for Larry and took him along on the trip for a serving man. The first night, the king's three sons stayed with an old woman who shook hands with the two oldest brothers but kissed the youngest. They had no knowledge that this was a token, and they paid her kissing no mind.

The old woman and the king's sons made three parts of the night. In the first part they just talked, in the second part they told tales, and in the last part they were eating and sleeping a sound, sweet slumber.

In the morning the old woman told them that the Green Knight's champion had stole her daughter and carried her off to the Terrible Valley, where the Green Knight lived. She had an idea this was the same man that knocked three teeth out of the King of Erin. She never said, "Will you?" or "Won't you?" She just gave Larry fine armor and a sharp sword and a white horse and told him to go bring back her daughter.

He said he would do that; but he said no bragging, boasting words. He took his brothers up behind him on the white horse and rode off in the direction of the Terrible Valley. They went down in a basket to the land of the Terrible Valley. What become of the white horse I never did hear tell. I reckon they took the bridle off and turned it loose to go back to the old woman.

Larry's two brothers came right back up from the Terrible Valley. They were too scared to stay down there. "We'll wait here for you," they said to Larry, when they let him down in the basket.

Larry explored around. He put on his armor and took his sharp sword and killed all the Green Knight's champions. He piled up one heap of their heads and another heap of their feet. Then he went to find the old woman's daughter. I don't know how he got her away from the Green Knight. The tale don't tell. I reckon the Green Knight put up a big fight, though.

Before the girl got into the basket for Larry's brothers to draw her up out of the Terrible Valley, she gave Larry a finger ring to keep. The brothers saw how pretty she was, and they wouldn't let down the basket for Larry. They went off to the King of Erin's castle and fooled him into thinking they killed the Green Knight's champions. They dared the girl to tell on them for lying.

Larry traveled about in the Terrible Valley till he found a way to get back home to the King of Erin's castle. The same day he got there, the king was going to make the girl get married to Arthur. But, when Larry showed her the finger ring she gave him in the Terrible Valley, she went and told the King of Erin the truth about how Larry killed all the Green Knight's champions and piled up their heads in one heap and their feet in another heap. Then the king was glad to let her marry with Larry. And, when her mammy came to the wedding, she shook hands with the King of Erin and his two oldest boys, but she kissed Larry like she had done the first time they met.

My mammy told me the tale called "The Terrible Valley," not for no occasion but just to pleasure me a-listening to her tell.

THE FISHERMAN'S SON

A FISHERMAN had a wife and one boy. The boy weren't too bright, and it was a hard matter for him to learn anything at all. The fisherman gave up trying to get the boy to learn in books so he could be a lawyer or somebody of high degree.

"I reckon I'll just have to learn him to fish," the fisherman said to his wife. "Then he can earn his own living."

One day when he was out in a boat trying to show the boy how to catch fish and the boy not learning much about it, another boat met up with them.

It wasn't a fisherman in the boat but a man of high degree. He said to the fisherman, "You won't never make a good fisherman out of that boy. Let me have him for a year and a day and see what I can make out of him."

The fisherman thought that sounded like a good idea, but he didn't know what his wife would say. "Wait now," he said to the man of high degree. "Wait till I go home and ask the boy's mammy to give her consent."

The man of high degree said, "No, I ain't got time to wait around. The boy belongs to you, and you ought to have the say-so over him without asking any woman. Make up your mind quick, for I got to be a-going."

It seemed like too good a chance for the boy to miss, so the fisherman let him go. He made the man of high degree promise to bring the boy back home in a year and a day.

I'll just pass over the big fuss the fisherman's wife made and get to where the man of high degree comes back in a year and a day. The fisherman was out in a boat when he saw a boat coming with two men in it. One man was his boy. The man of high degree wanted to keep the fisherman's boy another year. He looked better and smarter than the year before, and the fisherman said, yes, he could stay another year. He forgot to make the man of high degree promise to bring the boy back in a year and a day.

His wife made him remember, though. She fussed and scolded all the year long. When the year was up, the fisherman set out a-walking to find his boy and bring him back home.

After he had walked all day, he came to a little house with the front door open and an old woman sitting by the fire smoking her pipe. She made him welcome, and she told him her youngest boy was with the same man. In the morning, she showed the fisherman the right road, and she told him how to know his boy when he got where he was going.

"You will see twelve white doves," the old woman said. "One dove is your boy. You will know him, for he will be the one that hops about and makes a ring around all the other doves."

That was the way the fisherman got his boy back from the man of high degree. When his wife saw her boy back home again and looking bigger and smarter, she took the fisherman back in her favor again. But they were as poor as ever, and the boy never had learned to fish.

One day the fisherman and his boy slipped off and went to the horse races. He had no cash money to bet on the races. "I wish I had two dollars," the fisherman said. "I'd bet on that bay horse and win me a pile of cash money."

"I got a better idea," the fisherman's boy said. "I'll turn myself into a race horse, and you ride me in the race and win a bigger pile of cash money."

The fisherman misdoubted his boy's plan, but it turned out

that way. After the race, men crowded around wanting to buy the fine, new race horse. The fisherman didn't know what to do. "Go ahead and sell me," the race horse told him, "but be sure you keep the bridle. Then, after you are a piece of the way home, shake the bridle and I'll come back to you in my own shape."

The fisherman had his misdoubts, but he took his boy's advice. A man paid him a big price for the race horse and let him keep the bridle. A piece of the way home he shook the bridle, and his boy came back in his own shape. After that they had plenty of money, and the fisherman quit fishing for a living. And he bragged all over the country how smart his boy was, though he never did tell how his boy one time turned into a race horse. Even his wife never did know that part.

HEART, LIVER, AND LIGHTS

THAT makes me think of a tale about a farmer's boy that couldn't remember things and used to get all mixed up on what he was told to do. One day in the summer time, when the men folks were busy in the crops, the farmer's wife sent this here boy to town to buy meat to cook for dinner. Heart and liver and lights were cheap, and good, too, the way she cooked them.

The farmer's wife gave the boy some money and she said to him, "Buy that much worth of heart, liver, and lights." She pinned the money in his pocket so he couldn't lose it. Then she said, "Now, can you recollect what to buy?"

No, he couldn't recollect the first thing. "Well," she said, "Just keep saying it over and over all the way to town: 'Heart, liver, and lights.' That way it can't slip your mind what to get."

The boy started off to town saying, "Heart, liver, and lights." Over and over he said it, till, halfway to town, he met a man. The man slapped him in the face because what the boy was saying made him think of butchering time with the looks and the stink of the insides of things being butchered and it made him want to puke.

"Don't say that no more," he told the boy. "Say, 'May they never come up.' "

On the boy walked towards town, saying, "May they never come up. May they never come up." It had no meaning to him, and he was trying so hard not to forget what to say that he never noticed that he was passing a field where a man was planting Irish taters. "May they never come up," the boy went on saying. The man in the field thought the boy meant the crop he was planting, and he beat the boy for making such a bad wish.

"Say 'three hundred this year, four hundred next year,' " he told the boy. The man meant bushels of Irish taters, but the boy started saying it without inquiring what meaning the words had.

Next he passed a graveyard where a woman was putting some flower blooms on her man's grave and doing some grieving after him. She heard the boy passing by saying, "Three hundred this year, four hundred next year." Her mind was fixed on death and dying, and she thought the boy was wishing for that many people to die each year. She flew at him in a rage and beat him with a stick for being so mean. "Say, 'Peace be with him,' " she told the boy. And he went on down the road saying, "Peace be with him."

He passed by a farm just about the time a red fox ran off with a fine laying hen. The farmer and his work hands chased the fox across the fields, but he got away in the woods, and they turned back. "Peace be with him," they heard the boy saying. To their minds he meant the red fox. They were too wore out with chasing the red fox to beat him. "No, that's wrong," they told the boy. "Say, 'Hang the brute.' " And the boy took up that saying.

While he was saying, "Hang the brute," he met up with a
woman taking her drunk husband home from town. "Hang the
brute," seemed too harsh to her. "No, no," she told the boy.
"That's too harsh a way to treat a man for having a little dram
of liquor. You ought to say, 'May they never be parted.'"

That sounded good enough to him, so he started saying it.
Next he came to a well where two men had fallen in. They
didn't want the boy to wish them never to be parted, for that
would mean to stay in the well. They told the boy to say,
"One out; may the other soon be out."

After that he met up with a man that was blind in one eye.
"One out; may the other soon be out," he was saying. The
man thought the boy was wishing his other eye out. The tale
don't tell whether he beat the boy. It just says he told the boy
to say nothing at all.

The boy mistook him to mean that he was to say the words,
"Nothing at all." What the man meant was for him to keep
still and say no words at all.

When the boy got to town, he was still saying, "Nothing
at all. Nothing at all." That didn't make any sense to the
butcher. He tried to find out what the farmer's wife sent the
boy to buy. "Try to remember," he coaxed. "Try to remember
what she told you to say."

The boy tried with all his might. His mind went back to
all the things he had been told to say, starting with the last.

"Nothing at all."

"No," said the butcher, "I know you been sent to buy something or other."

"One out; may the other soon be out," the boy's mind
reached back to the men in the well.

"No, that ain't it. Try again."

"Hang the brute," the boy said.

"Now, the farmer's wife never said that," the butcher objected.

The boy went back to other sayings: "Peace be with him."

"Three hundred this year, four hundred next year." "May they never come up." But his mind couldn't reach back and get hold of "Heart, liver, and lights."

The butcher got madder and madder with the foolishness the farmer's boy was saying, and he gave up and chased the boy out of his place of business. "Go on back home," he hollered after the boy. "Go on back home. Maybe you can recollect the way back home. Tell your mammy the butcher said you're a fool."

The farmer's boy went down the road toward home saying, "The butcher said you're a fool. The butcher said you're a fool." He didn't chance to meet anybody on the way home. So he was saying that same thing when the farmer's wife asked him why he didn't bring the heart, liver and lights for dinner.

"The butcher says you're a fool," was all the boy could remember.

The farmer's wife got ramping mad at the butcher and said things that won't bear telling. Then she said to the boy, "It's too late to cook them things anyhow, for they take a long time. Just you go catch me a young frying chicken and kill it and get it ready to cook while I make two dried apple pies."

The boy forgot what she said about a young frying chicken, and he caught the old dominecker rooster and fixed him ready to cook. And the longer he was fried, the tougher he got. Nobody could chew him, and the farmer's wife had to fry some side meat for dinner. And to this day the farmer's boy can't remember what kind of meat they had for dinner that day.

An old miller told me about the farmer's boy that couldn't remember heart, liver, and lights when he went to buy meat. The miller was poking fun at me for not remembering all the news the neighbors used to send to him, and him back to them whenever I would take a turn of corn to the mill. It learned me not to forget what I was told.

OLD SHAKE-YOUR-HEAD

It's purely a shame how jealous some folks get over their
younguns at school and the foolish or mean things that being
jealous will make them say and do. It puts me in mind of a
tale about the King of Ireland's son that was in the same school
with the sons of the King of Spain and the King of France
and the King of Greece. These other three kings got jealous
because the King of Ireland's son was smarter than theirs and
stood higher in his books.

They figured their sons never could make a good show of
being smart as long as the King of Ireland had his son in that
same school. So they plotted mean things to do. Banded together, they had the power to tell the King of Ireland that
he had to get rid of his boy or get him out of that school and
out of the country somehow.

The King of Ireland couldn't fight the kings of three
countries. So he took his boy out of school and let him go
out in the world to seek his fortune. He gave the boy five
pounds of cash money—I don't know how much that would be
worth, for I never did see cash money weighed out that way.

The king's son put his cash money in his pocket and his
clothes in a suit satchel and set out a-traveling—a foot, I reckon,
for it don't make no mention of a horse.

He traveled past a graveyard way off from nowhere. The
noise of a big tussle made him stop and look, though he was
too scared to stand still. He saw four men fighting over a
coffin with a dead man in it. Two men wanted to bury the
man in the coffin; two men raised objections. The two men
that objected said the dead man owed them five pounds in
cash money, and they aimed to take his corpse and make soap
grease out of it and sell his coffin to somebody that was poor
and would trade for a second hand coffin.

The king's son listened to how things stood. Then he pulled
his five pounds out of his pocket and paid the dead man's

debt. The two men that had been fussing about what was owing set to work and helped the dead man's two brothers bury him.

With his pockets plumb empty, the king's son walked along. Pretty soon a red-haired man whose head doddled about when he walked or talked caught up with the king's son. He said to the King of Ireland's son, "Let me be your serving man and help you seek your fortune. You can call me Old Shake-Your-Head."

The King of Ireland's son took Old Shake-Your-Head for a serving man and let him carry the suit satchel. After a day's traveling, they came to a giant's castle. Old Shake-Your-Head told the giant about another giant that aimed to do him harm and showed him how to protect himself. The giant liked Old Shake-Your-Head for his kindness and offered him some gold from a big pile under his bed.

Old Shake-Your-Head said, "No, I'd a heap rather have that light black horse iffen you want to do me a favor."—I don't know how black a light black horse would be, but color made no manner of difference to Old Shake-Your-Head. This was a magic horse that would carry out of all danger anybody that would throw a leg over his back, and that was what made Old Shake-Your-Head want the light black horse.

In the same manner Old Shake-Your-Head got a two-handed sword at another giant's castle and a cloak of darkness from the last giant's castle.

"Now, we're fixed to travel," Old Shake-Your-Head said to the King of Ireland's son. "How would you like to travel to the King in the Golden Castle and ask him for his daughter?" That suited the King of Ireland's son fine.

The King in the Golden Castle was willing to marry his daughter to the King of Ireland's son, but the girl had set her heart on a black-haired giant that lived in the next country. She thought up ways to get out of marrying the King of Ireland's son.

She gave him her thimble that he had to keep all night

and give back to her in the morning. Her serving maid turned into a rat and got the thimble away while the King of Ireland's son was asleep. She gave it to the giant, and he flung it away in the high weeds. Old Shake-Your-Head didn't sleep, so he saw what went on. He crawled around in the high weeds and found the thimble and gave it to the King of Ireland's son, and he gave it to the king's daughter in the Golden Castle.

The girl tried the same trick with her comb. And in the same way it got back to her in the morning. Maybe she aimed to think up some more tricks, for she still wanted the black-haired giant. But the King of the Golden Castle said to her, "Now stop your foolishness and marry the King of Ireland's son. He is a smart boy and he is our kind of folks." And he said to the King of Ireland's son, "I wish you would kill that big rascal, for he aims to make trouble after you get married."

The King of Ireland's son took his two-handed sword and chopped off the giant's head. Then he married the Princess of the Golden Castle. After the wedding he never did see the red-haired man that had been a help to him. Old Shake-Your-Head had gone back to his coffin in the graveyard and lay down to rest in peace till the Judgment Day.

"Old Shake-Your-Head" is one of Grandpap's tales. He favored tales with graveyards and ghosts and all manner of scary things. Tales to make people laugh he liked too.

GILLY AND HIS GOATSKIN CLOTHES

GRANDPAP would laugh fit to kill when he told my mammy about Gilly to cure her of sour looks when she was a girl. When she would tell me about Gilly, she would laugh as much as the king's daughter that saw Gilly wearing goatskin britches and making people dance to his magic flute.

A widow woman was so poor she never had cash money to buy wearing clothes and nothing to trade for cloth. Her boy named Gilly wore out his clothes down to the last strip of cloth tied around him to hide his shame. In the winter when it was freezing cold, the widow woman made Gilly lay on the hearth; and she covered him over with warm ashes.

Some man gave the widow woman's Gilly a crippled goat. It was a nanny goat and gave milk. And it slept by the boy's side and kept him warm. The widow woman stayed poor, and the boy still didn't have britches nor other wearing clothes.

One day some hunters came along and their dogs killed Gilly's crippled goat. The widow woman had the butcher to dress it, so's they could eat the meat. Out of the goat skin she sewed Gilly a pair of britches and a jacket. He was proud as Lucifer and wanted to go somewhere and let folks see how fine he was dressed up.

The widow woman gave him a piece of rope and sent him to cut some wood. He walked along, feeling big and stout. He met a giant and pitched into fight. The giant bragged on how good Gilly could fight and made him a flute that would make people dance when they heard dance music played on it, no matter if they wanted to dance or not. Gilly said, "Thank you, sir," and went home with a big turn of wood.

He went to cut wood another time and the first giant's brother picked a fight with him. Then the giant's brother bragged on Gilly's fighting and gave him some salve to put on the places where he got hurt in the fight. He told Gilly to keep the rest of the salve and to rub a little on himself in time of danger, and nothing could do him any hurt. Gilly said, "Thank you, sir," and went home with a big turn of wood.

The last time he went to cut wood another giant picked a fight and then made him a present of a good stout club. "Now you never can be conquered in a just cause iffen you use this here club to fight with," the giant said. Gilly said "Thank you, sir," and went home with a big turn of wood.

The king's herald came riding by the widow woman's house. He said the king's daughter had not laughed for a good many years, and the king was plumb wore out with her sour looks. He said the king would give her for a wife to whoever could make her laugh, but if anybody tried and failed the king would have his head chopped off.

The widow woman's Gilly thought he might as well try, for he recollected how folks laughed and made fun of his goatskin clothes. So he put on his goatskin britches and jacket with the box of salve in his pocket. He carried the flute and the club in his hands. He was barefooted and bareheaded but he walked along proud, like he owned half the world.

It never helped his looks none when he had to fight with three champions by the king's front gate. Gilly used the giant's club and killed all the champions but one, and that one crawled off in the bushes to hide. Gilly never come to no hurt, but his looks got right badly messed up. He weren't a pretty sight when he stood under the window where the king's daughter was looking out. He stood there a-playing on his flute that was a present from the giant, and everybody began to dance. They danced all over the place and couldn't help it and couldn't stop till Gilly stopped playing on his flute.

It was the funniest sight the king's daughter ever saw in all the days of her life, and she laughed and laughed till she nearly fell out of the window.

Gilly stopped playing his flute and the dancing stopped. The king's daughter laughed and begged him to play some more. But that was enough for one day, and he wouldn't.

The next day some soldiers picked a fight with Gilly. He greased his arms with the giant's salve and knocked all the soldiers down senseless in a pile. Everybody that weren't knocked down got so scared they ran off and wouldn't come back for a week. The king's daughter laughed and laughed. Then she brought Gilly into the castle and waited on him till he got rested. She dressed him up fine and got rid of his funny-looking old goatskin britches. His jacket had got torn up in the first fight he had at the king's front gate.

The king had a fine wedding dinner for his daughter and

Gilly, and he hoped that Gilly would make her laugh every day of her life and not let her wear sour looks any more. The king sent for the widow woman to come live in the castle, but she just came for a visit and then went home again.

THE KING OF SPAIN'S MAGIC COW

ACCORDING to my best recollections, the first olden tale the Irishman told me was "The King of Spain's Magic Cow." At the time, I had a heifer calf that I was raising a pet, and I bragged a lot about what a fine cow she would make. One night, after I had bragged on her all through supper, the Irishman told me about the King of Spain's cow. I figured he told it to shame me for talking so much about what a fine cow I would have. But he said, "No, oh no, I was just trying to show you what to expect. You're going to hurt the feelings of that heifer and make her mad enough to break out of the cow lot and run off, iffen you don't set a higher opinion on how much milk and butter she'll provide and how rich she'll make you—barrels of milk, tons of butter. You'll be rich as the King of Spain."

This here magic cow belonged to the King of Spain, and she gave so much rich milk—barrels of milk every day and it thick with cream to make butter—that she made rich whoever owned her. But she was a contrarious cow, and got mad at the least thing. Whenever she got mad, she would break out of the pasture and roam the wide world and not come home at milking time. The King of Spain got tired of fooling with her, and he was rich anyhow. And he wanted to learn the magic cow a lesson.

He said he would give the magic cow for a wedding dowry with his daughter to any man that could make the magic cow stay in the pasture. Thousands of men tried and couldn't have success. So the King of Spain chopped off their heads.

Then an Irishman named Eli wanted to try. He made swords to earn his living, and his neighbors told him he better just keep on making swords, for it was a safe enough job of work. They said not to fool with the King of Spain's magic cow. But nothing would do him but to try.

He just talked gentle to the magic cow and persuaded her it would be the best for her to stay in the pasture with good things to eat. The magic cow was gentle natured and took kindly to soft words. So she minded Eli and stayed where he coaxed her to stay. He married the King of Spain's daughter and quit making swords, so he could have time to look after his magic cow.

After a few years, the King of Munster needed a new sword. He sent his boy to keep the magic cow in the pasture to give Eli time to forge a sword. The King of Munster's boy talked rough to the magic cow, and she got mad and ran off to Spain. The King of Munster's boy took out after her, and it took a year's fighting with giants and champions to get her back for Eli.

When he got old, Eli hired a man to herd the magic cow. That worked out very well for a time. Then the magic cow got mad and ran off again to Spain. That time the King of Spain wouldn't give her up to Eli, for the King of Spain had run clean out of butter while the magic cow belonged to Eli. So Eli went back to Ireland and had to be satisfied with common cows in his pasture.

FOLKS THAT GROWED FUR TO KEEP WARM

MAYBE you won't like a tale about some mighty rough times back in Old Ireland. Tain't nothing but an idle tale, though, and the Irishman said his granny listened to old men tell it to each other of nights in the winter. She said she was little then, and it seemed real in her imagining.

A wicked, mean-hearted king killed the King of Ireland and tore down his castle and ran his queen and her three little boys off into the woods. They had to live in the woods for seven years and eat just whatever they could lay their hands to. They never dast show themselves for fear they would get killed. Their clothes wore plumb out and dropped off in little raggedy scraps. To hide their nakedness and to keep warm, they growed a suit of fur like wild beasts in the woods.

After seven years' time—somehow with magic, I reckon—the Queen of Ireland got a castle again and civilized things to eat and wear. Her two oldest boys went off to Scotland and got to be great champions. When they first came out of the woods to live like folks again, her youngest boy couldn't walk nor talk. His brothers nicknamed him The Big Fool, and they said he never would be any good to anybody but just a burden on the family.

But the Queen of Ireland said he was not but seven years old and lived deep in the woods all his life and never had no civilized raising. She said he was the king's son, and he would turn out fine if folks would only have patience and let him learn how to live in the wide world.

After the other boys went off from home, the Queen of Ireland and the man that herded her sheep worked with The Big Fool and he learned to walk and talk and was stout, and he was smart too. One day he caught a mad dog and killed it. And another time—three times it was—he had a fight with a cow herder that drove his red, white, and blue cattle on the Queen of Ireland's farm, and they ate up and tromped down her crops. The last time he beat the cow herder so bad that he never did come back, nor his red, white, and blue cows neither.

Along about that time the Queen of Ireland told the Big Fool—the Irishman told me the Irish word for Big Fool sounds right pretty—about how the wicked, mean-hearted king killed the King of Ireland and tore down his castle. That made the Big Fool so mad he went right straight to that wicked, mean-hearted king's castle and killed everybody in his golden castle but one pretty girl; and he married her. He went back and got his mammy to come live in the golden castle and keep his wife company while he went off to find his two brothers.

On the way he had to fight giants and other fearsome things. One time he lost his legs off up to his knees, but he smeared them with some herbs the Queen of Ireland learned about when she lived in the woods, and his legs healed back onto the stumps and were stouter than ever before.

The next thing, he had to fight two champions; and he beat them till they had scarcely breath for living. It turned out the champions were his brothers, and they all three went back to Ireland to live in the golden castle. On the way a ship with a green cat the size of a man met up with them and carried off the Big Fool's brothers. Then he went on back to Ireland and lived in the golden castle and was the king—and maybe he forgot about the years when he lived in the woods and had fur growing on him to hide his nakedness and keep him warm and no house of any kind, living in a cave, maybe. Leastways, I hope such bad times faded out of his remembrance, and he could take pleasure in his golden castle and fine silk wearing clothes.

COLD FEET AND THE LONESOME QUEEN

MANY a time, when a person has a good solid name, he never hears nobody call him that name a dozen times in his life. That was the way with a man named John in a tale the Irishman told me one time. This here man got nicknamed Cold Feet, and that was the only name he ever did hear anybody call him by. He got that nickname from growing so fast and so big when he was still a boy that only a part of him could get into the house at one time. With his head and shoulders in the warm house and the rest of him outside in the weather, he was always complaining about his feet being cold. That was how come he got the nickname of Cold Feet, and seems like folks plumb forgot his name was John.

Naturally, a boy that big and still a-growing would eat up creation. It come to the time when his mammy just couldn't make a living for him. So he left home to seek his fortune.

He hired himself out to a knight in a castle to herd cows for a year and a day. The cows never made any trouble for Cold Feet but grazed all day peaceful as could be and went home at milking time in the evening.

Four giants lived in the same country as the knight in the castle. Every day one of them would come and threaten to do Cold Feet harm lessen he left the country. He was bigger than the giants and still a-growing, and they were afraid he would damage their reputation for size. They were different from other giants, for they had lots of heads instead of just one.

The first giant had four heads, and he threatened Cold Feet with four mouths all talking loud and mean at the same time. Cold Feet got enough of his sass and up and killed him and hid his four heads under some big rocks. It was the same way for three days after that with a giant that had six heads, then one with eight heads, and at the last a giant with a dozen heads on his shoulders and all his dozen mouths saying mean and threatening things to Cold Feet. His heads were soon off and hid under big rocks. And that was the last of the four giants.

But on the fifth day the giants' mammy came to threaten Cold Feet. She was a fearsome old hag with fingernails and toenails of steel, and each fingernail and toenail weighed seven pounds. Cold Feet was no match for her and she put him under a spell to go to the Land of the Lonesome Queen and bring back the sword of light, the loaf of bread not tasted, and the bottle of liquor that nobody ever drank from. To make it harder for Cold Feet to get these things she shrunk him down to natural size.

Cold Feet gave up his job herding cows and collected his wages and left for the Land of the Lonesome Queen. He was three days and nights on the way, and each night he stayed with a different old man, and each old man gave him a set of directions about how to get one of the things he was going after. The Irishman that told me the tale never gave me the directions. But what the old men told Cold Feet worked, and he got the sword of light and the loaf of bread nobody ever tasted and the bottle of liquor never drunk from.

Then he found the Lonesome Queen asleep in her castle—musta been a spell of some kind, for Cold Feet slept with her all night and loved her like a husband, and she never woke up at all even when he stole one of her golden garters to remember her by.

On the way home Cold Feet got cheated out of the things he had been sent after. How he got cheated I never heard tell. He was afraid to face the giants' mammy that sent him on the journey to the Land of the Lonesome Queen, so he went back to his own mammy.

Shrunk up the way he was now, he could live in the house with her; and he ate no more than any common man. He herded cows and hired out to the neighbors. He managed to make a living but had never a penny to lay by.

Enduring this time the Lonesome Queen woke up, and she guessed somebody had been in the bed with her, for in the course of time she had a fine boy baby.

The boy looked pine-blank like Cold Feet; but the Lonesome Queen couldn't know that, for she never did see Cold Feet. When he was nearly grown, Cold Feet's boy set out to travel the world and find his pap. On his way, he got back all the things that Cold Feet had been cheated out of years before and carried them along with him. After a time, he came to the house where Cold Feet lived, and he stopped by the spring to get a cool drink of water.

The boy's granny came to the spring to get a bucket of water and she saw that this here boy favored Cold Feet, so she asked him to go home with her to wait till Cold Feet came in home from work. The Lonesome Queen had given her boy the other golden garter that she had on when Cold Feet stole one. She told him his pap would have the garter to match. And it turned out that way.

Cold Feet took the golden garter out of his pocket and matched it with the one the Lonesome Queen's boy had. Cold Feet and the boy's granny made over him a lot, and he made them a present of the loaf of bread that nobody ever tasted, and the sword of light and the bottle of liquor never drunk. Then they all went to the Land of the Lonesome Queen, and she never was lonesome after that.

A CURIOUS LAW ABOUT ASKING IN MARRIAGE

IN times past they musta been some curious laws about courting and marrying. The Irishman told me a tale that started off with a curious law about asking in marriage. It said if a girl's folks wouldn't give her to a young man that asked for her—providing he was a decent young fellow, not no robber nor other wicked kind of man—like I started to say, if he was a decent young man and asked for a girl to marry him and her folks wouldn't agree to it, then he could give her death by the law. Curious kind of law, but then you know what queer turns the laws can take.

It was in the time of this curious law about asking in marriage that a king had a boy named Arthur and a girl named Esther—sounds like twins, but the tale don't say so. A tinker's boy fell in love with the king's girl. One day, when the king's family was eating dinner, the tinker's boy came and asked the king to let him marry Esther. The king said he would rather see her die than see her marry a poor tinker's boy and live a hard life. The tale don't say what the girl thought or said about the matter, and I wish I could know.

Anyway the king hung the tinker's boy till he was dead. Then he cut him up in seven pieces and flung him in the ocean waters.

He had a kind of coffin made for the girl and put in it water and things to eat. Then he set it in a big box that wouldn't leak and fastened the lid on tight and shoved it into the water. He watched it float away. It grieved him but he had to get rid of the girl some way. The law said so, and the king would a heap rather not kill her in cold blood but let her float away to perish on the ocean waters.

Somewhere the box with Esther in it floated to land. A man found the box and pried it open and saw the pretty girl inside. He had thought at first the box would have gold in it but he would a heap rather have the pretty girl than gold. He jumped over a cross and married her. She turned out to be a good wife, and they got rich.

Being rich was a new thing to the man, though not to the king's girl. They made some bad mistakes but the worst one was when they invited a rich robber to dinner. The man got mad because the dinner turned out bad and hit his wife. A girl from a king's family was not used to being knocked about, and she grieved and cried about the way her man treated her.

About that time her brother Arthur chanced to come along. He fought with his sister's man and carried him back to the King's Castle to ask the king what to do with him.

The king gave him a good talking to and sent him back home to treat his wife better after that. Arthur went back with him, because he liked to play cards with Esther's man. Arthur played with enchanted cards and he always beat whoever played against him. The king sent Esther an enchanted cup but the tale don't never say no more about it.

When Arthur and Esther's man got home they found out that the rich robber had stole Esther and run off with her.

Arthur killed the rich robber and brought Esther back to her man. Then he stayed for a seven years' visit with them.

When the seven years were up, he left to find a man as good as himself. He played cards with a stranger that turned out to be a giant. The giant quarreled about the enchanted cards, and Arthur grabbed the giant's sword and cut off his head.

Then he played cards with the giant's head. The head cheated, and Arthur flung it in the fire. Then the giant's brothers came with all their giant neighbors. Arthur put them all in a pile and he killed the old woman who tried to bring them back to life. He kept on a-traveling after that, for he hadn't found a man as good as himself.

WHEN FINN WAS A BOY

NEVER was one bit of use to caution young folks not to marry. When they see somebody they love good enough to marry and get the notion to marry, they aim to do it. Nothing nor nobody won't keep them from it. Take Mally, now, over on The Mountain. She'd been cautioned not to marry. Crippled up like she was, she would die a-borning a baby, granny-women told her. But she married anyhow, and last week she died a-borning her little boy baby. It lived, though, and seems like it's healthy a-plenty.

That calls to my mind a tale the Irishman told me about a man that had been cautioned not to marry. Some kind of token told him he would die the next day after he married. His mammy guessed the reason why he stayed single, but nobody else had any hint about the matter. He stayed single some years past the time most folks marry, not wanting to die the next day.

Then he met a king's daughter that was the prettiest thing

he ever did see. He couldn't stand not to have her, so he married her in secret.

The next day he had to go off to war. He told his mammy about marrying; and she said she would look after his baby, for a token had come to her that he would have a son by the king's daughter.

A witch told the king that his daughter's baby would grow up and take his kingdom away from him. To keep such a thing from happening, he flung the little boy baby into the ocean waters. The boy baby rose to the top of the water holding a fish by its fin. His granny on his pappy's side of the family got him out of the water. She took the fish away from him and flung it back into the ocean waters. But he held on to a piece of fin that broke off from the fish. That was the reason why his granny named him Finn.

The king heard tell that the baby didn't drown in the ocean waters, and he gave orders for all the little boy babies to be killed, thinking that would settle the matter. But his granny left the country with Finn, and in some other country made them a home inside of a big oak tree. She got him a dog, and she let it live in the tree with them, so Finn would be content to stay hid.

She made Finn stay in the oak tree day and night and never venture out. What they lived on and any such details and particulars the tale don't tell. But it does tell that Finn couldn't walk a step when he was seven years old. He had stayed scrouged up inside of the oak tree and never had used his feet and legs.

When he was seven years old, his granny learned him to walk and then to run up and down hills. She would switch his legs with a limber twig to make him run faster, for she wanted him to be the fastest runner that ever was in the whole world.

I don't know how old he was when he won a running match, but still a boy. By the time he was a man grown he could travel thirty miles at one fast, wide step.

Then the king heard tell of the fast runner and guessed

who it was. He aimed to kill Finn and sent fast runners and dogs after him. Somehow Finn's granny managed for him and his dog to get away, but the king's dogs overtook her when she mired down in the mud.

Finn and his dog traveled on till they came to a cave. They went in and Finn was fixing to cook supper when a mean, old one-eyed giant came in and said this was his cave. The giant gave orders for Finn to cook a fish for supper and not to scorch it the least bit. Then the giant stretched out in the cave and went to sleep.

Finn burned his fingers while he was cooking the fish for the giant's supper. He put his finger in his mouth, and it hurt so bad that he gnawed it down to the marrow. That worked magic till he could know all the things in the world to know. He could know how to get away from the giant.

He put out the giant's eye while he was still sleeping sound. He killed a goat and crawled into its skin. That way he got out of the cave. The giant flung a gold finger ring after him, saying it was a present for not scorching the fish. But when Finn put on the gold finger ring, it told the giant where he was, and the giant came after Finn. The finger ring stuck tight to his finger and wouldn't come off. So Finn cut off his finger to get rid of the finger ring and to keep the giant from knowing where he went to. He called up his dog, and they left the giant's country.

In another country Finn killed three champions, though his dog helped some. He fixed a bottle of medicine out of roots and herbs and such things that would bring an old woman back to life.

And he married a girl that could cook the best stir-about that he ever did eat. She musta been a king's daughter and pretty too. That would be my guess.

FINN'S SEVEN HIRED MEN

ONE time the King of Spain sent Finn an invite to come and see him. Finn and his seven hired men made a ship and put it in the ocean waters that looked toward Spain.

But maybe it would be a good idea to tell before the tale goes any further how Finn got his seven hired men. It happened when Finn was a young man and nobody with him at all. One day he was resting in the shadow of a high mountain when seven young men—they said they were brothers—came out of the mountain. They told Finn their names, but I don't know what their names might have been. I never been told, and I ain't no hand to fix up things in a tale that's been norated to me. Anyhow, Finn liked their looks and their ways; and he hired them for a year and a day—though they musta stayed longer from all I've heard tell of Finn's hired men.

Well, Finn and his seven hired men went to Spain, and the King of Spain told the reason why he sent for them to come. His Queen had in the past birthed three boy babies, but each time a big hand with a long arm reached down the chimney and snatched the baby up the chimney. That was the last that was heard tell of the baby. Three times it had happened that way.

Now the Queen was near her time with another baby, and the King of Spain thought Finn and his hired men could save this baby from being snatched up the chimney. Finn watched day and night with his seven hired men. The minute the Queen birthed her boy baby, Finn and his hired men saw a hand coming down the chimney. One of the hired men grabbed the hand, and it dragged him up the chimney. He pulled and tugged with all his might, sliding up and down the chimney all night long. Along about daybreak the hired men tore the arm off at the shoulder joint, and the giant went off howling bloody murder. After that things got peaceful, and the King of Spain's new baby was safe from harm.

A few days after they got rid of the giant with the long arm down the chimney, Finn and his hired men promised to find the King of Spain's other boy babies, and they set out to try and do that. After a heap of traveling in strange country, they found the King of Spain's sons carrying water to pour on the giant's shoulder with the arm tore off. The water maybe cooled the fever in the giant from such great hurt.

Finn and his hired men saw this from peeping over a high fence that couldn't be seen through. They fixed a ladder, and one of the hired men climbed over the fence in the dark of night and carried off the King of Spain's sons. When they got back to the King of Spain's castle, he offered Finn and his hired men a whole ship full of golden treasure. Finn said, no, he wouldn't take none; he figured it all belonged to his hired men.

The old giant with one arm off came a-ramping and a-raging to get the King of Spain's sons. But Finn's hired men all jumped on him at once and tore him in pieces too little to see.

Then Finn and his hired men sailed home to Ireland with their golden treasure. The hired men sat down to count up their money, and Finn went a-walking.

He met an old woman that wanted to play cards with him— he oughta been careful about playing cards with rank strangers, but he took the chance. They sat down to play. He won a game of cards. Then she won two games of cards. She put a spell on Finn to bring her a giant's head, and she wouldn't let him have but one helper, and that one couldn't be one of his seven hired men.

Finn had won a game at the first, so he had the power to put a spell on her to stand with her back to the wind and nary a bite to eat while he was gone to get the giant's head. Pretty soon Finn met a red-haired man and hired him to help get the giant's head.

It was a good bargain, for the red-haired man could go seven miles at a jump and three miles at a step. He took Finn on his back and they soon came to the western world.

They knocked on the door of a high castle and asked for some bread. "Wouldn't give you even the leavings," was all the answer they got. Going along, they met the baker's boy with a big basket full of bread. The red-haired man took three loaves and divided with Finn.

They had no wine to drink, so they knocked on another castle door and asked for some wine. "Wouldn't give you dish water," was the only answer they got. Going along they met a wine boy. The red-haired man took three bottles and divided with Finn.

When they came to the next castle, a giant came out and wanted to fight. The red-haired man cut his head off and put it in a basket, and they started back home. On the way home Finn found out that the red-haired man was a brother to his seven hired men that went with him to the King of Spain.

They went to the old woman that played cards with Finn. She begged for the giant's head, but they wouldn't give it to her. The red-haired man took his sword and chopped her head off. He flung her head and the giant's head into the bushes, and their two heads set the woods afire.

Musta been some more to the tale that the Irishman left out of his telling. Even in an idle tale, it don't seem right to go off and leave a fire you set in the woods. But I never said nothing to the Irishman about it, for he might think I was finding fault and not tell me no more tales about Finn. The Irishman had touchous feelings.

OLD WOOLY BACK

WAY off, on yon side of the world, I reckon, they was a land where wild people lived. They would kill strangers that chanced to come to their country and roast the strangers like an ox and boil up their bones in a big pot to make soup. Makes me want to puke to think about it.

Well, one time Finn and his hired men chanced to be in the wild people's country. They shut Finn and his hired men up in a house and barred all the doors so they couldn't get out. But Finn weren't no man to just sit there and get boiled up in the soup. He roused up his hired men to fight their best, and they killed most all the wild people and buried them before dark.

Then Finn's hired men, all but one, went out to cut bushes to make pallets of brush to sleep on. It don't say about Finn. I reckon he sat and rested a spell. One of the wild men came back with Finn's hired men that went to cut the bushes. He said he wanted to be with Finn and live civilized, but Finn wouldn't have him amongst his hired men.

The next day Finn and his hired men set out to kill all the rest of the wild people. The queen and her daughter wanted the king killed. They told Finn to be careful so the king's head wouldn't jump back on his body and be alive again. The queen wanted Finn to marry her daughter, but Finn wouldn't have her. He never killed the queen and her daughter, though; he let them go off in the bushes and stay alive.

Finn and his hired men left the wild people's country and went to live in a house. It don't say what place. A beggar died at their place, and a horse and wagon came from yon side of nowhere to haul his corpse to the graveyard. Finn lifted the corpse up into the wagon, and his hands stuck to the corpse. Different ones tried to pull him loose, and they stuck to him or to each other. So they went along all stuck together. Somehow they got loose and buried the beggar in the graveyard.

After the burying, they sat down to eat supper, and the beggar's ghost came and made them stick to the benches they were sitting on. One man was laying down on a bench by the fire, and he stuck to the bench longways. Finn took some magic salve and rubbed it on, and they all came loose from the benches—all but one. The salve got used up before he had rubbed any on the man laying down on the bench.

So Finn and his hired men all took hold and pulled him

loose. His hide on his back from the neck down tore off and
stayed stuck to the bench. His whole back was raw and sore.
Finn took a long, wide strip of fresh sheep's hide and laid it
on the man's back to cover up the raw place. The sheep's hide
growed to him like it were his own skin. After that he always
had wool on his back like a sheep, and everybody called him
Old Wooly Back.

The Irishman would laugh about Old Wooly Back and say
he wondered if his wife would shear him in the spring of the
year and spin yarn to weave cloth for Old Wooly Back a pair
of britches or her a warm petticoat. He would say Old Wooly
Back always had a soft seat to sit down on—and a heap of
foolishness like that.

THREE MEN NAMED THREE DIFFERENT COLORS

I RECOLLECT another tale the Irishman told me. This is how it
went.

A man named Finn was in the woods a-hunting with seven
other men. They had been right lucky, and had their hunting
bags stuffed full of squirrels, and I reckon they were thinking
about the good squirrel meat they would eat for supper.

About that time, along came three strange men through the
woods. They said they had been trying to find Finn for seven
years, and they wanted to take service with him. Finn asked
the strange men what their names might be, and they said they
were named three different colors: Black, Gray, and Brown.
Then Finn said he was glad to have them for his work hands.
He said their first job of work would be to watch through
the night, one at a time. Each man would watch as long as it
took a log to burn in the fireplace. They agreed to that.

Black took the first watch. He put his log on the fire and
went out in the dark to walk up and down and around the

castle and keep guard. He let Finn's dog named Brownie go
with him. A good piece of distance off from the castle he saw
a big house with lights a-shining from all the windows. He
made the dog wait by the outside door, and he went in to see
who was there and what was taking place.

It was a big play-party, but all strangers to him. Everybody
was drinking from a big silver cup. Black had knowledge about
the cup, and he eased into the crowd, and none of the play-
party folks paid him any notice. He aimed to get the cup,
for it was a magic cup that somebody stole from Finn a hundred years before. The magic was that no matter how many
folks drank from Finn's cup it never got empty.

Black waited till his turn to drink, and then he put Finn's
magic cup under his coat and slipped out. Finn's dog scared
anybody that started to follow after. When he got back to
Finn's castle, his log had burned out. He gave Finn the magic
cup and woke up Gray to take the next watch.

Gray put his log on the fire and went out, Finn's dog following after.

He saw the same big house with a fearsome racket coming
out of it. The men were fighting over a magic knife that somebody stole from Finn a hundred years before. The magic was
that when the knife cut on any old bone good meat would
come. The men quit their fighting and took turns trying out
the knife. When it came Gray's turn, he ran off with the magic
knife the way Black had done with the magic cup. When he
got back to Finn's Castle, his log had burned out. He gave the
magic knife to Finn and woke up Brown to take the last watch.

Brown put his log on the fire and went out, Finn's dog not
following after. This time the big house had one dim light and
was full of dead people. An old hag with one arm and one leg
and one tooth went around and took three bites out of every
corpse and then went to sleep. Brown hit the old hag with his
sword, and she died in her sleep.

Then three giants came—maybe kin to the old hag, I don't
know. Brown killed two giants, but tother one got away.

Maybe if Finn's dog had come like with Black and Gray, he would have caught the last giant. When he got back to Finn's Castle, his log was burned out.

In the morning, Finn wanted to know all about what happened, and the watchmen told their tales. Then they had a fine breakfast with Finn and his hunters and no work to do, no trouble with cooking. They just used the wine cup that couldn't be empty and the knife that would cut good meat off of any old bone. They worried some about the giant that got away.

Later in the day, the giant came and said he wanted to hunt with them. So they all hunted in the woods for twenty-one years. Then the giant died. He told Finn where he wanted to be buried, and Finn promised. It took twelve men to carry his coffin to the place. They buried the old giant by a church, and then Finn and his hunters went into the church and sat down.

When they wanted to get up and leave, they couldn't, for they were stuck fast to the church benches. They sat and they sat for seven days, still stuck fast to the church benches. Finn got so tired and worried that he took to chewing his thumb. Unbeknownst to him, that was magic. When he chewed his thumb, it made magic for him to know what to do to get unstuck from the church benches. The magic was to blow in his hands. Then they all come loose from the church benches and rose up and went back into the woods to Finn's Castle.

CONNIE'S THUMB RING

THE Irishman said he never did like the story about Connie, but he told me about "Connie's Thumb Ring." First time I ever heard tell of a thumb ring.

Times when a man goes off to war, he can't stay and live out his lifetime with a woman he takes up with in the place where he fights battles. It was that-a-way with a man from

Ireland that was the biggest fighter amongst all the soldiers. He went off to war in some other country, and he took up with some king's daughter, but he had to leave when the war was over and go back to Ireland.

The king's daughter grieved to see him go off to Ireland before she birthed his baby. She promised him it would be a boy baby. Whenever he left, he gave her a golden thumb ring, and he said to her, "Keep this here golden thumb ring for my boy. As soon as ever it fits him, then I aim for you to tell him about me and send him off to Ireland to find me. Tell him to fight any man that offers to fight, so he won't be counted a coward. And caution him not to tell his name to anybody till he finds me."

She promised him, and he got in a boat and sailed off to Ireland. She named the baby Connie and dreaded the day when he would go off and leave her. But the golden thumb ring was the size for a man grown, and so she thought she would keep Connie with her for a good long while. Strange to say, though, he growed uncommon fast; and, when he was just turned seven years old, the golden thumb ring was a good fit—or maybe the ring shrunk up, for in the rest of the tale seems like Connie is boy-size.

Anyhow, he set out in a boat on the ocean waters to cross over to Ireland. No mention of anybody being with him, so I reckon he made the trip all by himself. It tells how he shot water birds with a sling shot and always took true aim.

Over in Ireland some soldiers stood on the edge of the ocean waters and watched him a-coming. They went down to meet the boat and asked him who he might be. He wouldn't say. They picked out a soldier to fight him, and Connie knocked him down with his sling shot. Same way with two other soldiers that come at him.

Then they said the soldier that was Connie's pappy would have to fight this boy. A token of some kind warned the soldier that this boy was his own born son, but he paid no mind.

Connie had no knowledge who the man might be, and no token come to him to give him warning.

Connie was so little he came only up to the man's waist. So he had to stand on a big rock to be high enough to fight good. He fought so hard that his feet sank way down into the rock and his tracks show on that rock to this very day.

Then they tried to drown each other in the ocean waters. Connie got the best of the fight till the soldier that was in truth his pappy used a secret kind of trick. Then Connie told who he was, and in his last breath found his pappy and gave him back the golden thumb ring.

A TALE TOO SAD FOR TELLING

ONE olden tale I've pondered on ever since I was a boy and the Irishman told it to me. Leastways, he told me as much as he knowed. He said his granny would try to tell him this here tale when he was a boy, but she never could tell to the end. She would break down and put her apron over her head and cry. And she would say to him, "It's a tale too sad for telling." And he never did meet up with anybody else that knowed the tale that was too sad for telling. Somebody told him it might be set down in a book, but he never knowed if that were the truth. He couldn't read nohow.

The tale too sad for telling was about a girl named Deirdre. The Irishman used to make me say the girl's name over and over till the way I said it suited him. He said his granny couldn't bear to hear the girl's name called wrong. The tale started with a man that had seen a token that told him he would have a girl baby. He had no faith in it, for he never had no family but his wife, and through the years they had lost hope.

He asked a druid—the Irishman told me its meaning, and seems like a druid was some ways like a preacher and some ways like a witch man—anyhow, he asked a druid about the token. And the druid said, yes, the man's wife would have a girl baby, and it would be the cause of great sadness in the world, and blood, and men fighting each other and getting killed. And his girl not meaning any harm in all her life. It would be just a thing that couldn't be helped.

The man worried his mind over the druid's words, and his wife did too. They never told about the girl baby, and after its birthing they never showed it to nobody. The druid came to visit them; and he saw the girl; but then, he had knowed about it before they did. He named it Deirdre and said that meant sadness and sorrow. And the druid was full of sadness for what was bound to come to such a pretty little girl baby when it was a woman grown—and sadness to all the land she lived in.

At the first, the man had in mind not to let the girl baby live. But it was so pretty and healthy, so sweet and good that him and his wife couldn't bear to do away with it. They had always wanted a girl baby and never had no kind of a baby before. So they hid the baby in their own house and took loving care till it was big enough to wean but not big enough to remember.

Way off in the woods and mountains, a far piece from nowhere, they fixed a little house for her to live in. The back of the house was against the mountainside and hid from that direction. Around the front and sides they planted orchard trees higher than the little house and thick flower bushes. They put sods of grass on top of the roof, and the grass got green and the flowers bloomed, and the roof of the little house looked like a little bit of a meadow down amongst the trees.

They found a woman that was kind and good and had a heap of knowledge and hired her to live in the little house with Deirdre and raise her. They told her they would furnish nice things to wear and a-plenty to eat. The main thing was to keep Deirdre happy and make sure and certain nobody would ever lay eyes on her. Maybe they went to see her sometimes. The Irishman's granny had an idea they did.

It went on that way till Deirdre was old enough to marry, sixteen, maybe. But she had no thought of marrying, for she never heard tell of such a thing. And she never had seen any men in all her life. She had a heap of knowledge about dainty work for a girl and about birds and the woods with flower blooms and all kinds of pretties. She was happy living in her little house hid away in the woods and mountains a far piece from nowhere. Ideas about any other way of living were outside her knowing.

One night, though, a hunter got lost in her woods. He was hungry and scared with being lost and he hollered for somebody to come and help him. Deirdre heard him holler, and she asked the woman that lived with her about it. She made some excuse about how it was nothing but a noise natural to the woods. Two more times she made excuses; and then Deirdre said she knowed what it was, for she had a dream in the night about a lost hunter. She got up and let the hunter in at the door.

The woman was mad and scared, too; and she let the hunter know that he weren't welcome. Deirdre said he must be starved, and he said she was so pretty that seeing her made him forget how hungry he was.

What the druid said had come true. Deirdre was far and away the prettiest woman or girl in all the land forevermore. She was shy, though, and blushed pink and pretty if anybody looked at her, and that made her prettier than ever, being modest like that.

The hunter promised the woman that lived with Deirdre that he never would tell about the little house in the woods and mountains a far piece off from nowhere. At the time, he aimed to keep his promise. Then he got to thinking how the old king lived lonesome without a wife and how he would find favor with the king if he told him about the prettiest girl in all the land that was hid away from sight. So he told the king. And the king gathered up some soldiers and went to where Deirdre lived. He was old, and the hard trip over the mountains and in the woods well-nigh wore him out.

The woman wouldn't open the door to Deirdre's house till he said it was the king of the land. Then she never had no choice. So she opened the door, and the king thought Deirdre was far and away the prettiest thing he ever saw or dreamed on. His soldiers carried Deirdre and the woman back to his castle, him following after. That was much as the Irishman's granny ever could bear to tell, for the rest of it was a tale too sad for telling. I've pondered on it now and again ever since I was a boy.

THREE | TOLD BY *Uncle Tom Dixon*

TALES WHERE THINGS GO IN THREES

Uncle Tom Dixon

Uncle Tom Dixon

WHAT I remember best of Uncle Tom Dixon is his beautiful speaking voice lingering on some old tale that he was fond of telling. Now and then he could be coaxed to sing ballads or other old folk songs, but he much preferred to tell tales. For tale-telling there was never any need to coax him. His favorites were tales "where things go in threes," though he was also fond of local tales of ghosts, ha'nts, and other supernatural beings. He had a flair, too, for family and community history. And—whatever the tale—he took plenty of time in the telling.

"I love to linger on the telling," he said, "and give all the details and particulars. I love for ary other tale-teller to do likewise, and I fault anybody that whittles it down to nearly no tale at all. Many a fine tale has been plumb ruint that-a-way. My ownself, I won't never tell no tale without them that belongs to listen gives up the time to set a spell and take it resty."

The very location of the Dixon homeplace was in effect an invitation to "give up the time to set a spell and take it resty."

Uncle Tom lived on what had for generations been the family homestead on the top of the mountain that lay halfway between the school at Gander and the Village of Blackey—the nearest railroad stop—four and one half miles from the school.

The Dixon's sturdy old log house sat well back from the road across the mountain. It was surrounded by a stout picket fence to keep out stray cows or pigs, and well-nigh hidden by trees and flowering shrubs. The wide front porch that stretched the length of the house was shaded in summer by vines and brightened by rose moss and other flowers growing in old pans and buckets on the porch and in beds in the yard. The chairs on the porch sagged from use through the years by visitors who had accepted the invitation to "set and talk a spell" and have a cool drink of spring water or, in winter, to warm by the fireplace.

With Uncle Tom lived his daughter Suzanne and a granddaughter whose mother had died at her birthing. I do not recall seeing him often away from home. "The old place has a fine sense of home about it," he once said to me; "and, old or young, I've always claimed it for my favoritest spot on top side this earth." It was a gentle, quiet household with a ready welcome for visitors.

Going or coming, on the way between the school and Blackey, I nearly always stopped at the Dixon homeplace: to ask if Suzanne wanted me to take her eggs and butter and do any trading for her; if I was walking, to rest from climbing the mountain or to borrow their horse—a good horse, not a nag—to ride the rest of the way to Blackey. Coming back, I could think up plenty of reasons for stopping at the Dixons. Whether I had any other reason or not, I was always eager to see if Uncle Tom had some tale to tell that I had not heard before.

Besides stopping over on the way elsewhere, I sometimes was especially invited to the Dixons for meals or to spend the night. "We ain't got no lavish," Uncle Tom would say, "but such as we got, you're more'n welcome to." Suzanne and the little girl would echo his words and add their own, "We give you eager welcome."

Though he was around eighty in the early 1930's, Uncle Tom had a look of strength and dignity. He had worked hard all his life, but neither hard work nor age had bent his tall, erect body. Renters now tended his larger, low-lying fields, but Uncle Tom still cared for the garden and orchard trees, and tended "the patches of taters and truck near the home-place." The outdoor chores of morning and evening were his, except for feeding the chickens and other fowls and doing the milking—those were woman's work.

While he did his chores or if Suzanne was sitting with us at any time other than after supper, he was likely to leave us to what he called "woman's talk" and let the telling of olden tales wait. At such times Suzanne often talked with me about her weaving, about home remedies from "roots and yarbs and such." Or she and the child might be coaxed to sing or to tell riddles for me. Uncle Tom could never resist joining in on the riddling, with new and harder riddles each time. When Suzanne was busy about outdoor or indoor chores or cooking, at which she would ask the child to help but never allowed any help from me, then Uncle Tom would be 'minded to tell some tale that he had been saving up till I came again.

After supper, Suzanne and the child joined us on the front porch or by the big fireplace in the "front room," according to the season and the weather. Though they had heard Uncle Tom's stories many times, Suzanne and the little girl seemed as eager for them as I was. "It's the God's truth, I know the tales Pap has been telling all these years—maybe I *know* them as good as he does," Suzanne once said. "But Pap's got a fine sleight at tale-telling and I ain't. So's I love to hear him tell."

The child also knew the old tales. One evening when Uncle Tom was called outside the house in the middle of a tale, we waited a long time for him to come in and again pick up the thread of the story. When the waiting seemed too long, the child took up the telling at the exact word where Uncle Tom left off, and finished the story—lingering on the telling and putting in all the details and particulars. She had just finished when Uncle Tom returned and, not knowing what had happened, resumed his story.

Listening to him, we became increasingly aware of how closely the child had imitated his manner of telling, using precisely the words he was now repeating. When we burst out laughing and would not tell him why, he pretended to be very angry. "Dog my cats!" he said, "iffen I aim to tell ary tale to a passel of womenfolks that makes light of me."

As to the sources of his tales, especially what he called "olden tales from across the ocean waters," Uncle Tom was seldom very specific. He might say, "I learned it from my foreparents that used to tell it, gathered around the hearth of evenings." Perhaps he would say, "It comes from way back in the generations of my family," or "Just a tale I always knowed; don't recollect who told it to me way back in time." Maybe he would reach back still further and say, "It's been told in the generations of my kin, way back to the old country across the ocean waters." From wherever or whomever the olden tales came to Uncle Tom Dixon he made them his own and gave them something of the flavor of his personality in the manner of his telling. He wondered if the father of the donkey that was really a boy ever saw his son after he became a human being permanently. "It don't say; the tale don't tell" was no satisfactory answer to the question of characters that dropped from sight. Uncle Tom felt an intimate concern for the characters in his tales.

THE JAY BIRD THAT HAD A FIGHT
WITH A RATTLESNAKE

IN a mort of old time tales, people and things, along with what they done, go in threes. From my foreparents I learned the tale about the jay bird, where things go in threes, learned it by heart and nary a word missed in the telling.

To start off, a jay bird and rattlesnake were having a fight in the woods when the king's son came through the woods a-hunting. The rattlesnake weren't putting up a fair fight, and it made the king's son mad—he hated snakes like poison anyhow—and he took out his sharp pocket knife and cut off the snake's head and left him there a-wiggling till sundown.

The jay bird told the king's son that all the other woods creatures had been gathered around to watch the fight, but they ran off in the underbrush when they saw the king's son a-coming through the woods.

The jay bird took the king's son on his back and flew around over the country to show him the sights. The first day he showed the king's son seven mountains and seven bens—I ain't no idea what a ben might be. When it came night, the jay bird lighted down to earth and said, "See that house yonder? My oldest sister lives there and she will make you welcome to stay all night. If she asks you about the battle with the rattlesnake, say you was there. And if she asks you did you see me say, yes, you did. And meet me right here in the morning."

It turned out the jay bird's oldest sister treated him mighty fine and made him freely welcome. She fixed him a good supper, and het up warm water to wash his feet and gave him a soft bed to his sides.

The next day the jay bird flew over the country and showed him seven mountains and seven bens different from the ones on the first day. When it came night, the jay bird lighted down to earth and said, "See that house yonder? My middle sister lives there, and she will make you welcome to stay all night. If she asks about the battle with the rattlesnake, say you was there. And if she asks did you see me, say, yes, you did. And meet me right here in the morning."

It turned out the jay bird's middle sister treated him mighty fine too and made him freely welcome. She fixed him a good supper and het up warm water to wash his feet and gave him a soft bed to his sides.

The third day the jay bird wasn't there at all. He had turned into a good-looking young man. "I am the jay bird," he told the king's son. "A mean old witch put me under a spell to be a jay bird. Go on a piece further till you come to my youngest sister's house and she will make you freely welcome. In the morning she will give you a budget of something and you take it and turn back. Stop to take the night at my middle sister's house and at my oldest sister's house like you done before. And now I got business of my own to tend to."

The king's son went on to the jay bird's youngest sister's house and she treated him every bit as good as his other sisters did. And in the morning she gave the king's son something tied up in a budget.

"Now don't you untie this budget," she told him, "till you get to where you want to stay."

The king's son took up his budget and turned back over the road he had traveled. He stayed of nights with the jay bird's sisters like he done before. When he come to a place where he thought he wanted most to be, he untied his budget; and a big castle with a fine big orchard all around it built itself right before his eyes and him not turning his hand to do any work on it. But it was a mighty bad place to put up a house, for a giant came along and said this was his country, and he aimed to kill the king's son for trespassing on his land. Then he bargained with the king's son that he would let him go if he would give the giant his first boy in seven years.

The king's son made promise, thinking surely to God he could find some way to get out of his bargain. He tied up his budget, and the big castle went out of sight. Then he traveled on a piece till he was in the country where he wanted the most to stay.

He untied his budget and the big castle with a fine big orchard all around it built itself right before his eyes. A mighty pretty girl come out of the castle, and the king's son married her, and they set up housekeeping and settled down to live there. They had a boy baby, and that made them mighty happy.

Then in seven years the giant came to claim their boy according to the promise the king's son gave the giant seven years before. To keep their boy safe they dressed the cook's boy up in fine clothes and gave him to the giant, making like it was their own boy. The giant traveled a piece and then he stopped and asked the boy some questions to try him out. The boy gave it away that he was the cook's boy, and the giant took him right back home to the cook.

After that the king's son dressed up the butler's boy in fine clothes and gave him to the giant, making like it was his own boy. The giant traveled a piece and then he stopped and asked the boy some questions to try him out. The boy gave it away that he was the butler's boy, and the giant took him right back home to the butler.

The third time the king's son had to give his own boy to the giant, and the giant went off with him. The giant raised the boy like he was his own. When he was growed to be a man, the boy of the king's son wanted to marry the giant's girl. She was of a natural size and mighty pretty. She dressed fine, too, with a golden sash around her waist and a green shawl around her shoulders and a silver feather in her green hat.

The giant said the boy could marry her if he could do three big jobs of work. The first job of work was to clean out the cow lot where a hundred cows had been for seven years. The boy tried but it was too big a job of work. Then he heard sweet music, and the giant's girl came and worked magic, and got the job done before morning.

The next job was to patch a house roof with bird feathers of birds he had to catch and take no more than one feather from each bird before he let it go. The boy tried hard, but he couldn't catch so many birds. He heard sweet music, and the giant's girl came and worked magic and got the job done before morning.

The last job was to get bird's eggs from the top of a tree five hundred feet tall. The boy tried hard but he couldn't climb up to the bird nest. He heard sweet music, and the giant's girl came and worked magic and got the bird's eggs for him. But she lost one of her fingers up in the tree. "Look at that," she said. "Lost my finger up in the tree, climbing after bird's eggs. Well, anyhow, that way you can tell it's me."

They got married with all the ladies at the wedding dressed so's they looked like the bride. After the wedding, the giant said, "Now pick out the bride from amongst all these ladies." And the boy knowed her by the lost finger. "This is her," he said, and it was, for a fact. And the giant flew mad.

That night they had to get away from the giant, so they took the finest horse from the giant's stable. And they cut an apple up in three pieces. One piece they put at the head of their bed, another piece by the window, and the last piece outside the kitchen door. And they slipped off and left, riding the giant's fast horse.

The giant woke up in the night and aimed to kill them. "Have you gone to sleep yet?" he asked them.

"Not yet," said the piece of apple at the head of the new married couple's bed.

He went back to sleep and woke up again. "Have you gone to sleep?" he asked another time.

"Not yet," said the piece of apple by the window.

He went back to sleep and woke up again. "Have you gone to sleep?" he asked for the third time.

"Not yet," said the piece of apple outside the kitchen door.

Then he knowed the young folks had run off. He got up and put on his britches and took out after them on his next to the best horse.

The young folks saw him coming way off; and the girl, riding behind her man, took a twig out of her apron pocket and dropped it behind her. It turned into thirty miles of thick woods that the giant couldn't ride through.

He went back home and got his chopping ax and chopped

him a path through the thick woods. Then, being stingy, he took the chopping ax back home, lest somebody steal it or even use it. And the young folks got ahead of him.

When they could see him coming, the girl took a little round rock out of her apron pocket and dropped it in the road behind her. In a minute it turned into twenty miles of rocky mountains that the giant couldn't ride through. He went back home and got a pick ax and made a way to travel through the rocky mountains. Then, being stingy, he took the pick ax back home, lest somebody steal it or even use it. And the young folks got ahead again.

When they could see him coming again, the girl shook a drop of dew off a leaf into the road behind them, and it turned into ten miles of deep water the giant couldn't swim through. He tried to anyhow, and he sunk down under the water and drownded.

Then the boy wanted to go see his folks that he hadn't seen since he was seven years old. His bride, the giant's girl, said, "I'll just wait here by the spring, and you come back and get me so's I can visit with your folks, too. But don't let anybody kiss you or you will forget all about me."

His folks didn't know him at first and never done no kissing. But his old dog knowed him from the first and run to meet him way down the road and jumped up on him and lapped and licked—and that passed for kissing—and the boy forgot all about the giant's girl waiting for him by the spring.

The girl got afraid and climbed up a tree by the spring and sat there in the tree looking down at the spring.

Not a far piece from the spring where the giant's girl was waiting, a shoemaker had his house. He got thirsty for a drink of water, but the water bucket was plumb dry. So's he told his old woman to go to the spring and tote a bucket of cool water so's he could have a good drink.

When the shoemaker's old woman bent over to dip her bucket in the spring, she saw the pretty face of the giant's girl up in the tree looking down. But the shoemaker's old woman thought it was her own face in the smooth water of the spring that made a looking glass. "Well, I never knowed I was that good-looking," she said to herself. "And young-looking too. And me doing slavish work, toting buckets of water for an ugly old shoemaker. I won't do it no more. I aim to hold up my pride." And she left the bucket by the spring and went back to the house and sat down in the rocking chair and took her rest like she figured a good-looking and young-looking woman like she thought she was had a born right to do.

The shoemaker was still thirsty for a cool drink of water, and he told his girl to go to the spring and tote a bucket of water so's he could have a cool drink. When the shoemaker's girl bent over to dip the bucket in the spring, she saw the pretty face of the giant's girl up in the tree looking down. But the shoemaker's girl thought it was her own face in the smooth water of the spring that made a looking glass. "Well, I never knowed I was that good-looking," she said to herself. "And me doing slavish work, toting buckets of water for an ugly old shoemaker. I won't do it no more. I aim to hold up my pride and fix myself prettier so's I can marry me a king's son or some other man rich and high up in the world."

By this time the shoemaker was nigh about starved for a cool drink of water. He never quarreled with his womenfolks, but he just went to the spring to get him a cool drink and tote a bucket of water. When he bent over to dip his bucket in the spring he saw a pretty girl's face in the looking glass of the smooth water. But he knowed it weren't his own face. And he looked up in the tree and found the giant's girl that had been hiding up in the tree all this time and looking down.

The shoemaker told her to come on down and not be scared, for he wouldn't let nothing hurt her. And he took her to his house with him when he went back toting his bucket of water. And she made herself handy around the house while his old woman and his girl rocked in a rocking chair and fixed to catch a king's son or some other man rich and high up in the world.

One day two men that were gentles came to the shoemaker's house to get him to make some shoes for the king's son in their country. They never paid no mind to the shoemaker's girl, but the giant's girl was so pretty they wanted to marry her, and they told the shoemaker—each of them made his own separate bargain—that they would give two hundred dollars if they could marry the pretty girl that was staying at his house. But the girl said, no, she wouldn't marry them at all, not even for a heap of money. She didn't want to marry nobody, for she was married already to a king's son, but she never told nobody her secret.

The shoemaker sent word when he had the shoes ready for the king's son, and two different men came to get the shoes for the king's son. The giant's girl begged them to let her go back with them, just so she could see what a king's son looked like. And they said she was so pretty she could go anywhere she had a mind to with them. And, if she didn't favor the way the king's son looked, they'd be more'n glad to marry her.

When they got to the king's castle, the king's son still didn't remember the giant's girl that he married some time back. He was fixing to marry some other girl not noways as pretty as the giant's girl. But he asked the giant's girl would she sit down and eat supper with him, for he could see mighty plain that she was a sight prettier than the girl he was fixing to marry. They sat down to eat supper, and three silver pigeons perched themselves on the back of the chair the king's son was sitting in, and they told him a heap of things he had plumb forgot. And he remembered the giant's daughter and knowed who it was setting there eating supper with him and looking so pretty. And he wanted to stay married to her. And he took the giant's girl to the king and told him how things was, and the king married off the other girl to one of the men that went to the shoemaker's to get the shoes for the king's son. And the king's son stayed married to the giant's girl, and they lived together many a year.

THE THREE GIRLS WITH THE
JOURNEY-CAKES

LET me get you a cool drink of spring water. Then you sit
here on the porch and rest from climbing the mountain.

While you are a-resting, I aim to norate two tales matched
up in pairs that come from way back in the generations of my
family. My grandpap loved to tell "The Three Girls with the
Journey-Cakes," and my granny would tell "The Three Boys
with the Journey-Cakes" soon as he finished up telling. In my
mind, them two old time tales always been together. I can't
no ways think about them separate.

A widow woman that could make good journey-cakes had
three girls. Be they pretty or ugly, I don't recollect. Anyhow,
they lived at home till they got to be women grown and
thought they could make their own way in the wide world.

The oldest girl said one day, "I aim to go out in the wide
world to seek my fortune. Could you fix me a snack to eat
on the journey to wherever I aim to go to?"

Her mammy baked two journey-cakes. "You can have your
rathers," she said to the oldest girl. "Will you take the biggest
journey-cake with my curses or the least journey-cake with
my blessings?"

"I aim to take the biggest journey-cake," was what the
oldest girl said she wanted. And she wrapped it up in her
Sunday best plaid shawl—blue and red and yellow it was—and
set out on her long journey. Whenever it was time to eat,
the birds and the other woods creatures gathered round where
she sat down under some trees to eat. They asked polite as
you please would she give them a crumb, maybe two. "No,"
she said, "I won't give you none. I ain't got hardly a-plenty
for my own self." So she kept all her fine big journey-cake for
herself, and the birds and the other woods creatures went
hungry.

She traveled on till she come to a house where she hired

herself out to watch by the side of a dead man of a night, so his sister that had waited on him till he died could get some sleep. Her wages were named to her—a peck of gold and a peck of silver and a bottle of liniment that would even cure a dead person.

All through the daytime she slept in a soft bed with a silk coverlet spread over her. When night came on, she sat down by the dead man to watch. She went to sleep on the job, and the dead man's sister hit her over the head and killed her, throwed her out in the high weeds and grass in the meadow.

Time passed by and the oldest girl didn't come home to the widow woman's house. So the middle girl said, "I aim to go out in the wide world to seek my fortune. Could you fix me a snack to eat on the journey to wherever I aim to go to?"

Her mammy baked two journey-cakes. "You can have your rathers," she said to the middle girl. "Will you take the biggest journey-cake with my curses or the least journey-cake with my blessings?"

"I aim to take the biggest journey-cake," was what the middle girl said she wanted. And she wrapped it up in her Sunday best plaid shawl—all green and blue it was—and set out on her long journey. Whenever it was time to eat, the birds and the other woods creatures gathered round where she sat down under some trees to eat. They asked polite as you please would she give them a crumb, maybe two. "No," she said, "I won't give you none. I ain't got hardly a-plenty for my own self." So she kept all her fine big journey-cake for herself, and the birds and the other woods creatures went hungry.

She traveled on till she came to a house where she hired herself out to watch by the side of a dead man of a night so his sister that had waited on him till he died could get some sleep. Her wages were named to her—a peck of gold and a peck of silver and a bottle of liniment that would even cure a dead person.

All through the day she slept in a soft bed with a silk coverlet over her. When night came on, she sat down by the dead man to watch. She went to sleep and the dead man's sister hit her over the head and killed her, throwed her out in the high weeds and grass in the meadow.

Time passed by and the middle girl didn't come home to the widow woman's house. The widow woman got worried and cried some when she lost two of her girls out in the wide world. The least girl was gentle-natured and she said, "Please, mammy, hush up your crying, and I'll go and look for your two girls that's lost. And I'd be much obliged if you would fix me a little snack to eat along the way on my journey out in the wide world."

Her mammy baked two journey-cakes—a big one and a little bitty one with the scrapings of the dough. "You can have your rathers," she said to the least girl. "Will you take the biggest journey-cake with my curses or the little bitty journey-cake with my blessings?"

"I wouldn't set out on no journey without your blessing," the least girl said. "And the little bitty journey-cake will be plenty big for me."

She wrapped the little bitty journey-cake in her second best old gray shawl and set out on her journey—no telling how long.

When it was time to eat, she called the birds and the other woods creatures about her before she unwrapped her journey-cake and sat down to eat. "Won't you have some?" she said and passed it around till she had no more than a crumb or two left for her own self. Then she got up and walked on, and the birds and other woods creatures went along with her, though they kept hid in the edge of the woods and didn't show themselves on the public road with the least girl.

It turned out that she hired herself to do the same job her sisters had tried their luck with. Her wages were named to her—a peck of gold and a peck of silver and a bottle of liniment that would even cure a dead person.

All through the day she slept in a soft bed with a silk

coverlet spread over her. When night come on, she sat down by the dead man to watch. The little birds—the night birds—sat outside the window and kept her awake. After a time the dead man rose up in the bed. "If you don't lay down and stay dead, I aim to hit you with this strap," she said. And he laid back down. Time passed and the dead man rose up again. The least girl hit him with a strap and made him lay down dead. Three times he rose up and the last time he jumped out of bed, and she took out after him.

The woods creatures that were big enough carried her on their backs fast as the wind through the woods. The little birds whirled about the dead man's head and the little woods creatures got under his feet and tripped him up so's he got left behind, and after a time he gave up and laid down and stayed dead. And the least girl went back to his sister's house and collected her wages—a peck of gold and a peck of silver and a bottle of liniment that would cure even a dead person.

She hunted around in the high weeds and grass in the meadow till she found her sisters laying there dead. She rubbed the liniment on them till they come to life. Then they all three went home again, and the widow woman made them welcome and they lived off the least girl's wages—all their lives, I reckon. A peck of gold and a peck of silver would last a mighty long time if a person never spent lavish.

THE THREE BOYS WITH THE JOURNEY-CAKES

A KING had three girls that liked to go out a-walking. The king had cautioned them not to go too far a piece from home or no telling what might happen. They never paid him much mind. One day they found lots of pretty flowers in a far-off woods and they wandered about picking flowers till they got into the edge of the giant's country. And three giants stole the king's three girls and went off with them to someplace, no telling where.

The king hunted for his girls and he paid people wages to keep on hunting. Then a witch told him that couldn't nobody ever find his girls without they had a ship that would sail on land or sea. The king promised he would give one of his girls to marry any man who would furnish him with a ship that would sail on land or sea, so he could get his three girls back.

It turned out that a widow woman that could make good journey-cakes lived in the king's country with her three boys. Her oldest boy took it into his head to try to build a ship for the king that would sail on land or sea. It was a long journey to the edge of the ocean waters where he aimed to build his ship.

The widow woman baked two journey-cakes and cooked a chicken too. She said to her oldest boy, "You can have your rathers. Will you take the biggest journey-cake with my curses or the least cake with my blessing?"

The oldest boy said, "I aim to take the biggest journey-cake and the chicken too, for I got to go a long journey and do a hard job of work when I get there." And he put the journey-cake and the chicken in a big knapsack and started off from home. Whenever it was time to eat, the birds and other woods creatures gathered round where he sat under some trees to eat. They asked polite as you please would he give them a crumb, maybe two. "No," he said. "I won't give you none. I ain't got hardly a-plenty for my own self." So he kept all his fine big journey-cake for himself, and he kept all the chicken too, and the birds and the other woods creatures went hungry.

After so long a time he came to the woods by the edge of the ocean waters. He set to work to cut timber to build a ship that would sail on land or sea. But fast as he could chop down a tree, it straightened up and growed right back like it was when he started chopping. He couldn't make no headway cutting timber so he gave up and went back home. The middle boy tried his luck next. His mammy baked two journey-cakes and cooked a chicken too. She said to the middle boy, "You can have your rathers. Will you take the biggest journey-cake and my curses or the least cake with my blessings?"

The middle boy said, "I aim to take the biggest journey-cake and the chicken too; for I got to go a long journey and do a hard job of work when I get there." And he put the biggest journey-cake and the chicken in a big knapsack and started off from home. Whenever it was time to eat, the birds and other woods creatures gathered round where he sat under some trees to eat. They asked polite as you please would he give them a crumb, maybe two. "No," he said, "I won't give you none. I ain't got hardly a-plenty for my own self." So he kept all his fine big journey-cake for himself and he kept all the chicken too and the birds and the other woods creatures went hungry.

After so long a time he came to the woods by the edge of the ocean waters. He set to work to cut timber to build a ship that would sail on land or sea. But fast as he could chop down a tree it straightened up and growed right back like it was when he started chopping. He couldn't make no headway cutting timber so he gave up and went back home.

Then it was the youngest boy's turn. His mammy baked two journey-cakes but he wouldn't let her kill no chicken. "Give me the least journey-cake," he said without her asking him what was his rathers. "It will be a-plenty if you give me your blessings to tote along with me to keep me safe on this journey." He never bothered with no knapsack, for the least journey-cake would go in his pocket. He told his mammy and the other boys good-bye and whistled to call up his dog and went off down the road.

Whenever it was time to eat, he sat down under some trees and his dog came sniffing his pockets. The birds and other woods creatures gathered round. They never had to ask

for a bite or crumb. "Come and get your share of this journey-cake," he said and every last one of them got as much as
he had, maybe more. And the journey-cake got bigger till
there was a-plenty for the last one of them, even an old woman
that come along while he was dividing out the journey-cake
amongst his dog and the birds and other woods creatures.
After the journey-cake was all gone, he got up and went
along the road again, his dog following after. The old woman
faded back into the woods, and the birds and other woods
creatures went out of sight.

After a time, not so long, neither, he came to the woods
by the edge of the ocean waters. He took his chopping ax
and started to cut timber to build a ship that would sail on
land or sea. The old woman came and sat down on the first
tree he chopped down. She told him to go back home and
stay a year and a day and be a help to his mammy and then to
come again to this place where he had chopped down a tree
by the edge of the ocean waters.

I don't know the details and particulars of how he got
home again nor what he done there in a year and a day nor
how he got back to the edge of the ocean waters. Anyhow—in
a year and a day he went back to the place where he had
chopped down a tree. There was the ship already floating on
the ocean waters, waiting for him to come. No sign of the
old woman, but the ship had some men on it to sail the ship
for him and they sailed away over land or sea—it never made
no difference which.

They sailed along and they saw some curious sights. One
was a man drinking up all the water in a big river. He stopped
and went along with them on the ship that would sail on land
or sea. Another place they saw a man eating up all the meat
of a big herd of cattle. And he went on their ship too. Then
they saw a man with his ear to the ground to hear all the news
of the world before anybody else knowed it. He went on their
ship too.

After that they came to the land that belonged to the

giants that stole the king's three girls when they went a-walking a far piece from home.

The widow woman's youngest boy bargained with the giants to give back the king's three girls. The first giant said, "I'll give back the girl I stole if anybody can drink as much water as I can." The man that was drinking up a river when the youngest boy's ship came along set out to drink with the giant. When the man was still thirsty, the giant bust wide open with all the water he drank and the girl he had stole was set free.

The second giant said he wanted to see somebody eat as much meat as he could. And the man that was eating up a herd of cattle beat the giant and the king's second girl was set free.

Then the last giant said he wouldn't give up the girl he had stole unless somebody could tell him what was going on yon side of the wide ocean waters. The man with his ear to the ground just leaned down a little closer and then he told the last giant the news from yon side the wide ocean waters and the last giant had to give up the king's girl that he had stole.

The widow woman's youngest boy gathered all the girls on his ship and sailed over land and sea till they came to the king's country, and the king was mighty glad to get his girls back home, and he let the widow woman's youngest boy take his pick of the girls he brought back safe from the giants. And the youngest boy picked the youngest girl to marry. And I don't know what took place after that.

THE GIRL THAT MARRIED A FLOP-EARED
HOUND-DOG

THAT old flop-eared hound-dog laying there on the hearth with his head to the fire 'minds me of a tale my foreparents used to tell of evenings gathered about the hearth. While we wait for Suzanne to call supper, I aim to tell you the old time tale called "The Girl That Married a Flop-Eared Hound-Dog." Musta looked pine-blank like that old hound-dog laying right there by the fire.

They was a man—a king maybe—that had a fine castle and lands that stretched from here to yonder. His wife died and left him all lonesome. One day when he was out in the woods, not hunting but just walking around nearly about to lonesome to death, a fine hound-dog with long flop-ears come up to him wagging its tail and acting friendly. The king thought maybe it had got lost from some folks hunting in his woods. So he sat down on a log and called the dog up to him and said to it, "What you doing here, flop-eared hound-dog? How come you got lost from hunting? What you want me to do for you?"

He never thought a breath about no answer. He was just making friends with a good hunting dog. But the flop-eared hound-dog set itself down in front of him and said, "I want to marry one of your girls; that's what I want and I can take good care of her and keep her happy if she's a-mind to have me."

Well, the king was so addled in his mind with hearing a hound-dog speak out that way that he said, "Come along home with me, and I'll let you ask one of my girls will she marry you, and I'm willing if she is."

The flop-eared hound-dog asked the oldest girl first would she marry him. She flew mad and screeched and screamed, "No I won't marry no flop-eared hound-dog! I won't marry nothing but a natural man! Who ever heard tell of such an idea!"

Then the flop-eared hound-dog asked the middle girl would she marry him. And she had a bigger fit than the oldest girl done had. And she wouldn't marry him neither.

When he asked the youngest girl would she marry him, she said she would if she could come back home now and again to see her folks. She never 'peared to feel no shame about who she was marrying but asked a big passel of folks to the wedding just like she was going to marry a natural man. And she fixed a heap of fine wedding clothes.

Then the very minute of the wedding ceremony when the sisters had their eyes covered up with their hands, for they couldn't bear to see a flop-eared hound-dog stand up and marry their sister in front of a whole crowd of folks that never had no hint that she weren't marrying a natural man— well, that very minute the groom came in, and it weren't no flop-eared hound-dog no more but a good-looking young man dressed up in his Sunday clothes. A mean old witch had put him under a spell till some nice girl was willing to marry him of her own free will. He was so good-looking and rich that the oldest girl and the middle girl turned mighty jealous. And folks said it was the best wedding they been to that season.

After the wedding frolic was over, the bride and groom went to their fine home in some place a far piece off. I don't know where it was nor no more about it. It was just a fine big house and they lived happy together.

Then in a year and a day the girl hankered to go see her folks, and she wanted to stay there till she birthed her baby. Her man was willing for her to go on a visit to her folks, but he cautioned her not to tell his name to nobody even if they begged mighty hard. If she told that his name was Sunshine on the Dew, she wouldn't never see him no more.

Well, she had the baby at her old home place, and it was a mighty pretty boy baby. When it was two days old, in the night folks heard fairy music; and in the morning the baby was gone. Whoever had stole the baby left sweet cakes and wine at the head of the bed. But no trace of the baby.

The sisters blamed the baby's daddy and they tried to find out what his name was—but the youngest girl shut her mouth up tight and wouldn't tell. Her man came in a month's time and took her home with him.

Another year and a day passed by and the youngest girl

hankered to visit her folks again and stay till she birthed her baby. Her man cautioned her again not to tell his name to nobody or she wouldn't see him no more. When the second baby—a girl this time—was two days old, they was fairy music in the night. And the baby gone—nobody could guess where. Whoever had stole this baby had put sweet cakes and wine at the head of the bed like the time before.

The sisters blamed the baby's daddy again and tried to find out his name. But the youngest girl shut up her mouth tight and wouldn't tell. In a month's time her man come and took her back home with him.

Three times the youngest girl went home to visit her folks and stayed till she had birthed her baby—the last one another boy. Three times her man cautioned her not to tell his name or she wouldn't see him no more. But the sisters threatened her with her life if she wouldn't tell. So she said in a low whisper that his name was Sunshine on the Dew.

When the last baby was two days old the fairy music in the night came again. And the next morning—no baby—no sweet cakes nor wine at the head of the bed neither. And no man come to take her home with him no matter how long she waited.

After she waited some months for her man to come and he never showed up, she set out on foot to go to her married home. Nobody home when she got there. No sign of nobody. So she set out to travel till she found her man. She traveled all day till she had holes in her shoes. At nighttime she saw a little house in the woods. The door stood open and a fire was blazing in the fireplace. An old woman in a rocking chair by the hearth made her welcome. She said her man with three babies different sizes had been there three nights before. The old woman gave her a good supper and warm water to wash herself and a soft bed to her sides. In the morning she gave the girl some scissors that she said would cut by themselves whatever the girl wanted her cloth to be.

The second night at the same kind of little house an old

woman made her welcome and said her man with three babies different sizes had been there two nights before. This old woman gave her a good supper and warm water to wash herself and a soft bed to her sides. In the morning she gave the girl a thimble that would sew by itself.

The last night another old woman in a little house made the girl welcome and told her her man with three babies different sizes had been there just the night before. The girl wouldn't stay for no supper nor no warm water to wash herself nor no soft bed to her sides. She wanted to hurry on and try to catch up with her man. The old woman tied up a snack to eat in a budget and gave it to the girl along with a needle that would sew fine things by itself.

The girl went on till she came to a fine big house with a crowd of folks gathered about. It was her man fixing to marry again. But the girl swapped her magic sewing tools that could cut and sew fine things without no help from any person. She swapped them things to the other girl to give back her man to her. I don't call to mind the details and particulars of how it come about—but when the man that had been a flop-eared hound-dog saw his first woman, it all come over him again how he loved her with all his heart; and he gave the fine new house to the woman he wasn't going to marry, and took his babies three different sizes and the girl that had birthed him the babies and they went back to their own home place to live out all the days of their life.

THE SNAKE PRINCESS

You and Suzanne been talking woman talk till I ain't told you no tale this time. While Suzanne's gone to the spring, I'll tell you a tale about a rich sailor's boy. It's called "The Snake Princess."

A rich sailor had a ship full of goods to sell in far-off lands.

He hated to sail off across the ocean waters and leave his little, bitty baby, but he had it to do. He got in his ship and sailed away. A big wind made his ship sink and all his goods in it. He somehow got to land in a place where some little black men lived. He talked to the little black men and told them how he was poor now because his ship full of rich goods had sunk in the ocean waters, and he was a far piece from home.

The little black men said, "We can help you get home and make you rich again, but we got to be paid back. We'll do it if you will give us the first thing that rubs against you after you get home."

The sailor thought about his little dog that always rubbed against his legs when he got home. His little, bitty baby never entered his head in that connection, for it weren't big enough to walk or even crawl when he left home. I reckon he forgot how long he'd been gone from home.

"I hate to give up my pet dog," he said to the little black men, and they just grinned. "But it's a mighty good trade, and I promise."

The little black men wished him at home and he was there. His little bitty baby had got big enough to crawl and pull itself up to hold onto things. It rubbed against his legs, crawling, and pulled up, holding to his britches legs. He fainted dead away when the knowledge came over him of the meaning of his promise to the little black men. He came to after a bit, but he never could get the worry off of his mind.

And, besides, the little black men had promised he would have money, and he hadn't found any money yet, though he had hunted all over the place. After a time, he did find a pile of money when he was rummaging up in the loft of his home. He got richer, but he got a more worried mind too—thinking how he had promised away his boy to the little black men.

The boy got to be twelve years old and big enough to take notice how peaked and pale his daddy looked. He asked questions till the sailor had to tell him his secret worries.

The sailor's boy said, "Well, I reckon you got to keep your

promise to the little black men. They kept their side of the bargain, and you always did deal honest up to now."

The sailor sent word to the little black men, "I'm ready to keep my promise I made." And he named the day they could come get his boy.

One little black man came in a boat to get the sailor's boy. The sailor looked at the boat and he said, "You oughta have a big ship to sail the ocean waters. That little old boat won't never make it."

The little black man made him no answer. He took the sailor's boy into the little old boat and started off. The sailor stood on the bank and watched. Just like he thought, the little old boat couldn't make it through the ocean waters. It turned over, and the little black man and the sailor's boy fell in the water.

The sailor turned his back. "I can't bear to watch," he said to himself. And he died from grieving there on the banks of the ocean waters.

The little old boat turned right side upwards again, but with only the sailor's boy in it. It floated to a big, high castle and the sailor's boy got out of the boat and went into the castle. Nobody in sight and the rooms all empty—no beds nor chairs, no cook stove, no nothing. All he could ever find in the castle was a big snake coiled up in the main room of the castle.

The big snake was by rights a girl that was witched. The snake raised up its head and talked to the sailor's boy. "I waited twelve years," it said, "and I'm mighty proud to see you. I'm mighty tired of being a snake, and I aim to tell you how you can help me get turned back into a girl."

The sailor's boy said he was right willing to hear.

"You have to watch three nights in the castle," the snake girl told him. "The little black men will come and torment you and try their best to make you talk. Don't dare to say even one word no matter what they do to you, and that will break the charm and lift the spell on me, and I'll be a girl again."

Three long, dark nights the sailor's boy watched. It's untelling how the little black men tormented him, but not even one word would the sailor boy say, no matter what. The last night he died toward morning, but not even one word. The charm broke and the spell lifted and the snake turned into a pretty girl—a princess she was, the princess of the Golden Mountain.

First thing after she turned into a girl, she worked with the sailor's boy till she brought him to life again. They just naturally got married to each other. Then all the housekeeping things came back into their castle, and they ruled over the Golden Mountain.

After nine years the sailor's boy got homesick. He had no way of knowing his daddy had died. Maybe had other kinfolks back there. Anyhow he said, "I'm lonesome to see the old homeplace. I wish I could go for a little visit with my folks."

The snake princess said, "You can do it easy as not with my wishing ring that I aim to let you borrow." She took off her wishing ring and put it on his finger. "Now, just so you don't wish me away from my castle on Golden Mountain. Don't ever do that."

He promised he wouldn't, and he turned the ring around on his finger and wished himself back at his old homeplace. No more than said till he was there.

He told his kinfolks and neighbors about what happened in the nine years he'd been gone. They couldn't believe it weren't some fixed up tale. He had on old clothes and he didn't look like a rich man that was married to the princess of the Golden Mountain.

The sailor's boy got all out of patience. "I wish my princess was here, and I'd prove it to you that I'm telling the God's truth." In a minute she was there and that proved he was telling the true facts. But it broke his promise not to wish her away from her castle on the Golden Mountain.

They sat by the shores of the ocean waters and the snake princess wept and cried. She soothed him to sleep with his head in her lap, and then she took her wishing ring and wished herself back to her castle on the Golden Mountain.

No sign of her when he woke up, and he had no idea how to get back to her castle on the Golden Mountain. He just wandered about over the world till he came to where three giants were quarreling over their inheritance—three things: a pair of shoes that would take the person that wore them any place he wanted to go to, a sword that would kill anybody if the person that had the sword would say, "Everybody's head off but mine," and a cloak that would keep whoever wore it from being seen.

The giants were supposed to take one thing apiece, but each one of them wanted all three of the things. So they had been quarreling for years over their inheritance and making no use of the magic things at all.

They wanted the sailor's boy to help them divide things amongst them. He said, "I'll have to try them out first to see if they're all in good shape. It wouldn't do for one of you to be left with some old thing with the magic all wore off." They thought that sounded reasonable enough.

So he took the sword in his hand and felt of it. Then he put on the cloak and the giants couldn't see him nor their sword. They began to holler for him to come back. "I'm just trying out things like you wanted me to," he said. Then he took a good hold on the sword and said, "Everybody's head off but mine," and it chopped off the three giants' heads.

The sailor's boy kept the cloak and the sword for himself, and he put on the magic shoes and wished himself away to the castle on the Golden Mountain.

The snake princess was having a feast and she asked him to come in. He lived there after that, and he had more magic things than the snake princess had.

THE CABBAGE HEADS THAT WORKED MAGIC

OLD Mandy, that old mule you been riding, looks a mite like somebody I used to know, not naming no names. Puts me in mind of a tale about turning human people into donkeys. Just a tale I always knowed, don't recollect who told it to me way back in time.

It starts with a hunter being neighborly with an old woman he met up with when he was in the woods a-hunting. He helped her out somehow and she said, "Now I aim to do you a good turn to show my thanks."

She told him to go along through the woods till he came to nine birds fighting over an old cloak and about to tear it in pieces. She said for him to shoot amongst the birds and make them drop the cloak, and then for him to grab it, for it was a wishing cloak.

And then she said, "Pick up the dead bird and cut it open and swallow down the bird heart without chewing it up, and a piece of gold money will come under your pillow every night."

It worked out like she said. Every morning of the world a piece of gold money under his pillow. He saved up the gold money and got rich. He wanted to travel and see the wide world.

One day, a-traveling, he came to a castle with a pretty girl looking out of a high window. He couldn't see that an old witch woman was standing close behind her. Nor he couldn't know that the old witch woman told the pretty girl about the bird heart that made a piece of gold money come under his pillow every morning and about the wishing cloak.

The old witch woman made the pretty girl promise to get both of his magic things. They acted sociable with the rich hunter and gave him wine to drink. It had herbs in it that would put him to sleep and make him puke up the bird heart. When he puked up the bird heart in his sleep, the pretty girl washed it off good and then she swallowed it. After that, no more pieces of gold money under his pillow. It was under the pretty girl's pillow, but the old witch woman took it away from her.

After that, the pretty girl went on a far journey with him on purpose to trick him out of his wishing cloak. The old witch woman made her do it. She put on the cloak and wished herself back at her own castle, leaving him on a high mountain in a far country.

He rode down off of the high mountain on a big, thick cloud. He landed in a garden patch with big heads of cabbage. He liked raw cabbage, and he was hungry, so he ate a head of cabbage. It worked magic and turned him into a donkey. He wanted some more cabbage, but he ate it in a different part of the garden patch, and it worked magic to turn him back into a human person. That gave him an idea.

He gathered some heads of both kinds of cabbage and put it into a big poke. Then he went back to the pretty girl's castle. He took some juice of walnut hulls and made his face brown, so the old witch woman and the pretty girl wouldn't know who he was. He showed the old witch woman his fine cabbage heads. "I'm a fool about cabbage," she said and she bought some. He sold her donkey cabbage; and, soon as she ate a few bites, she turned into a donkey. Same thing happened to the cook at the castle.

He gave the pretty girl some donkey cabbage for a present, and she turned into a pretty young donkey. Then he had three donkeys. He drove two of them down the road, him riding the old witch woman donkey. He met a farmer and sold him the cook donkey and the old witch woman donkey. The old witch woman donkey acted contrary and wouldn't do no work, and the farmer beat her to death. I never heard tell what became of the cook donkey.

The hunter gave the pretty girl donkey some of the other magic cabbage that would change her back to a pretty girl. He made her give back his wishing cloak and he made her puke up his bird heart. He washed it off and swallowed it, and then he married the pretty girl. After that a piece of gold money would be under his pillow every morning, but the pretty girl would wake up first and get it and hide it. He let her do it, for he could use his magic cloak to wish his gold money away from her when he was a-mind to.

THE DONKEY THAT WAS A BOY

AND another olden tale about a donkey person has been told in the generations of my kin, way back to the old country across the ocean waters. I always knowed it, though it's been years since I sat down and norated it to anybody.

It's about a king and a queen that had waited a long time for a baby, a-wishing and a-hoping all the time that they'd have one. After the space of a good many years, the queen had a boy baby that looked like a donkey. Soon as she laid eyes on it, the queen fainted dead away, and she like to a-never come to. She wanted to throw the donkey baby away and be shut of it.

But the king was more tender-hearted. He said, "No, I aim to keep it, for it's a heap better than no baby at all. I aim to raise it like my true-born son and train it to be king after me and sit on my throne with a crown on its head. That's what I aim."

The queen said, "Folks will poke fun at our donkey boy on account of his looks, and they'll make this life a misery to him!"

"They won't dast do a thing like that," the king said. "I am the King, and I'll make a law to kill anybody that gives our donkey boy any hint that he is a donkey or anything funny about him. Folks have got to treat him like he was a natural human person. I'll see to that."

The king called all the people together and showed them the

baby that looked like a donkey. He said to all the big crowd of folks, "It is my true-born son, and I look for you to treat him according. I don't aim to say no more about it."

The crowd agreed with the king that was the right way to do and have faith things would work out for the best in the end.

From then on, nobody so much as hinted that anything was wrong with the king's son. The tale don't tell if they dressed him up in clothes for a boy or if they let him go bare in his donkey skin. Other ways, though, they treated him like he was a natural boy.

He loved music, and he wanted to learn to play on the harp. The king got a good musicianer to show him how. The king's son didn't know he was a donkey, so he learned to play on the harp. He would sit on his haunches and set the harp between his hind legs and let it lean back against his shoulder. Then he would pick the strings with his front hoofs. He got to be a fine harp player and seemed like he was right happy.

Then one day he chanced to look down in a well. The clear water in the bottom of the well was like a looking glass, and he saw that he was a donkey. It made him heartsick and ashamed to find out he didn't look like a natural human boy. He got his harp and left home.

He traveled a week, and that much traveling brought him to the gates of a castle. Nobody opened the gate for him, and he sat down and started to play on his harp. The gate keeper rushed off to tell the king of that country that a donkey was sitting at the front gate playing on a harp.

Everybody laughed at the gate keeper's big lie. Leastways, they figured it was a lie.

"Just you come to the front gate and see," he said to all the crowd around the castle. They came to the front gate, and there sat the donkey still playing on his harp. They opened the gate and asked him in. They took him to the king, and the king said he could eat supper with the serving men.

The donkey said, "Thank you kindly, no. I was raised to eat at the king's table."

The king let the donkey eat with him and his daughter, and the donkey ate dainty like a true-born prince. He stayed a long time at the king's castle, and he took to looking mighty sad. The king tried to find out what the donkey was sad about.

"Do you want some gold?" the king asked him.

"Thank you kindly, no," the donkey said.

"Do you want to go home?" The king thought that might be it.

"Thank you kindly, I'm not homesick," the donkey said.

"Do you want my daughter for a wife?" the king asked.

"Thank you kindly, yes. I would love to marry your daughter." And the donkey quit looking sad.

"I'm willing," the king said, "but I'll have to ask my daughter if she wants to."

The king's daughter said, yes, she loved the donkey—only she called him a prince, and never named the word donkey—and she wanted to marry him, for he had fine manners like a true-born prince, and he could play music on a harp.

They had a big wedding; and, after the wedding when the bride and her husband were by themselves, he found out he could take off his donkey skin. Ho took off his donkey skin and hung it over the foot of the bed. Then he was a fine looking young man and he loved his bride till morning.

The king thought his daughter would be sad with a donkey husband, but she looked happy as a lark. The king's serving man spied on them to see a donkey husband love his bride, but he saw the husband take off his donkey skin and be a natural man. He ran to tell the king, but the king thought 'twas a big lie the serving man fixed up.

The next night the king spied on his daughter with her husband, and the king found out his serving man had told the God's truth. The next morning, before the young folks woke up, the king slipped and grabbed the donkey skin and put it in the fire. It burned up, and after that the donkey husband stayed a natural man and was happy with the king's daughter.

I wish I knowed if he ever got lonesome and went back to his homeplace, and if the king that was his daddy ever got to see him a natural man. The tale don't tell.

THE PRINCESS THAT WORE A RABBIT-SKIN DRESS

MANY a time I've heard women sing to a baby about a rabbit skin to wrap the baby in. But I like the tale about a rabbit-skin dress better.

A king died right after his queen had a girl baby. She married again, and that king died. Then she married another time, and the last time she made a mighty bad choice. He was mean to her, and she pined away and died. After she died, that king wanted to marry the dead queen's daughter by her first king. His stepdaughter had sooner die than marry him and she was scared witless that he would compel her to do it.

Her little mare saw how worried the princess was and gave her good counsel on what to do.

"Ask him for a silver dress," the mare told her, "and tell him you won't answer till the dress is done. I'll get the fairies to bother the dressmakers and make the work slow."

It took a year and six months to make the silver dress, and then the princess said, "I won't tell you if I'll marry you till I have a golden dress." The mare told her to say that.

It took two years and six months to make the golden dress. Then the princess said, "I won't tell you if I'll marry you till I have a dress with diamonds and pearls." That was the mare's counsel too.

It took three years and six months to make the dress with diamonds and pearls. The princess said, "I'll tell you in the morning." Then she ran straight to the mare to find out what to do next.

The mare gave the princess a dress of rabbit skins patched together and told her to make her face brown with walnut juice. Then the mare said, "Now put your side saddle on my back and ride me off into the deep woods."

The princess minded what the mare told her to do. In the middle of the woods they lay down to sleep, and that was the last time the mare was heard tell of for a long time.

Some hunters with their hound-dogs came through the woods, and a prince was along with them. They found the girl in the rabbit-skin dress and took her along when they went back to the castle. They told the housekeeper to give her a job of work.

All the people that worked at the castle poked fun at her. They said, "She's a rabbit all but the ears. Why don't you grow you some long ears and be a rabbit all the way?" All manner of rude things they said to her.

One serving man tried to handle the princess in the rabbit-skin dress like he thought she was a public woman. She slapped him a-winding. That learned him she was modest and decent, and he better keep his hands to himself.

She had to do all the slavish work and sleep on a pallet behind the cook stove. One night, when the princess went outside to tend to nature before she went to bed, her little mare came to see her.

The mare told her the prince was going to have a play-party at another castle the next night. "I would love for you to go to the play-party," the mare said. "I will help you get dressed up to go, and you can put your side saddle on me and ride me there and back.

The next night the mare gave the princess a nut that opened up with the silver dress. She helped the princess pull off the rabbit-skin dress and fix up fine in the silver one.

The prince mirated over the princess but he couldn't find out who she was before she left the play-party.

The next night the mare brought her a nut that opened up with the golden dress. The prince still couldn't find out who she was before she left the play-party.

The last night the mare brought her a nut that opened up with the dress with diamonds and pearls. Though he still didn't know who she was, the prince put a golden ring on her finger when he danced a set with her. Then she ran off from him again.

She loved the golden finger ring and kept it on her finger when she put back on her old rabbit-skin dress. That was how the king could tell who she was when she took him some water in the morning to wash his hands and face. He asked her to marry him and she said, "I will and gladly," and ran back downstairs to dress up like a princess.

THE GIRL WITHOUT ANY HANDS

SOMETIMES maybe what a person dreams does have a meaning for them to follow—'minds me of a tale—

A king married again after his queen died, and he made a bad choice. The new queen had a head full of meanness to do to the king's boy and girl by the dead queen. Behind the king's back the stepmother queen treated them meaner and meaner till she done the worst she could do.

One day, when the king was off away from home, the step-mother queen poisoned the king's little pet dog. When he came home, she laid the blame on his girl. She had made the girl promise not to tell what happened to anybody christened with a name in the church.

The next time the king was off away from home, the step-mother queen killed his little boy and left him lay where the king would find him. When he came home, she laid the blame on his girl. This time, too, she had made the girl promise not to tell what happened to anybody christened in church.

The king said the girl would have to be punished for killing her brother. He sent a serving man into the woods with her and told him to cut off her hands and leave her in the woods and bring back her hands to the king. The serving man followed out the king's orders.

The king got a splinter in his foot and couldn't get it out. His foot festered up and got sore and all swole up. He put poultices on it, but that never done no good.

In the woods, the king's girl wandered about with her hands chopped off. The stumps of her arms made a great misery, and she was hungry, and she was scared of her life. She got so wore out that she dozed off to sleep and dreamed about the dead queen. In her dream, the dead queen told her to be good and say her prayers. In the morning, she said her prayers and washed herself at a spring. She was hungry but no breakfast she could lay her hand to.

A girl came to the spring eating bread and butter and got a bucket of water. The girl without any hands was up in a tree by the spring where she climbed to hide when she heard somebody coming. I can't see how she could climb a tree without any hands, but that's what the tale says.

The girl eating bread and butter stooped over to dip up her bucket of water and saw the image of the girl up in the tree showing in the water of the spring like a looking glass. She thought it was herself she saw in the spring. She thought to herself, "I am so pretty I ought to marry a prince. I won't pack water from the spring." She said that to the older woman that sent her to pack water. The old woman locked her up in a dark cellar and fed her nothing but bread and water. Two more girls acted like that when they saw the girl in the spring water and thought she was them. The old woman locked them up on bread and water.

The girl without any hands was still up in the tree when a good-looking prince came along. He stooped over to drink out of the spring and saw a pretty girl's picture in the spring, but he knowed it weren't his picture. So he looked up in the tree and found the girl without any hands. She couldn't tell him things, for she promised not to.

He pitied her poor arms and he loved her. He took her home to his castle and married her. They had a boy baby and before it was christened in the church the prince had to go off to war.

The girl without any hands had another dream about the dead queen, her mother. The dead queen told her about the king's sore foot with the splinter and told the girl what would cure it. The remedy was water from the spring where the prince found the girl without any hands. The dead queen told the girl to wash her arms in the spring. Washing her arms in the spring made her hands grow back on.

Then she took her baby and a bottle of the spring water and went to try and cure the king's foot. The king didn't know her because she had hands. She cured his foot washing it in spring water.

One day the prince rode by the king's castle going home from the war. He never had seen his wife with hands on, but he could tell it was her by the baby. She told the baby the tale about her chopped-off hands and all the stepmother queen's meanness. She could tell the baby because the prince went off to war before the baby was christened in the church. The king and the prince heard her tell and that straightened things out in their minds. They got rid of the stepmother queen in the worst way they could think of. Then they lived safe and happy in their castles.

THE BOY THAT WAS FOOLISH-WISE

WHAT I'm starting to tell now ain't much of a tale. Mostly it's just a pack of foolishness about a boy that hired out to a farmer and acted foolish-wise and outsmarted the farmer. The boy's two brothers had been hired out to the farmer for a year and a day, and they came back home all wore out and sick from slaving in the garden and corn patches—and no wages in their pockets. The farmer cheated them out of the last penny.

The boy that had stayed at home and worked around the place got mad. "I'll show that farmer," he said. "I'll collect your wages for you, and I'll outsmart him so he can't cheat me out of what will be owing."

He went and hired himself to the farmer, and he laid down a hard bargain. He said, "You'll have to pay me twenty pounds for a year's working, and some more things I want to set straight; it's a bargain that every time I won't do what I can do I lose a month's wages, and every time I'm stopped from doing what I was told to do you pay me an extra month's wages."

The farmer agreed, thinking all the time that he'd figure some way to get out of living up to what he promised.

The first day the boy worked, he never got much to eat. He stole a half a goose and made out to keep from starving.

The next day he had a scant bite for breakfast, so he called for his dinner and ate it right after his breakfast. He asked for his supper and ate that too, along with breakfast and dinner. Then he went out and asked the farmer, "What do you tell your work hands to do after supper?"

The farmer said, "I tell my work hands to go to bed after they eat their supper."

The boy went to bed and lay there all day, resting up from slaving the day before. The farmer found out he weren't working, and hunted and found him in the bed.

He made the boy get up out of the bed, and the boy collected an extra month's wages according to their bargain, for the farmer had told him to go to bed and then made him get up.

The day after that, the farmer told the boy to keep the old brindle cow out of the corn patches. There he sat all the morning minding Old Brindle, and keeping her out of the corn patches while the other cows and the sheep and hogs were tromping down the young corn.

The farmer saw how things were, and he hollered at the boy, "Leave Old Brindle be and chase them other critters out of the corn patches!"

The boy let Old Brindle alone for a while and chased the other critters out of the corn patches. He collected another extra month's wages for being stopped from doing what he had been told to do.

Another day the farmer told the boy to make a path across a swampy place. The boy said, "What made the path over the mountain?"

The farmer said, "Sheep's feet made the path over the mountain."

The boy sharpened his pocket knife and started to cut off the sheep's feet, saying, "I reckon sheep's feet made a path over the mountain, they can make a path across a swampy place. Reckon I'll just have to cut off all the sheep's feet and strow them along in the miry places, like filling up mudholes with rocks." The farmer made him stop, and that was another extra month's wages.

Things went on like that for some time, with the boy collecting an extra month's wages every day of his life. The farmer couldn't stand it no longer, and he told the boy he was fired. The boy said he wouldn't quit, but the farmer begged him to. After some time, the boy agreed to go home if the farmer would pay him the wages owing to his brothers. The farmer paid the brothers' wages, and then he said, "Now you are fired. You got to quit working for me and go home."

"There goes another extra months wages," the boy said. "You hired me to work for you, and now you're making me stop what you hired me to do."

And the farmer was bound to pay.

THE FARMER'S BOY THAT GOT EDUCATED

A FARMER'S boy got educated in books, and it ruined him for working on the farm. He felt like a man of high degree and above milking the cows and chopping up stove wood and doing such chores. He said, "I'll just leave the farm and live in a town and take my station in life."

So he took his books and a sword with him and went up to Edinburgh to live. He lived in a room in a woman's house and he hung his sword up on the wall and he read in his books like an educated man of high degree.

One day the woman said, "I wish you would leave for a while; I need to let some of my company sit in your room and talk to each other."

He said, "I can't do that, for I don't know the town. I'll just go to bed and be out of the way when your company sits and talks to each other." So he went to bed to read in his books.

Some tinkers came in and sat down to talk to each other. They talked about the Queen of Rome, and pretty soon the farmer's boy stopped reading in his books, for he wanted to listen. The tinkers had traveled the wide world and they had seen all the queens in all the countries. "The Queen of Rome is far and away the prettiest queen of all," they said, "and the lovingest." They talked on into the night about the Queen of Rome and the farmer's boy listened to every word they said. He fell deep in love with the Queen of Rome, just from listening to the tinkers talk about her. He couldn't think about nary thing but the Queen of Rome.

He took down sick, and the doctor said he was sick in love. He would be cured iffen he found the woman he was in love with. The doctor said, "And it ain't the Queen of Rome. She's too high above your station in life, and you just a farmer's boy come up to Edinburgh from the country."

The farmer's boy got mad at the doctor and sassed him back.

"I got educated," he told the doctor, "and I aim to be a man of high degree. And I am, too, in love with the Queen of Rome, and I aim to find her."

So the farmer's boy that got educated went to London. He left his books behind in Edinburgh, for he quit reading in his books after he got sick with the love of the Queen of Rome. He took his sword with him to London, though; he figured he might need it to fight with. And it turned out that-a-way.

Some soldiers came in after he went to bed and quarreled at him. They said he had to pay for liquor for them to drink. He said he would pay for a share but not all of the liquor. So they picked a fight with him, and he got his sword down off of the wall and cut off all the soldiers' heads and left them lay.

He got on a ship and said he wanted to go to Rome. The captain said that ship went to France, but that would be a piece of the way to Rome. So the farmer's boy stayed on the ship. Some soldiers got on the ship and wanted to kill him for cutting the heads off of the soldiers that quarreled at him in London. But the captain of the ship pushed the soldiers off of his ship into the ocean waters.

The farmer's boy got to France on the ship and traveled on to Rome somehow. The tale don't tell. In Rome he hired himself to the Emperor, and the king liked him for a work hand. When it was a year, he fixed to leave and the Emperor couldn't make him stay. He sent for his wife to beg the farmer's boy to stay, for she had coaxing ways.

It turned out she was the Queen of Rome that the tinkers talked about in Edinburgh till the farmer's boy fell in love with her. She fell in love with him and he stayed without being coaxed. They plotted how to get rid of the Emperor so they could marry. But he was right accommodating and died in a natural way. After they waited a decent time, the Queen of Rome married the farmer's boy that got educated, and she made him the ruler of Rome. And he put a crown on his head and said, "Now I am a man of high degree."

Got no use for any such a tale as that, throwing a slur on

farmers' boys getting educated. It stands to reason if getting educated ruins a person for work and sets him to hankering after the Queen of Rome, then he never were much good for work nor had much gumption before he ever seen inside a book.

THE BOY THAT WAS TRAINED TO BE A THIEF

A WIDOW woman had a boy that was idlesome and shifty. He wouldn't do a hand's turn, not even on an easy job of work. He just lay around the widow woman's house and ate up creation. She never had no easy time making a living for him. One day she said, "I do wish to goodness you would stir about and be something or other."

He lay around a week or more just thinking about what he would be. Then he said he would be a thief, for that seemed like the easiest way to make a good living.

The widow woman said, "Well, that ain't my choice, but if you aim to be a thief, I aim for you to be a good one."

So she hired the Master Thief to train her boy. He trained the widow woman's boy till he could steal from the Master Thief and not get caught at it. The Master Thief said the widow's boy was a good enough thief to get hanged.

For a time they practiced stealing together. Then the widow woman's boy tricked the Master Thief. He took all the gold and silver and cheese and hid out, and set the people to chasing after the Master Thief with big clubs and rocks. When he got back together with the Master Thief, he said, "I'll show you I'm an honest thief." And he divided up the gold and silver and cheese with the Master Thief, though if he gave the Master Thief an even share, I don't know.

After that the widow woman's boy practiced stealing without no partner. One day he met a boy going to a wedding with a young sheep for a present to the bride. He figured how he could steal the sheep easy.

He traveled up the road a piece ahead out of the boy's sight. Then he took off one of his shoes and left it in the middle of the road. The boy with the sheep came along, and he saw the shoe. He thought to himself, "One shoe won't do me no good without its mate. No, I won't bother to pick it up."

The widow woman's boy slipped back through the bushes along the road and got his shoe. He put it down again ahead of the boy and hid to watch. The boy with the sheep saw the shoe in the middle of the road and he thought to himself, "That's the mate to that shoe back down the road a piece. I'll just go back and get it and then I'll have me a pair of shoes."

He put the sheep down and went back down the road. The widow woman's boy stole the sheep and tied it out in the woods. He picked up his shoe and hid in the bushes to watch.

The boy came back up the road without finding the shoe, and he noticed his sheep was gone. He hunted around for it, and then went back home to get a goat for a present to the bride. Pretty soon the widow woman's boy saw him coming with a goat. He made a noise like a goat from where he was hid back in the woods.

The boy put down his goat, for he thought to himself, "Now, I'll get that goat in the woods and then I'll have two goats for a present to the bride. Two goats will be good as one sheep." Whenever he went back in the woods to catch the goat that weren't there, the widow woman's boy stole his goat and ran off home with it and the sheep he had already stole. The boy just gave up and went back home and stayed away from the wedding.

Another time the widow woman's boy coaxed the Master Thief into playing at hangings only he tricked the Master Thief and hung him dead. The Master Thief's wife thought the widow woman's boy was so clever that she wanted him to marry her, but he wouldn't. He just ran off and never even helped her to bury the Master Thief.

THE DEVIL FOR A HUSBAND

A PERSON'S got no business making a bad wish that they don't mean, for it might come true. You never can tell. It turned out that way with a woman that got mad at her daughter and made a bad wish. What I aim to tell is nothing but a tale, but such as that does happen.

In the olden tale about a bad wish that come true, a woman got mad at her daughter and said, "I wish you had the devil for a husband." She got over her mad spell and never gave her bad wish another thought.

A short time after that a strange gentleman came to their town. He said he was from a far country. He was tall and dark-complected and he was rich. Anybody could tell that from the fine clothes he wore—a long red silk cloak and other fine things. He always wore a stylish cap; nobody ever saw him bareheaded. Even in the house he wore his cap, though he had nice manners other ways. He called himself Ned.

The young folks liked him, for he could play music for their dances and play-parties, and he liked frolics and fritter-minded things. And he was agreeable to whatever they wanted to do.

The older folks had their misdoubts about him. They said, "I don't like that look in his eyes whenever he thinks nobody's watching him." They reminded each other, "He don't never go to church meeting. And he don't look like he ever done any work in his whole lifetime. Look at them white hands of his."

But the young folks liked him. One girl was in love with him, the daughter of the woman that got mad at the first of the tale and made a bad wish for her daughter. The woman was ugly and had a bad temper, but she was smart. She had her misdoubts about the gentleman courting her daughter, though she had forgot all about her bad wish. She had an idea his stylish cap might cover up horns.

Before the wedding she told her daughter to cover up all the openings to her room, even the keyhole and right after she was married to switch her husband good with a peach tree limb that had been prayed over in church.

The bride followed out her instructions right after the ceremony. Her husband took off his long red silk cloak, and she could see that he had horns and a tail. He shrunk up till he could go through the keyhole.

But he was no match for the woman. She had the mouth of a bottle, holding it to the keyhole. He crawled into the bottle, and the woman put the stopper in right quick. The devil kicked and screamed; then he made promises. But the woman wouldn't let him out. She buried him in the bottle deep in the ground on the highest mountain.

That got shut of the devil for a time, not just for the woman and her daughter that had the devil for a husband, but for the whole blessed world. With the devil out of the way there was a whole year of peace, and everybody was happy the wide world over.

Then some travelers rode over the highest mountain, digging for gold. And they found an old bottle with a black spider or some other bug inside. Leastways, it looked like a black bug to them. By rights it was the devil.

The devil begged to get out. He said he would give the travelers their dearest wish if they would let him out of the bottle. The travelers put no faith in a black bug in a bottle giving them their dearest wish, and they went off and left the bottle on the mountain.

One traveler got to studying about it, though, and he went back and picked up the bottle and put it in his pocket. After he got to the foot of the mountain, he took the bottle out of his pocket and he said, "My dearest wish would be to marry the princess, but she is bad off sick, and I don't know if she would have me anyhow."

The devil said, "I can cure the princess in an hour's time and make her want to marry you. But you will have to let me loose in the world first."

The traveler took out the stopper and the devil crawled out of the bottle. He got bigger till he was back to his old size, stylish cap and red silk cloak and all. He went with the traveler to the castle where the princess was bad off sick.

The devil made out like he was a fine doctor with new cures for the princess. The king and the traveler started to go in with him, but he said he would have to be with the princess by himself or his curses wouldn't work.

One hour passed by and the king and the traveler looked in where the princess lay. "She was a heap worse off than I thought for," the devil said. "It may take me three hours to get her cured." And he shut the door and left them outside. In three hours the girl would be dead. The devil was sure of that much. Then he would shrink himself up and get away before anybody could find out he didn't cure the princess. The devil couldn't cure the princess to save his life, for it was outside his nature to do any good in this wide world.

One more hour passed by, and the king and the traveler were getting bad worried. Then the woman whose daughter had married the devil came to see how the princess was, knowing she was bad off sick. The king and the traveler said the doctor was in the room with her, and she would be well in three hours.

"Where in this wide world did you meet up with such a fine doctor?" the woman wanted to know.

The traveler told her about the bottle he found on the highest mountain.

"You'll have to do something mighty quick," the woman said. "You got the devil himself doctoring the princess and he'll kill her before he's through. I don't think we could figure any way to catch him again, but we've got to scare him off."

She thought a minute about what to do to get rid of the devil the quickest. "Ring all the church bells," she told the king and the traveler. "He can't stand to hear church bells ring. It purely scares the life out of him."

All the church bells started to ring. The devil got so scared he opened the door to ask what was the matter, and run right into his mother-in-law. He just vanished away from there in a big hurry and left his fine red silk cloak behind. Some say he always wore a black cloak after that.

Anyhow, the princess got well and married the traveler. They tried to get shut of the fine red silk cloak but it wouldn't even burn up in the fire. The tale don't say how they ever managed to do away with what the devil left behind.

THE GOLDEN ARM

THE man that told me "The Golden Arm" never had much sleight at tale-telling. The way he told it the tale was whittled down to nearly no tale at all. I like for a tale-teller to linger on the telling and give the details and particulars. But I never did hear no better telling of the tale of "The Golden Arm," and I'm bound to tell it like it was told to me.

The way he told it, a man had a golden arm, born with it that way or not, he didn't say. The golden arm was a bother to him and a satisfaction too. The boys at school made fun of him for having a golden arm. And all his life long, folks tried to steal his golden arm, thinking they'd sell it for cash money. So he learned to keep his golden arm hid. He would wear long thick coat sleeves and on the golden hand a thick glove. When anybody found out about his golden arm, he would go off to some other place to live.

He found out he could cure sick folks with his golden arm just by touching his golden hand to their forehead. He never would take money for making sick folks well, though, for he felt like he never earned money with just a touch. Mostly he cured the ones that were too poor to have a doctor that charged cash money.

But he could not cure his own ailments with a touch from his golden hand. He had to let a doctor dose him. Towards the end of his time, he got bad sick. The doctor told him he couldn't live. Then he begged the doctor to bury him in secret, lest somebody find out about his golden arm and dig him up and steal it. He showed the doctor his golden arm and told him how it had been a bother to him and a satisfaction. He told the doctor it gave him the weak trembles to think about grave-robbers stealing his golden arm and leaving him go up to heaven one-sided on the Judgment Day.

The doctor promised to bury him in secret. He died, and the doctor buried him way back on the mountain, and nobody could ever know where. Then the doctor got to studying about it. He thought that solid gold arm must be worth a million dollars, melted down to make into money. He thought about it and he thought about it. After a time he dug up the corpse and cut off the golden arm and went home with it under his coat.

He hid it under the bed till he could get a chance to melt it down and sell it for a million dollars. That night a voice from under his bed kept saying, "I want my golden arm; I want my golden arm" till he went plumb crazy and never did have enough mind to doctor any more. He buried the golden arm back, but he stayed crazy to the end of his days and couldn't sleep for thinking he heard somebody saying all night long, "I want my golden arm; I want my golden arm."

FOUR | TOLD BY *Doc Roark*

TALES PICKED UP ALONG
WITH DOCTORING

Doc Roark

Doc Roark

It was from Nelt that I first heard of Doc Roark. "We just ain't had much dealings with regular doctors," Nelt said soon after the opening of the school at Gander. "They's been doctors in the towns ever since the railroads came into the mountains, but they ain't been over in the back country much. We ain't got much roads nor cash money for doctoring. But old Doc Roark he rides by whenever he gets around to it and doses them that needs it. He's a mighty good hand at doctoring stomach ailments and rheumatiz. Old Doc ain't no regular doctor, though. He just picked up doctoring, mostly by hisself.

"Mostly we just make out, a-doctoring ourselves with remedies made out of roots and herbs and such. Whenever a body's sick, all the kin and neighbors are willing to come and sit up all night to wait on the sick person or do nigh anything to help out.

"Old Doc says they ain't no use paying out good cash money for doctoring whenever it's something you can cure your

179

ownself. Granny always kept a nation of herbs on hand to
mollify different ailments. I bear in mind a lot of her ways of
homemade doctoring. One I favored was Granny's tonic made
out of sassafras roots in whiskey. She made everybody in the
family take a dram every morning in the spring of the year,
just to give them more get-up."

As late as the early thirties it was literally true that practi-
cally the only medical service available to the people in this
area was that of old Doc Roark, a native doctor, who rode
about the country on horseback, his saddle pockets stuffed
with drugs and other doctor's trappings. He proudly admitted that he had "mostly just picked up doctoring" by himself. He also admitted his lack of whole-hearted belief in the
existence of germs. "I ain't got much faith in germs" was his
way of putting it.

Old Doc never hurried, was never too busy to stop and talk
at places where there was no need for his professional services.
Seldom was he to be found at home, for his rounds of visiting "the puny and the bedfast" took him all over the country.
He spent the night at whatever house was near when darkness
came. Everywhere he was welcome.

Doc Roark wasted no money on bottles and other con-
tainers for medicine. He preferred pills and powders because
they were easier than liquids to carry around in his saddle
pockets. The pills he counted out into a little dish or cup at
the home of the patient. The separate doses of powders were
measured out on the tip of the blade of his pocket knife and
each dose folded carefully in a bit of Sears Roebuck Catalog
paper. A woman who heard about this when she visited the
school sent pill boxes, etc., for Doc's use. He gave them to
children for play-parties and continued to use catalog paper.

Because he covered such a wide area, it was often a long
time between Doc's visits. Then people resorted to home
remedies. These simple remedies were frequently recommended
to the teachers and many of the older people could recite a
whole catalog of them. One old mountain woman once said

to me, "Shore now, they's a sight of cash money and trouble folks could be saved a-doctoring themselves, iffen they was a-mind to and not so God-Almighty scared of being took before their time." But, when she was "bad-off" sick, she sent for Old Doc.

In school, I heard about Doc Roark before I even saw him. Mallie Ingle sang for the physiology class a song old Doc had taught her one time when she was sick, "The Ballad about a Body's Bones." Other children told me they had "heard tell of Old Doc Roark's big, thick doctor books." When some parents were dubious about pictures in the "healthy book" their children used at school, Old Doc set matters straight by saying, "I own up that a body's insides ain't no pretty sight, but a body gets a heap of respect from his insides from knowing how they act and do."

In appearance, Doc was a rather small old man of uncertain age. Some one who had known him all his life said in 1931, "Doc is way up in seventy, but he won't never own up to it." Doc kept his hair and beard dyed jet black. When age was mentioned, he claimed to be "not far from sixteen." His twin brother, who made no effort to remain youthful in appearance, was sometimes present with Doc, his grizzled hair and beard a remarkable contrast to Doc's. People laughed good-naturedly and "allowed Doc never fooled nobody but hisself."

When I was invited to the wedding supper for Doc's second marriage at the bride's home on Montgomery Creek, I met him for the first time. He showed me his big, thick doctor books and told me he had, more than forty years before, gone out to Louisville for only a few months "to pick up some regular doctoring." He told how he saw doctors "carve up dead folks to see how they looked inside and maybe figure out what ailed them." At another time I heard him tell of autopsies and operations to a larger audience. One women said it made her "sick enough to puke." Another, who enjoyed the recital, said, "It's as good as tales about ghost spirits and such."

On the evening of the wedding supper, Doc told me enough

local ghost and hant tales to make me pretty well acquainted
with supernatural inhabitants of Montgomery Creek.

Doc usually stopped at the school at Gander when his trips
brought him through that neighborhood. He came to chat with
the teachers and to ask whether anyone out in the "level
country" had sent any more "biled shirts and swallow-tail
coats." Early in the history of the school, friends outside the
mountains had sent in a package of clothing what Doc called
"biled shirts"—the kind that had stiff bosoms and that buttoned
down the back—and a "swallow-tail coat." We had wondered
at first what to do with such apparel, but Doc was delighted
to have them to wear as "a sign of my profession."

Along with his doctoring, Doc said that he had picked up
many old tales and other "old time things." He knew all the
folk remedies current in the area, and all sorts of superstitions,
beliefs, and practices that had to do with matters of health. He
said that he "never done no child-fetching," but he was well
versed in the lore of midwifery. His store of ballads was large,
though he could seldom be persuaded to sing except to please
some sick child.

His long repertoire of tales ran heavily to local legends,
ghosts—human and otherwise—"hanted" places, and "other
scary things to tell." He said he more often had been a listener
than a tale-teller. People often told tales, he said, when they
sat up nights with the sick. That custom was fading out in
the mountain country. He had no use for women who either
told or listened to what he called "blackguard tales." When
one of the tales he was telling me got to the point where he
considered it unfit for me to hear, he stopped right there and
explained why he was not finishing the story.

There was no use insisting, for once before, when I had
asked Doc a question about the three "public women" in the
community, he had refused to answer. "They's no reason why
a young girl, pure and good and natured to live decent ought
to know such things. It's none but them bold doctor persons
out in the level country would name such traffic to a lady."

So my collection of "tales picked up along with doctoring" contains nothing Doc Roark considered "not fitten to tell."

THE WATER OF LIFE

SOME tales I picked up along with doctoring; some I just always did know. This tale I learned from somebody I doctored years ago. Ain't heard it told in many a day. It's a tale about doctoring—in a manner of speaking.

A king lay dying. The doctor said the only thing that would cure the king was the Water of Life. He cautioned them that it was hard to find—half across the world, and a big risk to a person's life to try to get. The king's oldest son offered to go, but the king said he would rather die than have his son take such a risk to his life.

The oldest son started out anyhow. In the mountains he met a dwarf, a queer little hunched-up man. He made fun of the dwarf in a mean way, and it hurt the dwarf's feelings. The dwarf pulled the mountains together, so the king's oldest son couldn't get through but was hemmed in.

Same thing happened with the king's middle son.

When the youngest son met the dwarf, he took no notice of the dwarf's looks. He treated the dwarf like he would any other friendly man he chanced to meet a-traveling. He explained to the dwarf what he was looking for, and the dwarf said he would love to help him.

The dwarf gave him some bread and a sword. He told the king's youngest son he would come to a castle, and a touch with the sword would make the gate fly open. The bread was to feed two watch dogs by the gate, so they wouldn't bark at him or bite him. The dwarf said the Water of Life was running out of a spring at the castle. He cautioned that the gates locked shut at twelve midnight.

The castle gate opened to the touch of the sword. A

princess at the gate made the dogs keep still, so he didn't
need to use the dwarf's bread. The princess promised to
marry him. After he went home and got the king well, he
would come back to her castle. He sat there courting the
princess till the gate was about to shut at twelve midnight. It
went shut on his heels as he went through and mashed the back
of his heels. He had the Water of Life in a big bottle.

He met up with the dwarf on the way home. He tried
to give the dwarf's bread and his sword back to him. The
dwarf said for him to keep the bread and the sword, and they
would make him rich. He asked about his brothers; and, just
to accommodate him, the dwarf pushed back the mountains
and let them go.

Along the way, they met a good king in trouble. The
youngest boy used the dwarf's bread and his sword to help
the good king out of his trouble. He said he would pay the
youngest boy back some day.

The brothers were jealous because the youngest boy had
a bottle of the Water of Life that would cure the king. When
he was asleep, they stole his bottle with the Water of Life.
They put in its place a bottle with common spring water.

When they got home, the youngest boy gave the king his
bottle of water, not knowing what his brothers put in place
of his true bottle. The king worsened every time he took a
sup.

Then the brothers gave him water out of the bottle they
stole from the youngest son. The king got well like magic.
He thought the youngest son had tried to kill him. He told
a man to take the youngest son out and kill him, but the man
let him live if he would leave the country.

On his way the youngest son met wagon loads of gold
coming from the king he helped with the dwarf's bread and
sword. He said to take the gold on to the castle where he
used to live and give it to the king. The drivers of the wagon
loads of gold told the king the straight of things, and he

wished his youngest son was alive. He drove the brothers off from home.

The princess back at the castle where the youngest son got the Water of Life was waiting for him. She made a golden road for him to ride on. His oldest brother came along and saw the golden road to the castle. He thought it was too fine to ride on. He rode to the left side of the golden road. They wouldn't let him through the gate at the castle. The middle brother rode on the right side of the golden road. They wouldn't let him through the gate at the castle.

The youngest son rode right up the middle of the golden road. The gates at the castle swung wide, and he rode straight through to where the princess was waiting to marry him.

THE DOCTOR THAT ACTED A PARTNER WITH DEATH

WAY back, when I first started doctoring, an old granny-woman liked to torment me. One way she tried to torment me was with telling tales on doctors. One time she told a tale on a doctor that acted a partner with Death. It hurt my feelings then, though it wouldn't make one hair's difference to me now.

She said a man had twelve boys and gave them all pretty names. Then he had another boy. He couldn't think of any name for it. His wife couldn't think of any name for it. Thirteen was just too many boys to think up names for.

A skinny, old skeleton of a man stopped at their house one day. They showed him their new boy baby. He asked what was its name. They said maybe he could think up a name. He said, if they would let him name it, he would watch over it and help out in its trade or profession. They agreed to that.

The boy learned to be a doctor. He learned all about roots and herbs and such things as would mollify folks' ailments. The skinny, old skeleton of a man that named him was Death, but the boy didn't know that till he got to be a doctor.

Then Death made himself known to the young doctor. He said he wanted the doctor to act a partner with him. He said he would stand at the head of a sick person, and that would mean the sick person would get well. Other times he would stand at the feet, and that would mean the person would die. The doctor could see Death, but other people couldn't. Then the doctor could say if the sick person would get well or not. It would always turn out the way the doctor said. That way he would get rich and famous, for he would be called a doctor that never made a mistake. Everybody would want him to doctor them and would give him big pay.

The doctor agreed to that, and from then on acted a partner with Death. He got a fine reputation for he never made a mistake when he said whether he could cure a man or not. And he got rich.

One day he got to studying about it. He counted up and found out that Death always claimed half of the people he doctored. That seemed like too many. Maybe he would get to be more famous if he cured more people, or if he could pick what people he would cure. He made up his mind to fool Death.

The next time he was doctoring a person about to die, he put the sick person's head at the foot of the bed. That way he fooled Death into standing at her head. The doctor said she would get well, and she did. Death pardoned the doctor for cheating and told him not to do it again.

Then the king's daughter got sick and was about to die. The doctor wanted to cure her, and he fooled Death again. The king's daughter got well. But the devil in the shape of Death had all he could stand of the doctor cheating. Death pulled the doctor down into a cave under the earth. Then he blew out the light, and that ended the doctor.

DOCTORS AIN'T SMART AS THEY THINK THEY BE

THE same old granny-woman that told me the tale about the doctor that acted a partner with Death, said, "Doctors ain't smart as they think they be." To torment me, she told a tale that she said proved she was right.

She said three doctors had such good success curing people that they got prideful about what smart doctors they proved to be. They got ambitious to try out their luck with cutting and carving on folks they doctored. They thought they better practice first on each other.

They would cut off one doctor's hand, and carve out one doctor's stomach, and gouge out one doctor's eye. Then they would put all them things back and make them grow and work like always. They set to work on each other. They cut off one doctor's hand, and carved out one doctor's stomach, and gouged out one doctor's eye. Then they got to feeling dauncy, and thought they would have a night's sleep and finish up doctoring each other in the morning.

They put the things they had cut and carved from each other on a high shelf. They told their serving man not to let the cat get in. The cat got in anyhow and climbed up on the high shelf. What it found looked to it like the trimmings from butchering time, and it ate every bite of it.

The serving man found the cat on the high shelf and the things gone. He guessed the worst, and was afraid of his life. He had to put back what would match the things in the cat's stomach. He found a thief dead from hanging and chopped off his hand to match the one the cat had for its supper. He got a hog's stomach where a farmer had been butchering, but no eye.

Then he had an idea. The old cat made all his trouble, and she could furnish an eye. So he gouged out one of the cat's eyes. He put all the things he had collected on the high shelf. He killed the old cat, and then he left the country.

In the morning the doctors put back the hand and the eye and the stomach, and never did know the difference. The things healed up, but they never did work like always before. The thief's hand made that doctor steal, and the cat's eye made that doctor see in the dark, and the hog's stomach gave that doctor an appetite like a hog. But the doctors never did guess the truth. They thought their nature had just changed.

THE SNAKE DOCTOR

BEST I can recollect, an old woman from over on Betty's Troublesome told me the tale about the snake doctor. She had a heap of knowledge about different kinds of leaves good to use for teas and poultices and other kinds of remedies to doctor with. She always used to say, "They's healing in the leaves."

A man married a girl that he loved so much he couldn't bear to think about ever being parted from her. He promised her if she died before he did, he would be buried in the grave with her coffin, and not be parted from her, even in the grave.

Not a long time after the wedding, the wife took sick and died. The man held to his promise. At the burying, he had the neighbors, after they lowered the coffin into the grave, to lay him down beside it. They thought it was a foolish idea even to show his love. They laid him down, but they didn't shovel on the dirt.

They went off and left the grave open. They said that way the man could climb out whenever he changed his mind and decided to go on living. He said, "No, I'll just lay here and starve to death, and then you can shovel in the dirt on me."

Laying there in the grave beside his wife's coffin, he noticed a dead snake. It had been cut in two by the neighbors that dug the grave. While he watched, another snake came crawling up with some leaves in its mouth. It rubbed the leaves on the two cut ends of the dead snake. Then it put the pieces together and they stuck together and the dead snake came alive. The two snakes wiggled off together and left the leaves lying there by the grave.

That gave the man an idea for trying to bring his wife back to life. He opened up the coffin and rubbed her with the snake leaves, but it didn't work. Then he thought maybe it was because the leaves had been used once for a cure. So he set out to find fresh leaves of the same three kinds the snake doctor had used. He was a town man and never had knowledge before that about things in the woods and fields.

So it took him a while to search out leaves that were a match for the three kinds the snake doctor used. After a time, he found all three kinds and went back to his wife's grave. He rubbed her with the leaves and she came alive. He helped her out of the coffin and up out of the grave. He filled up the grave like any burying.

His wife said she couldn't bear to face the neighbors that had buried her. They would just ask too many questions about how it was to be dead and come back to life. So the man took her to live way off in a strange country. Anyhow, they started on their way to a strange country.

On the way, the wife fell in love with a king that lived in a castle. She stayed with him and left her first man to go on by himself. He never would bring anybody back to life after that. He went off and lived in a far country and kept it a secret what he learned from the snake doctor.

THE BOY THAT HAD A BEAR FOR
A DADDY

A TALLY—you know what I mean, a foreigner—over at one of the coal camps where I was doctoring an old man one time asked me if a human woman could have a baby by any kind of a beast. I said it weren't no ways possible, but he kept on talking about it and told a tale of that nature.

He said a human woman had a baby by a he-bear. The woman was about to get married to a natural man, but the he-bear sneaked in the night before the wedding and lay with her. She tried to fight him off, but she weren't no match for a bear. In the morning the he-bear drug her off to his cave, and nobody ever heard tell what became of her.

She had the baby in the bear's cave. The baby looked like a boy, but it had a bear's nature. It ate like a bear, never could get enough. It wouldn't let the woman wean it. Still sucking when she died when it was seven years old. Just suckled her to death, drained her life away. It was stout like a bear. A little boy, wanting stick horses to ride, it pulled up whole trees by the roots and straddled them for a stick horse. Temper like a bear too. One time the he-bear brought home two rabbits for the boy's supper. Made him mad, for he wanted more. He grabbed up a big oak tree by the roots and beat the he-bear to death.

After that, he had to travel the world and earn his living. First he hired out to a farmer. He said he would work hard for as much of the crop as he could tote off. That would pay his wages. The farmer thought that was a good bargain.

The bear's son worked hard and raised a fine crop, the best the farmer ever had. But, when it came time to collect his wages, the bear's son toted off the whole crop.

Next he hired himself to a blacksmith. He hit so hard with the hammer that he mashed the anvil deep down in the ground. The blacksmith fired him.

Then he undertook to dig a well. The man he was working for took his spite out on him and flung a big millstone down in the well to kill the bear's son.

He flung it right back up out of the well and said, "Don't be scratching gravel down on me." When he got the well dug and came up out of it, he found out the millstone had hit the man and killed him. So he had to leave the country.

After a time, he came to a castle where a princess was getting married. From that place in the tale on, the Tally talked so much blackguard talk and made such a nasty tale of all the rest of it that it weren't fitten to tell.

THE BLACKSMITH THAT TRIED DOCTORING

A scotchman told me this tale. I don't remember his name, but I doctored him for the flux. His uncle followed the blacksmithing trade, though he never tried doctoring.

The Scotchman said once they was a blacksmith that could fix plows and put a good sharp edge on a mowing blade and mend other work tools. But he never had learned how to shoe horses. Nobody ever had showed him how, and he couldn't figure it out by himself.

Then one day a stranger, passing through and driving a good team of horses, stopped at the blacksmith's shop and asked if he could borrow the forge and anvil and other work tools of the blacksmith to shoe his horses. That was what the blacksmith wanted to learn how to do, so he said the stranger could borrow whatever he needed to.

The stranger pumped the bellows and hammered on the anvil and got the shoes ready. Then he took the legs off of his horses at the knees. He nailed the shoes on the horses' hoofs and put the legs back on and drove off.

That looked easy to the blacksmith and he wanted to try it himself. He caught his own horse out in the pasture and tied it by his blacksmith shop so he could shoe it. He fixed the horseshoes. Then he chopped his horse's legs off at the knees and nailed the horseshoes on the hoofs. They wouldn't stick to the leg stumps, and they sure wouldn't grow back on. His horse died, and he drug it off into the woods. He said to himself, "Better luck next time when I've learned how better."

Another time the same stranger driving the same team of horses came passing through and wanted to borrow the blacksmith's forge and anvil. He pumped the forge and hammered on the anvil, working over two old hags. Then he took them out of the fire and dropped them in an old wooden tub of water the blacksmith used to temper things. When he lifted the old hags up out of the water, it turned out he had made them over into pretty, young girls. They got into the wagon with him, and he drove off.

The blacksmith watched, and he thought he had learned how. So he told his old hag of a mother-in-law. She wanted him to make her young and pretty. He tried his best, but it was a failure. His mother-in-law didn't die, but she looked uglier than ever before. She blamed him for her worsened looks and got meaner by the day. To get away from her, the blacksmith went on a trip.

When he was off from home, he saw the same stranger that had borrowed his forge and anvil work a cure on the king of the country where he was traveling. The stranger cut off the king's head and stirred the brains around with a silver tool of some kind. Then he put the head back on, and the king was cured and gave the stranger some gold money.

After that the blacksmith tried to cure the king of England. He stirred the brains and tried to make the head grow back on, but it wouldn't. The blacksmith was in a fix. When the people found out he had killed the king, he would be hung. The stranger that had let him watch the curing of a king took pity on the blacksmith. He finished up the bad job as best he could, and the king lived. The stranger said to the blacksmith,

"Now you stick to blacksmithing after this. Don't never try to be a doctor nor deal with magic."

The blacksmith never did try no more extras again. But he had ruined the King of England. He got cured in his body, but his brains that the blacksmith had stirred the wrong way stayed addled and wouldn't work right. Always after that the Kings of England all had addled brains.

THE MAN THAT NEVER WASHED FOR SEVEN YEARS

WAY back when I was young, an old man that had been in the war, when he was hardly no more than a boy, told me a tale about a man that didn't wash for seven years. He said he learned it in the war. I never did hear anybody else tell it, and hadn't thought about it for years. So I may forget how it goes and leave out some.

A soldier came back from the war and tried to get a job of work. It was bad times, and money was scarce, and nobody hiring new work hands. The soldier figured he would sit down and starve to death, or he could go back to the war and get killed. No living choice that he could see.

One night, when he lay awake from being hungry, a little black man came to his bedside—the devil it was or maybe a witch man, don't make no difference which. The little black man told him he wanted to offer him a way to keep money in his pocket. He said if the soldier would wear an old bearskin instead of his soldier clothes and not wash himself nor comb his head for seven years, he would always find money in his pocket.

Far as the soldier could see, it was the only living chance he had. So he agreed to take the little black man's offer. The little black man left the bearskin on the foot of the soldier's bed. In the morning the soldier put on the bearskin and looked into the looking glass. He was well-nigh scared of his own looks. He was about to take off the bearskin and throw away his bargain with the little black man.

Then he found a secret pocket in the bearskin, and it had money in it. He went and bought himself the biggest breakfast he ever did eat. And he thought to himself, "It won't be no new thing for me to go without washing for a long time. A man can't live clean fighting in a war."

Still and all, even fighting in a war and not having chances to wash and to comb his head often as he was used to never gave him no idea how bad it would be to go nasty for seven years and have his hair all ratty for that space of time. After one year, he stunk worse than any skunk and looked bad enough to scare a dead man alive. Folks wouldn't put up with him, money in the pocket or no. And after that first money he spent out of the secret pocket he couldn't get the bearskin off. You might say it was like his own skin.

The places he went to and the things that he lived through have slipped my mind. But he wound up living with a man's family that was so poor they had to have the money he paid for his board. They put up with the way he stunk and his scary looks. Two of the girls made fun of him something awful. The youngest girl, though, treated him like he was a welcome visitor, never letting on to him that she smelt nor saw anything about him but the best.

When the family got in better circumstances, they told him they didn't need his board money, and he would have to leave. He broke a piece of gold money in two and gave the youngest girl half. He told her to keep it, and he would come back some day, and match halves with her, and that way she would know who he was.

When the seven years were up, the old bearskin dropped off, and the little black man came with a fine suit of clothes. And the fine suit of clothes had a secret pocket that always had gold money in it. The soldier washed and scoured and combed for six months and let the gold money save up. Then he put on his fine suit of clothes and went back to court the girl that he gave half of his piece of gold money to. He matched halves with her and they married, and every day of his life he washed himself and combed his head.

THE BIRD LIVER

TRAMPING through the woods, two boys caught a bird. A man came along and pulled out a feather from one of the bird's wings. He could tell from the feather that whoever would eat the bird's heart would marry the prettiest girl and whoever would eat the bird's liver would get rich. He said to the boys, "You cook this bird for me while I get a nap of sleep, and I'll pay you for it." He went off and lay down under a tree.

The boys roasted the bird good and done. They got so hungry they ate the heart and liver—not knowing it was magic. They were just hungry. When the man went to eat the bird, he looked for the heart and liver first. He got so mad—for he guessed what the boys had done—that the boys were scared witless and ran off through the woods.

They found an old woman's house and they lived with her a year. Every morning the boy that ate the bird liver found money in his shoe. The old woman told them the secret about the bird they caught. She saved their money, and she made them go to school every day.

After a year, they left the old woman's house and went to try their fortune. The one that ate the bird heart married a king's daughter. The one that ate the bird liver married a miller's daughter. Every morning there was money in his shoe, but he wouldn't tell his wife where he got it.

His mother-in-law found out his secret. She gave him a dose that made him puke up the bird heart. His wife grabbed it and swallowed it. Then they drove him off from home. His wife built herself a fine house.

He wandered over the world. Somehow he got hold of a wishing cap. He put it on and wished his wife with him. She was mad about being called away from her fine house. She made him climb up an apple tree to get her some apples. A big wind took his wishing cap off and sailed it down to the ground. His wife snatched it up and wished herself back home.

The man ate some of the apples he picked, and horns came on his head. He nibbled around on one thing and another till he found the right one and his horns fell off. He ate some kind of wild sallet and turned into a horse. Another kind of wild sallet turned him back to a man. He had fun sampling this and that, turning into one thing and another and back again.

He got on a boat and went home. His wife was putting on airs, living like a lady of high degree. He went to her fine house and sold her some apples that made horns come on her head. The doctors couldn't take them off.

The man coaxed the doctors into giving her some kind of dose to make her puke up the bird liver. He cleaned it good and swallowed it. Now he would have money in his shoe again every morning. He went off to yon side of the world and left his wife wearing her horns to pay her back for her meanness.

THE GOLDEN FILLY CHEST

A MAN's wife died, and he vowed he wouldn't marry unless he found a woman that could wear his wife's clothes. The only woman he ever found that his wife's clothes would fit was his own born daughter. He sent for her to come talk to him. He told her he wanted to marry her. She was too scared and too shamed to talk or even to think. She ran off to her uncle to get his advice.

Her uncle said the thing for her to do was to say she would marry him if he would give her her dearest wish; then to ask him for things he never in this wide world could get. That way she would get out of doing the sinful thing he wanted her to do with him.

The uncle said to ask for three fine dresses made out of things cloth couldn't be wove from. Then he couldn't get her dearest wish to give to her, and that would be the end of it.

The girl took her uncle's advice and asked for three dresses —her dearest wish. One dress wove of the feathers of a thousand different birds, one dress wove of the blue sky and the silver moon, and one dress wove of the golden sun and little stars.

The next day he sent for her and said, "Here's your dearest wish." He gave her the dress wove of the feathers of a thousand different birds, and the dress wove of the blue sky and silver moon, and the dress wove of the golden sun and little stars. All folded up in a golden filly chest.

The girl took the golden filly chest and ran to her uncle to get his advice on what to do next. Her uncle saw that his first advice didn't work out the way he had calculated. He told her she would just have to run away from home. He gave her a magic bridle and told her to shake the bridle and a horse with a sidesaddle for her to ride on would come.

She shook the magic bridle and rode off on the horse with the sidesaddle. She took her golden filly chest with her. Way off in some other country, she got off of her horse and took its bridle off. The horse vanished away. She hid her golden filly chest in some bushes. She went to a castle and hired herself out to cook.

Some days after that, the prince had a dance. The girl said she would like to go to the dance. The queen flung water on her and said she was too dirty to go to the dance.

The night of the dance the girl slipped out in the bushes and put on her dress wove of the feathers of a thousand different birds. She shook the magic bridle and had a horse to ride to the dance. The king danced with her till a woman got jealous and flung a candlestick at her. Then she left.

The next night she wore her dress wove of the blue sky and the silver moon. The king had nine men watching the door so she couldn't run off like the night before. She slipped by and the nine men never did see when she left.

The last night she wore the dress wove of the golden sun and the little stars. The prince danced with her all night. The next day after the dance he married her, and she didn't have to wait to get wedding clothes made. She had fine dresses a-plenty in her golden filly chest.

THE FARMER'S DAUGHTER

ONE time a farmer had a daughter that was the smartest thing you ever did see. No matter what hard questions anybody would ask, she could riddle out the right answers.

Then one day the king sent for this farmer to come to his castle. The king said to the farmer, "Now I'm a-going to ask you three hard questions. You can go home and riddle out the answers and come back and tell me tomorrow, and, if you don't give me the right answers, I aim to take your farm away from you."

The king asked the farmer three questions: "What is the fastest thing in the world? What is the richest thing in creation? What is the thing that I love the dearest?"

The farmer went home mighty bad worried. He couldn't think up answers that seemed like the right ones, and he was afraid he would lose his farm. His smart daughter noticed his worried looks and asked him what was the matter. He told her what the king asked him and how he would lose his farm.

The smart daughter pondered a minute and then she said, "I've riddled out the right answers, and I'll tell you, and you can say them off to the king. The fastest thing in the world is the light of the old sun-ball. The richest thing in creation is the earth—and I could prove it. The thing the king loves the dearest is to sleep."

The next day the farmer stood in front of the king's throne and said, "The fastest thing in the world is the light of the old sun-ball. The richest thing in creation is the earth. The thing the king loves the dearest is to sleep."

"You got the right answers," the king said, "and I won't take your farm away from you. But you ain't that smart your own self. Who riddled out the right answers and told them off to you?"

The farmer had to own up that his smart daughter told him the answers.

"Sounds like the smartest woman ever," the king said. "I want to see that girl. Send her to my castle tomorrow; and, just to try out how smart she is, tell her this is how I want her to come: not wearing her clothes and not going bare-naked; not a-walking and not a-riding, and with a present for me that won't be a present."

The farmer had misdoubts that his daughter could riddle that out. He told her what the king said, and she thought she could do it.

The next morning she wrapped herself up in a fish net. She got on the nanny goat to ride with her feet dragging. She had a live pigeon in her hand to give to the king for a present.

The king looked out of the window and saw her coming. He could tell that having the fish net wrapped around her was not wearing clothes nor going bare-naked. Traveling a-straddle of the nanny goat was half walking and half riding but neither one nor tother. He thought to himself, "What about the present that won't be a present? I've got her outsmarted on that."

The girl came in the castle and said, "Here's your present that won't be a present." She handed him the pigeon, but it flew out of the window and wouldn't be a present. So she had done according to all three of the king's riddling instructions.

The king said to the farmer, "That is the smartest girl I ever did see. I want to marry her."

The farmer was willing.

After the wedding, the king said to the farmer's smart daughter, "Now I own up you are the smartest girl I ever did see. That's the reason why I married you. But I don't want you butting into my business. I won't put up with it."

She did butt into his business, though. The king said, "Now I cautioned you, and you went right ahead and butted into my business anyhow. I won't put up with it. In the morning you got to go back to your daddy's farm and live. You can take along with you whatever you've got that you want the most to keep."

The smart girl fixed a big dinner with wine to drink. She kept on pouring out wine for the king till she got him dead drunk. Knowing he wouldn't wake up till morning, she carried him with her that night back to the farmer's house.

In the morning the king woke up in a strange bed and didn't know where he was at. The smart girl told him he was at the farmer's house. When the king asked how come he was there, she said, "You told me to take back to the farmer's house with me whatever thing I wanted the most to keep. The dearest thing to me and what I wanted the most to keep was the king that I was married to."

The king was so tickled to find out how much she loved him and how clever she could riddle out a way to keep him that he took her back to his castle to live out the years of her life. When she butted into his business, he just put up with it.

THE BEGGAR WITH THE BASKETS

A BEGGAR went around with a basket on his arm begging for a piece of bread. If a young girl offered the piece of bread that he begged for, he would grab her and put her in his basket and run off.

He acted that way at a place where they had three young

girls. The first time he begged for a piece of bread, a young girl handed it to him. He grabbed her and put her in his basket and ran off to his big old house.

The next time he went begging, he left her there. He gave her a key and told her one certain room she better not open. Soon as he was out of sight, she unlocked that room and went in. She saw some eggs and touched one. That left marks on it that wouldn't come off.

When the beggar came back home, he could tell she went in that room. He chopped her head off and caught the blood in a bucket. He cut her in pieces and hid the pieces.

Same way with the next girl in that family.

Then he carried off the last girl in his basket. He went off and left her the key with the same instructions. He didn't know that he had no power over her. She went in the room and hunted around till she found the pieces of her sisters. She dipped the pieces in the buckets of blood and stuck them back together again. The cuts healed up, and her sisters were as well and pretty as ever. She hid the sisters away.

When the beggar came home, he couldn't see anything wrong. He said he wanted to marry the girl. She said she wouldn't promise till he took two baskets of presents to her folks. He agreed to that. She put her sisters in two baskets and covered them over with presents. He complained about the baskets being so heavy, but he never guessed what they had in them. So he carried the girls back home safe to their parents.

The last girl had no idea of marrying him. She dressed up in feathers so he wouldn't know her if he met her on the road. He would think she was a monster big bird. And she went back home. No more was heard tell of the beggar with the baskets.

THE CONTRARIOUS PIG

THIS foolish tale I loved when I was little. What the old woman says to different things belongs to be said kinda quick and devilish.

An old woman was cleaning up her house, and she found a silver dollar that she had forgot she ever lost. When she was through cleaning up her house, she went to a farmer's house and paid him the silver dollar for a pig. She tied a rope on one leg of the pig and drove it along the way home. When she got to the stile across the fence, the pig was contrarious and wouldn't climb over the stile. It was too heavy for the old woman to lift, so she had to get help somehow to make that contrarious pig climb over the stile so she could get home by sundown. She tied the pig to the stile by the rope around its leg, and she went back along the road till she met a dog. She said to the dog:

"Dog, dog, bite pig,
  Pig won't climb over the stile,
  And I can't get home by sundown."

The dog said, "I won't do it." And she went back along the road till she met a stick. She said to the stick:

"Stick, stick, beat dog,
  Dog won't bite pig,
  Pig won't climb over the stile,
  And I can't get home by sundown."

The stick said, "I won't do it." And she went back along the road till she met some fire. She said to the fire:

"Fire, fire, burn stick,
  Stick won't beat dog,
  Dog won't bite pig,
  Pig won't climb over the stile,
  And I can't get home by sundown."

The fire said, "I won't do it." And she went back along the road till she met some water. She said to the water:

"Water, water, squench fire,
  Fire won't burn stick,
  Stick won't beat dog,
  Dog won't bite pig,
  Pig won't climb over the stile,
  And I can't get home by sundown."

The water said, "I won't do it." And she went back along the road till she met a calf. She said to the calf:

"Calf, calf, drink water,
  Water won't squench fire,
  Fire won't burn stick,
  Stick won't beat dog,
  Dog won't bite pig,
  Pig won't climb over the stile,
  And I can't get home by sundown."

The calf said, "I won't do it." And she went back along the road till she met a butcher. She said to the butcher:

"Butcher, butcher, kill calf,
  Calf won't drink water,
  Water won't squench fire,
  Fire won't burn stick,
  Stick won't beat dog,
  Dog won't bite pig,
  Pig won't climb over the stile,
  And I can't get home by sundown."

The butcher said, "I won't do it." And she went back along the road till she met a rope. She said to the rope:

"Rope, rope, hang butcher,
  Butcher won't kill calf,
  Calf won't drink water,

Water won't squench fire,
Fire won't burn stick,
Stick won't beat dog,
Dog won't bite pig,
Pig won't climb over the stile,
And I can't get home by sundown."

The rope said, "I won't do it." And she went back over the road till she met a rat. She said to the rat:

"Rat, rat, gnaw rope,
Rope won't hang butcher,
Butcher won't kill calf,
Calf won't drink water,
Water won't squench fire,
Fire won't burn stick,
Stick won't beat dog,
Dog won't bite pig,
Pig won't climb over the stile,
And I can't get home by sundown."

The rat said, "I won't do it." And she went back over the road till she met an old cat. She said to the old cat:

"Cat, cat, catch rat,
Rat won't gnaw rope,
Rope won't hang butcher,
Butcher won't kill calf,
Calf won't drink water,
Water won't squench fire,
Fire won't burn stick,
Stick won't beat dog,
Dog won't bite pig,
Pig won't climb over the stile,
And I can't get home by sundown."

The old cat said, "I will if you'll catch me a sparrow bird for my dinner. I'm too old to climb trees any more."

The old woman caught a sparrow bird,
She went back over the road and gave it to the cat.
The cat began to catch the rat,
The rat began to gnaw the rope,
The rope began to hang the butcher,
The butcher began to kill the calf,
The calf began to drink the water,
The water began to squench the fire,
The fire began to burn the stick,
The stick began to beat the dog,
The dog began to bite the pig,
The contrarious pig broke the rope and climbed over the stile, ran all the way to the old woman's house.

The old woman followed close behind, and she did get home by sundown.

FIVE | TOLD BY *Uncle Blessing*

TALES OLD MEN FOLLOWED TELLING

Uncle Blessing

Uncle Blessing

UNCLE BLESSING always felt that he was at a disadvantage as a teller of tales because he did not hear tales told at home when he was a boy growing up. Since tale-telling was not a part of his family life in his boyhood, he accounted for the tales he did know—and the number is considerable—by saying that when he was a boy he listened to "the tales old men followed telling."

Sometimes these old men were Regular Baptist preachers such as the one who told "The Jew That Danced Amongst the Thorns"—a respectable enough tale. But Uncle Blessing said some of the tales some preachers told were "too plumb filthy for any use." Of such tales he told me none at all. When the tale which he called "The Girl That Wouldn't Do a Hand's Turn" came to a certain point in the narrative, Uncle Blessing said that after that point it became a "long blackguard tale too nasty for telling"; and he ended the story right there. This was one of his tales learned from an old Regular Baptist preacher. He assured me that most Regular Baptist preachers told tales "clean a-plenty to suit anybody's hearing."

Most of his preacher legacy of tales that he considered fit for telling are local tales of ghosts and other supernatural manifestations. Some of these appear to be old saints' legends that have been localized, with the saints dropping out of the story and being replaced by local apparitions, usually the spirit of some one dead returning to punish or to help some person yet among the living. The tales Uncle Blessing credited to preachers also include a number of anti-Catholic tales, though he said no preacher telling such a tale in his hearing had ever met a Catholic.

He had some difficulty with forgetting parts of some of the longer tales, for example with "The Witch from the Ocean Waters" and "A Queen That Got Her Just Deserts." Of the latter he could not recall the beginning. Of the part played by the two brothers, the mare's colt, and other features of "The Witch from the Ocean Waters" he had only a "dim recollection that things goes along by threes."

One feature of Uncle Blessing's narrative style that differs from the others of the six narrators whose tales are included here is the moralizing contained in his comments on the tales he told. The very title "A Queen That Got Her Just Deserts" has a moralizing tone. In "Two Women that Turned to Niggers" he said the change of color was a judgment sent for the meanness they had done. In the end of this tale, which is a variant of "The Black and White Bride," Uncle Blessing has the two women remain black as an "everlasting judgment sent on them." In other tales, for example, "The Jew That Danced Amongst the Thorns" and "A Bunch of Laurel Blooms for a Present," he said, "That ought to a-learned them a lesson." Always it was plain that Uncle Blessing thought the wrongdoers in any tale got what was no more than they deserved.

Somehow I got the impression that Uncle Blessing considered the telling of tales simply for pleasure was a worldly indulgence, almost an outright sin. The moralizing style of narrations was perhaps an effort to give the tale-telling a more worth-while purpose in the sight of his own conscience.

Uncle Blessing was a most regular church goer, not only to the monthly Saturday–Sunday "meeting" in his home community but also at other Primitive Regular Baptists "meetings" in neighboring communities. Each Saturday Uncle Blessing could be seen quite early in the morning joggling along the road on his big horse with his wife up behind him on their way for a week-end visit wherever they had decided to go to "meeting." In 1930 his wife said to me, "Blessing has served the Lord faithful all his years—seventy-odd, I reckon. Going along with him on the nag, I can watch after him and hear a sight of preaching and see folks I never would see no other way. Seems like all the church meetings Blessing's been to in his lifetime and the way he's wore out his old ears listening to preachers oughta win a heap of favor with the Almighty and excuse some things Blessing does to help himself along in the world or just for nothing but pleasurement."

Then Aunt Mary laughed. "Talking about doing things for nothing but pleasurement, that's my main excuse for riding along behind Blessing on the nag whenever he travels about the country. It's the truth to tell that I love to hear some preachers—though not just any preacher sounds good to my old ears. And I love to watch over Blessing. But what I like the best of all on the trips with Blessing is just the pleasurement of riding about the country and seeing different places and different folks and eating other women's cooking besides my own. I do hope the good Lord will forgive me iffen that seems to Him fritter-minded. For many a year, starting when I was just a young girl, I washed and ironed and cooked and doctored for a big passel of younguns—a-skimping and a-saving and a-doing without things and not no chance to even go to meeting or to visit with the neighbors or kin that lived any piece of distance off. Now I'm old and my younguns are raised and married and a-living here and there. So's whenever Blessing saddles up the nag to go to meeting or to the voting place at election time or to trade a shearing of our sheeps's wool or wherever he aims to go, I just get up behind him on the nag's back and have me a trip somewheres."

By no means all the visiting was done by Uncle Blessing and his Mary. Their old house sitting in the shadow of a mountain and a little above the level of the creek-road was a welcoming place. The front porch, made gay by the colored magazine pages pasted on the outside wall was lined with chairs and an old bench or two, and was a favorite place for people who wanted to catch the mail boy on his trip down the creek and save the walk to the post office to mail a letter. And with its wide overhung roof and its shelter by the mountain behind the house the porch was a good place to sit on a rainy day and watch the creek rise. Any time, any weather, there was a welcome and Uncle Blessing might be coaxed into telling a tale. Or Aunt Mary might sing for the visitor. And, like as not, there would be a slice of Aunt Mary's gingerbread spread with applesauce. And, when there was preaching in the local "meeting house" once a month, Uncle Blessing and Aunt Mary expected company that would "take the night" and stay for Sunday dinner. "Meeting Saturday and Sunday," Aunt Mary said, "we spread up the company beds and put the big pot in the little one."

"That's the way we was raised to do," Uncle Blessing added, "to make preachers and other folks that comes to meeting freely welcome to such as we got. It gives me a sight a pleasurement and I learn a heap just listening around to the preachers talk and tell and the neighbors too. Though what I hear ain't always pure as Gospel, I do get a sight of pleasurement just listening to whatever is telling."

THE JUNE APPLE TREE

SEEMS like tale-telling never did run much in the generations of my kin. But, when I was a boy, I learned a heap of olden tales just listening around one place and another to the tales old men followed telling. I don't follow tale-telling no great sight, never had no good sleight at it. A right pretty tale comes to my mind, though, if you are a-mind to listen.

They was a woman took a fancy to an apple tree that was a-growing at her homeplace. She thought it was a sight how pretty in the spring with apple blooms all over, and in the summer it bore apples a-plenty to furnish all she could use up and some left over to divide with the neighbors. She would sit out under her June apple tree and wish she had a little boy to see the pretty apple blooms in the spring of the year and to climb up amongst the limbs and pick apples in the summer.

One day she was sitting out under her June apple tree, wishing she had a little boy and peeling apples to dry. Not thinking what she was doing, she peeled careless and cut her finger. It festered up and got sore and never did heal up.

The next spring she had a boy baby like she had been wishing for years. She died, though, and left the little bitty baby an orphan. The tale don't tell if she died from her cut finger or from the birthing. She wanted to be buried under her June apple tree. She felt like she wouldn't feel so lonesome in the grave if she lay under her June apple tree with apple blooms shattering down on her in the spring, and her little boy climbing up amongst the limbs to pick apples in the summer. And she would all times be close to her homeplace and her little boy. Some claims the dead don't watch over the living. I don't know. Anyhow, that was the way she felt about it, and her man buried her under the June apple tree.

Then, after a decent time, he married a woman with a little girl. Her little girl dearly loved his little boy, but the woman hated him like poison. She never dast do him harm when his daddy was at home, but she watched her chance other times.

She wouldn't let him climb up amongst the limbs of the June apple tree to pick apples. She got all the June apples herself, and she locked them up in a big old chest with a thick, heavy lid. One day, when his daddy was off from home, the little boy wanted an apple. The woman told him to reach down in the chest and get one. He reached, and he leaned his head down in the chest to see which apple he wanted. The woman shut the thick, heavy lid down on him and pinched his head off.

She fastened his head on somehow and set him up in a chair. The little girl came in and said something to him, and he didn't answer her back. The woman made her slap him, and his head fell off. The little girl thought she was to blame, and the woman let her take the blame.

The woman cooked the boy up into some kind of dish. When the man came home she told him the boy ran off to see some of his kinfolks. At the table the little girl cried and wouldn't eat a bite. The man had three helpings. After supper the little girl gathered up the bones and buried them under the June apple tree. After the burying of the bones, a pretty bird flew out of the June apple tree and went flying off out of sight. The little girl went home crying her eyes out for the little boy she dearly loved.

The pretty bird flew to a man that made golden jewels and sang a song to the man:

> My stepmother she killed me;
> My father he ate me;
> My sister she buried my bones,
> Tied up in her red silk apron,
> Buried them under the June apple tree.
> This pretty little bird is me.

The man that made golden jewels loved the pretty bird's song; and he said, "Sing that song to me again, and I'll give you a golden chain."

The pretty bird sang its song again for the man that made golden jewels. Then it flew off with its golden chain.

Next the bird flew to a weaver and sang its song:

> My stepmother she killed me;
> My father he ate me;
> My sister she buried my bones,

> Tied up in her red silk apron,
> Buried them under the June apple tree.
> This pretty little bird is me.

The weaver loved the pretty bird's song; and she said, "Sing that song to me again and I'll weave you a web of red silk."

The pretty bird sang its song again for the weaver. Then it flew off with its web of red silk.

Then this pretty bird flew to a mill. It sang its song to the miller:

> My stepmother she killed me;
> My father he ate me;
> My sister she buried my bones,
> Tied up in her red silk apron,
> Buried them under the June apple tree.
> This pretty little bird is me.

The miller loved the pretty bird's song; and he said, "Sing that song to me again, and I'll give you a big, heavy mill-stone."

The pretty bird sang its song again for the miller. Then it flew off with its big, heavy millstone. It flew back to its home and lit on the house roof. It sang its song:

> My stepmother she killed me;
> My father he ate me;
> My sister she buried my bones,
> Tied up in her red silk apron,
> Buried them under the June apple tree.
> This pretty little bird is me.

The man was happy. He had a good supper, and he loved to hear the pretty bird sing sitting on the house roof. The little girl loved to hear the pretty bird sing, but she was still crying and grieving for the little boy she dearly loved. The step-mother could tell what the pretty bird was singing; the others in the family couldn't make nothing out of it but a pretty bird's singing. She was scared of her life.

The father went out to see the pretty bird that was singing on the house roof. The pretty bird flew over him and dropped its golden chain around his neck. He went back into the house; and, when the stepmother saw the golden chain, she got scareder.

The little girl went out to see the pretty bird that was singing on the house roof. The pretty bird flew over her and dropped its web of red silk on her. She went back into the house; and, when the stepmother saw the web of red silk, she got too scared to stay there any longer. She rushed out of the house to get away from hearing the pretty bird that was singing on the house roof. The pretty bird flew over her and dropped its big, heavy millstone on her and mashed her into the ground.

After that the pretty bird changed back into a boy. The man and the little girl were mighty glad to have him back, and they dearly loved the June apple tree. They would sit under the June apple tree and think about the man's first wife buried there and the boy would sing, not like a pretty bird but like a natural boy. Seemed like to them, the woman buried under the June apple tree had watched over her boy and made him come back to life.

And they felt like the mean stepmother got her just deserts. They never did find any sign of her, no bones nor nothing. People that mean-hearted and mean-acting ought, by rights, to just vanish from the earth.

THE WITCH FROM THE OCEAN WATERS

You a-walking home from Blackey? Get up behind me here on the old nag. Just hold round my waist, so's you won't fall off. I know ladies like you from the level country can't ride sideways on a nag without falling off, lessen they hold on to something.

I noticed some boys fishing in the river back there a piece. Won't catch nary fish, for they ain't nary one in that stretch of the river. Puts me in mind of a tale about a man that never caught no fish one time. Would it pleasure you to hear any such a tale?

This here man went out in a boat a-fishing, though a river or on the ocean waters I never heard tell which. He fished and he fished but never caught even a crawdad. Then a witch rose up out of the waters—ocean waters, I aim to say from here on. This here witch promised him all the fish he wanted if he would promise to give her in three years his first boy.

He made promise and felt safe a-plenty for he never had no boys nor girls neither, and him and his old woman was too far along in years for any birthing. So's he promised.

Then the witch from the ocean waters gave him grains—wheat, maybe—I don't know—but grains tied up in threes. She said to him, "Give three grains to your old woman, and three grains to your mare, and three grains to your bitch dog, and plant three over back of the garden patch." Then she swum off and left him, and he caught a boatful of fish.

He traded his fish for a good price and then he went home. He put the money in the clock. He gave his old woman three grains and his mare and his bitch dog, and he scratched up the ground and planted three grains over back of the garden patch. Then things happened in threes. His old woman had three boy babies, and his mare had three black colts, and this bitch dog had three pups—a mighty puny sized litter for a good hound-dog bitch. And three trees growed over back of the garden patch.

His luck held out good, and he kept on catching fish and trading for cash money and things and made a good living.

Three years passed by, and one day the witch climbed in the man's boat and said, "Did you bring me your first boy like you promised?"

And he said, "Laws-a-mercy, I clean forgot all about it."

"Well," she said, "You 'pear to be mighty forgetful. But

I'll give you four more years. Then you bring me your first boy." And the witch went out of sight in the waters.

Ain't no use to tell all the same words again, so's I'll just say that in four years the fisherman forgot again and the witch out of the ocean waters gave him seven more years, and then he had to bring her his first boy.

When the seven years was nigh about gone, the fisherman got a worried mind. He couldn't forget about what he promised the witch out of the ocean waters and he couldn't figure no way to get out of his bargain. After a time he told his first boy how things was. The boy never had no worry. He just asked for a good stout sword, and three swords had to be made before he got one that satisfied him and that he couldn't break.

When he had a sword that satisfied him, he set out with his dog—it was one of the three pups I told you about a piece way back in this here tale.

After he traveled a ways he came across a buzzard and wolf with a dead sheep. He divided it amongst them and his dog, and they promised to help him if ever he had need.

He traveled on a piece and took a job with the king herding cows. His pay was to be according to how much milk the cows gave. Not much milk and low wages. So's he set out to find better pastures for the cows. He found a meadow with fine pasture and turned his cows in to graze.

Then along came a big giant, and they had a fight. The dog got on the giant's back and brought him down low on the ground, and the boy cut off the giant's head with his new sword.

Across the meadow was the giant's house with the doors open. But the boy didn't steal-take nothing. He just pastured his cows, and they had gallons of milk, and he got good wages.

When that pasture was grazed over, he went on till he found another meadow with good pasture. He had to fight a giant there, too, and his dog helped him, and he cut off the giant's head. He never tried to steal-take nothing from this giant's house, though the doors stood wide open. The pasture in this giant's meadow held out good.

But then came a giant with three heads that they had to give a girl to every year to keep him peaceable. This year he claimed he had to have the king's onliest girl. The girl's lover was supposed to save her from the giant that had three heads but he got scared and ran away.

So's the boy that herded the cows cut off the giant's three heads and tied them up in a budget. She gave him a pretty finger ring for his troubles. Halfway home, her lover came out of hiding in the underbrush and told her she had to tell the king he killed the giant with three heads, or he would kill her.

When they got to the king's house, the lover untied the budget and showed the king the three heads and said, "I done it."

Same thing over again with a giant with seven heads. And the girl gave the boy that herded the cows one of her earrings to pay him for his trouble. The girl's lover acted same as he done before.

Then it was a giant with nine heads. And the girl gave the boy that herded the cows the other one of her earrings for his trouble. And he kept the giant's golden clothes to pay himself back some more for his trouble. And the lover acted same way he done before. But the cow-herd boy showed the king the finger ring and the earrings the girl gave him back for his trouble when he killed all the giants with more heads than was natural. And the king said the cow-herd boy could marry his girl.

But she said, "I won't marry him in them old clothes that smells like cows." And he went off behind the door and put on the golden clothes from the giant with nine heads, and they had a big wedding frolic.

Seems like I ought to put the mare's colt in that belonged to this boy but I clean forgot. And they's some more to tell about the other two boys and how the trees withered and

was a sign and a token. But all that part has slipped my mind—
all but a dim recollection that things goes along by threes.

THE GIRL THAT WOULDN'T DO A
HAND'S TURN

WOULD you want to hear a tale about a girl that was a sight
how lazy? I learned it from an old Regular Baptist preacher.

Well, a farmer had two girls that were not well-favored for
looks but were plenty work brittle. His other girl was pretty
to look at, but lazy and idlesome. She wouldn't do a hand's
turn of work.

A man that was of the gentles, maybe a king's son, wanted to
marry the pretty girl.

The farmer cautioned him, "She won't do a hand's turn.
Maybe you better take one of her sisters."

The gentleman said, "I'll train her to work." And so he
married the lazy, idlesome girl that wouldn't do a hand's turn.

When they got to his house, he told the cooks to give the
work hands the things that belonged to be put on his table
and give him and his new wife what they cooked for the work
hands.

The lazy, idlesome girl saw the work hands eating chicken
and beef and cake and pie and candy, all kinds of good things
that made her mouth water. On the table for her and her husband just cornbread and beans. She complained about the work
hands eating better victuals than was on her table.

The gentleman said, "They ought by rights to have the best,
for they earned it. They work hard all day, and you don't
never do a hand's turn."

It went on like that for a week. Then the lazy, idlesome girl
said she was burnt out on eating cornbread and beans, and she
would learn to work if she could have good things to eat.

The gentleman said no he weren't ready yet for her to learn

to work. And the cooks went on giving them cornbread and beans.

In another week he had to go on a trip. He gave the cooks the keys and told them to lock up all the good things to eat.

After he left home, an old woman knocked on the door. The lazy, idlesome girl opened the door and let the old woman come in by the fire.

Some time after she let the old woman come in, she peeped in at a crack in the door. The old woman had pulled off her dress and was a man, warming his legs by the fire. She went in, aiming to ask him some questions.

He thought she was a serving maid, and he asked her what kind of work she could do.

She said, "I ain't never learned to do a hand's turn, and I don't do no work."

He grabbed hold of her and said, "A girl pretty as you don't need to learn how to do a hand's turn. She can find other ways to manage."

After that it gets to be a long blackguard tale too nasty for telling. I'll just say she never did learn to do a hand's turn of work.

A QUEEN THAT GOT HER JUST DESERTS

A QUEEN was trying to get rid of the king's son by his dead queen. The tale reaches further back in time than that, but I don't know that part that comes at the first, so naturally I can't start way back there.

Like I said at the start, a queen was trying to get rid of the king's son. She told him he had to bring a magic kind of wood to her—wood not bent nor straight. He left home not knowing what the meaning of her instructions might be.

He stayed all night with some of his kinfolks, and they riddled it out for him. They said the wood not bent nor straight was sawdust. So he went back to the castle and gave the queen a handful of sawdust.

She was plenty mad, for she thought he never could riddle out what she sent him after. So she had to think up some other dangerous thing for him to do. She sent him to find bramble briars and get some ripe blackberries for her in the middle of the winter.

He had no idea where to go to, but he walked along till he came to a giant's house. The giant set the dogs on him, but they just wagged their tails and made him welcome. From the way his dogs acted, the giant could tell the king's son meant no harm. So he showed the king's son where he could find some bramble briars and pick ripe blackberries in the middle of the winter.

He went back to the queen and gave her a handful of ripe blackberries in the middle of the winter. She was madder than ever, for she could tell he had made friends with the giant. No other way to find bramble briars and pick ripe blackberries in the middle of the winter. She was so mad she picked up a sword and cut the king's son's foot off.

He hobbled back to the giant's house. The giant stuck his foot back on and cured it. Then he gave the king's son a fine horse and his daughter to marry. After that the giant went to see the queen. He killed her, and so the queen got her just deserts to pay her back for the meanness she had in her heart.

THE WOMEN THAT TURNED TO NIGGERS

IT was a judgment sent on two women that turned to niggers for meanness they done. They's a tale about it, but I ain't followed telling tales for some years. And some tales kinda fades out of my recollection; some don't. Seems like they's places where this here tale fades out.

Best I call to mind, them two women turned to niggers after

they mistreated a stranger passing through. T'other girl—step-kin to them—treated him good and kind, and he let her have two wishes to show his thanks.

She wished that she would be pretty, and she wished she would go to heaven when she died. She got the first wish, and pretty soon she was the prettiest girl in the world. T'other wish she had to take on faith that she would go to heaven when she died.

Her step-kin that had turned to niggers hated her so bad they lay awake of nights thinking up ways to be mean to her.

Her own brother, not step-kin, was a good hand to draw pictures; and he made a picture of her that was true as life. He showed the picture to the king, and he wanted to marry her.

The king sent for her to come to his castle and marry him, and she went. The nigger stepsister went along, though what excuse she made I don't know. Along the way the nigger stepsister pushed the pretty girl into the deep waters, and the pretty girl turned into a white swan, swimming in circles on the deep waters.

The nigger stepsister went on to the king's castle and said she was the bride the king sent after. The king was mad, for he was certain in his own mind that he never sent for no nigger bride. But a mean old witch made him marry the nigger bride, much as he hated to.

After the wedding, the white swan would quit swimming in circles on the deep waters. It would walk up to the castle and sit by the fire in the cook room and ask questions. The questions the white swan asked are all faded out of my recollection. I do know that one time the white swan said she could be a girl if somebody would cut her head off.

The very idea of chopping off a white swan's head to turn it to a girl scared the cook so bad she went and told the king. The next time the white swan came to his cook room and sat down by the fire to ask questions, the king came downstairs and chopped her head off. She turned back into a pretty girl, and the king could tell who she was from her picture that was hanging on his wall.

She told on the nigger bride, and the king made her go back home. Both of the women that turned to niggers had to stay like that for the rest of their mortal lives. It was everlasting judgment sent on them for their meanness.

THE JEW THAT DANCED AMONGST THE THORN BUSHES

SEEMS like all the tales about Jews gives the Jews a bad name— greedy, grabbing for cash money, cheating their work hands out of their wages—I don't know what all. I never did know a Jew, never even met up with one. Back whenever I was a lad of a boy I heard an old Regular Baptist preacher tell a tale on a Jew. He told it to some more preachers—not to me. I chanced to be there and heard him tell.

The tale he told on a Jew was about a Jew that cheated his work hand on his wages. The man worked hard at slavish things, but for two years hand-running the Jew never paid him no wages. Said he was saving up the wages, so his work hand would have a bigger pile of cash money when he got paid.

The Jew tried to make it seem reasonable and right, but his work hand got the idea the Jew aimed to cheat him plumb out of his wages. So the third year the work hand told the Jew he would be bound to have his wages.

The Jew argued around about it and paid him three pennies—one for each year's wages. He quit his job of work and left with his three pennies in his pocket. He met a little old man that looked needy, and he gave him his three pennies of wages. The little old man thanked him kindly and said he would pay him back with three wishes.

He said he wished for a fiddle that would make people dance, and he got a fiddle. He wished for a gun that would hit what he aimed at, and he got a gun. He wished that anybody he asked a favor of would do it. He couldn't tell if he got that till he had a chance to try it out. The little old man went on about his business, and the Jew's work hand traveled on with his new fiddle and his new gun.

He chanced to meet up with the Jew that cheated him on his wages. The Jew wanted a squirrel that was up in a hickory tree, but he was too bark-tight stingy to use up a shotgun shell to kill it. The Jew said, "Shoot that squirrel for me." And the man with the new gun shot it. The squirrel fell dead down amongst some thorn bushes. The Jew went to get the squirrel, and the man tuned up his fiddle and started to play.

It was a dance tune, and the Jew started to dance in there amongst the thorn bushes. He begged the man to stop playing his fiddle, but he wouldn't. The Jew had to dance amongst the thorn bushes till the thorns tore his clothes all off and left him bare-naked. Then he had to give the man a pocketful of cash money to stop playing his fiddle.

The Jew took it to court, but the court wouldn't believe the Jew gave away money. They said the man was bound to rob the Jew if he got any money out of him. They said they would hang him for being a robber.

The day they were fixing to hang him, the man said he wanted to play his fiddle one more time. The Jew begged them not to let him, but they said it weren't too much for a dying man to ask for.

He tuned up his fiddle and started to play, for anybody he asked a favor had to do it or let him do it. Soon as they heard his fiddle playing dance tunes, the Jew and the court and all the people come to see the hanging started to dance. They woulda danced till they all dropped dead if the court hadn't give him his life to get him to quit fiddling. That ought to a-learned everybody a lesson, more especially the Jew.

THE CAT THAT WENT A-TRAVELING

BAD luck to kill a cat. Best just tote it off from home and turn it loose and leave it. A cat's a shifty creature, and it'll manage somehow to get a new place to live. Seems to me like I know where that stray cat on your porch came from, though I'm not naming no names. And, speaking of stray cats, from times when I was a boy I always knowed a tale about a cat that went a-traveling and got itself a new home.

This here olden tale says a cat heard an old woman say she was going to kill it, for no good reason but she hated cats. The old cat gathered up her kittens and set out a-traveling.

Down the road a piece she met up with a dog. She told the dog how come she was a-traveling. The dog said, "Think I'll just go along with you. Folks don't treat me too good where I been living. Won't let me lay by the fire in the wintertime."

The cat said, "Come along and welcome."

A little piece on down the road, they met up with a cow. They told the cow how come they were a-traveling. The cow said, "Think I'll just go along with you. Folks don't treat me too good where I been living. Don't feed me nothing but little, old nubbins."

They said, "Come along and welcome."

Next they met up with a guinea hen. They told the guinea hen how come they were a-traveling. The guinea hen said, "Think I'll just go along with you. Folks don't treat me too good where I been living. They hunt my nest in the high weeds and take out my eggs with a big spoon."

They said, "Come along and welcome."

After that they met a gander. They told the gander how come they were a-traveling. The gander said, "Think I'll just go along with you. Folks don't treat me too good where I been living. Pick all my feathers off of my back and sides to make them a featherbed."

They said, "Come along and welcome."

Then they met a rooster. They told the rooster how come they were a-traveling. The rooster said, "Think I'll just go along with you. Folks where I live don't treat me too good. Been talking about killing me to make a big pot of chicken and dumplings."

They said, "Come along and welcome."

They kept on a-traveling till nigh-dark. Then they found a little house. Seemed like nobody was living there. So they took up for the night. The dog lay by the fire. The rooster and the guinea hen flew up to the rafters. The cow stood behind the door. The gander squatted in a corner. And the cat and her kittens took the bed for their share.

In the night, all the animal creatures woke up with the voice of some men talking in the little house. They listened, and it was robbers counting the money they stole. The animal creatures were scared so bad they made their own noises as loud as they could. The cat and her kittens mewed, the dog barked, the cow mooed, the guinea hen pot-racked, the rooster crowed, and the gander screamed and hissed.

All the animal creatures named in this here tale are mighty noisy creatures, and all put together they scared the robbers so bad they ran off and left their money.

The cat said, "They'll be back. They won't give up the money they stole without trying." So the animal creatures planned out how they would scare the robbers so bad they would stay gone after that.

The next night the robbers came sneaking back to get their money. All at the same time and in the dark, the animals made their noises, and acted out what they planned. The cat and her kittens mewed and scratched. The dog barked and bit. The cow mooed and kicked. The guinea hen pot-racked and pecked at the robber's eyes. The rooster done the same thing and crowed. The gander screamed and hissed and beat the robbers with his wings.

Hearing all the different noises mixed together at the same time, the robbers had no idea what all it might be. And being come at in the dark with all them things trying to hurt them made the robbers scared of their lives. They ran off in the dark and left their money again and never did come back.

The cat took the little house for her home and let all the animal creatures live with her and her kittens. They used the money the robbers left to live on, for they had no idea who it belonged to and couldn't give it back. The robbers ought not had it, for they never came by it honest.

A BUNCH OF LAUREL BLOOMS FOR A PRESENT

BROUGHT you some laurel buds to make a flowerpot to pretty up your house. Mary always loved laurel blooms the best when they were still little, knobby, pink buds, kinda square-shaped. Giving you a bunch of laurel blooms puts me in mind of an olden tale about a girl that wanted laurel blooms for a present.

It starts with a man going off from home a far piece to tend to some business, and he asked his three girls what they wanted him to bring them back for presents. The oldest girl said she wanted him to bring her back a green silk dress. The middle girl said she wanted him to bring her a pair of gold beads. The youngest girl wanted him to bring her a bunch of laurel blooms for a present. Maybe they had moved down to the level country from the mountains, and she was used to seeing laurel blooms back where they used to live. I don't know. The tale don't say.

The man bought the green silk dress and the pair of gold beads as soon as he got to the far-off place. But he waited about the laurel blooms till he was ready to start back home, so they wouldn't get all wilted. Then he couldn't find any laurel blooms. He looked and he looked. After a time he saw some laurel blooms on the edge of a woods. Seemed like they didn't belong to nobody, so he picked some to give his youngest girl for a present.

After he picked the laurel blooms, and old witch came out of the laurel bushes and said they belonged to her, and she didn't aim to let nobody pick them. She said he had already picked some, and he would have to die. He told her the flower blooms were for a present to his youngest girl. Then the old witch said he could live if he would give his youngest girl to her.

He would rather die than do that. He begged the old witch to let him go home and give the presents to his girls. She said he could do that. He gave the green silk dress to the oldest girl and the pair of gold beads to the middle girl. They put on their finery and primped in front of the looking glass. He gave the laurel blooms to the youngest girl, and she hugged his neck and kissed him. Then she put her present of flower blooms in a flowerpot of water to keep them fresh. Her sisters made fun of her for asking for nothing but flower blooms when she coulda had fine things to wear.

The man told his girls he had to go live with the witch, and the youngest girl ran off in the night and went in his place to save him from the old witch. The old witch put her to live in a nice little house with an upstairs. A good supper was fixed and on the table waiting. The youngest girl saw two places at the table. Then in came the biggest toad-frog she ever did see.

It sat down in one chair, and she sat down in the other chair, and they ate supper together. The toad-frog washed up the dishes and told her to rest from the long journey. She went upstairs and found a room with a nice bed and lay down to sleep. In the night she could see by the candle the big toad-frog climbing into her bed. She went back to sleep; and, in the morning when she woke up, he was gone. He had breakfast ready when she went downstairs, and all the time he cooked and kept house. He treated her kind and good, but she couldn't like his warty old skin and his toad-frog eyes.

Living with a man-size toad-frog would give a girl the creeps, it seems like to me. But she learned to love his kind and help-some ways, though not his looks.

He picked laurel blooms every day and brought her for a present. She felt like she could live out her days with him, if only he looked like a natural human. One night she woke up thinking about it. In the moonlight she could see a hand-some young man laying in the bed beside her and the warty old frog skin hanging on a bed post.

She eased out of bed, got the warty old frog skin in her hands, and tipped downstairs. She flung the warty old frog skin into the fireplace and watched it crackle and burn. Then she went back to bed and slept sound till morning.

It was a handsome young man woke her up next morning. He told her he could stay a man now. Burning up the warty old frog skin had lifted the witch's spell on him. They lived there amongst the laurel blooms together in the nice little house with an upstairs.

Her sisters were jealous all their lives for her having such a handsome man that would cook the breakfast, and give her a house with an upstairs. Maybe they learned their lesson about being greedy and wanting costly presents and ending up with not as much as the youngest sister that asked for nothing more than a bunch of laurel blooms.

MY FAVORITEST OLDEN TALE

ENDURING the time I was a boy, my favoritest olden tale was the one I've been saving up till now to tell you. It starts with a boy and girl leaving home to get shut of a bad stepmother that treated them so mean they couldn't stand it.

All day they walked through a big woods without coming to any clearing or anybody's house. They got hungry and picked ripe blackberries from off some wild bramble briars.

They lay down to drink out of a running branch with good, clear water. The boy took a drink, and he turned into a little young deer. The girl figured she better go thirsty, so she never took no drink of branch water, and she stayed a girl.

She untied the long ribbons on her hair and fixed a halter to lead her little brother that had turned into a deer. That was one part I loved the best when I was a boy—the part where the girl leads the little deer gentle and easy with a halter made out of pretty ribbons. She loved her little brother even when he was turned into a deer.

I used to watch anybody leading a calf or a lamb or a colt, and I'd wonder if maybe the little animal creature was by rights a little boy. And, whenever I would drink water out of a branch, I would hunker down and drink water out of my hands, though most of it dripped through my fingers before I could get it to my mouth. I was afraid if I lay down flat on the ground to drink out of the branch I would turn to a deer.

The girl, leading the deer with the ribbon halter, walked another whole day in the woods till she found a little house. It had beds and chairs and other housekeeping things in it. All the time I was a boy, I used to think about having me a little house in the woods. The girl led the deer into the little house, and they lived there happy with each other's company.

In some olden tales a human person changes to look like an animal creature on the outside but keeps a human person's thoughts and ways. This here little boy that turned to a deer changed to a deer all the way through. He couldn't even talk. And most times in olden tales the animal creature turns back to a human person in the nighttime; and, then in the end, it changes back to stay a human person from then on. In this here tale the little boy stayed a deer, daytime, nighttime, and always and forevermore.

His sister lived with him in their little house and made a pet of him. But he had a deer's nature and wanted to be loose in the woods some of the time. She would open the door and let him out to roam the woods like a wild deer.

Then she would let him in when he came home again. She musta been mortal afraid that hunters would kill him, but she left him live according to his nature.

It was the king's woods, and sometimes he came there to hunt. One day when he was out with his hunters, he saw the prettiest little deer he ever did see. It got away, though, and ran off through the woods out of the king's sight.

The next day the king followed the little deer to the house where it lived. He saw it knock on the door with its right front hoof, and the door opened and let it go in.

The day after that, the king's hunting dog hurt the little deer. The king followed it to the little house. He waited around and saw a pretty girl open the door and let it in the house. Then she went out in the woods and hunted herbs to doctor the little deer's hurt. The king watched till she went back to the little house, and then he went to his castle.

The last day of the king's hunting, the little deer was back in the woods. The king tied up his hunting dog so it couldn't hurt the little deer again. He followed the little deer home that day and made himself acquainted with the girl. He asked her to be his queen and live with him in his castle. She said she would and gladly if she could take her little deer to live there too.

The king loved the little deer, too, though he didn't have no knowledge of how it got to be a deer. So the girl and her brother that was a deer went to live in the king's castle. When she was the queen, the girl fixed a soft pallet in the corner of her own room in the castle for the little deer to sleep on. She had a big, wide bed with silk coverlids and with curtains all around. So she slept with the king in private with the curtains pulled shut.

I used to lay in bed scrouged up, with other folks taking up all the room in the bed and snatching covers off of me. I would lay there and be scrouged and see folks doing things in other beds in the same room with me—things I didn't know the meaning of and a little boy ain't got no business seeing.

And I would wish I had me a big, wide bed with curtains all around so I could sleep private and have room a-plenty.

Well, the girl lived happy with the king and the little deer till the old mean stepmother found out where she was at. Then she sent her own ugly, mean daughter to kill the queen and be queen herself. The mean, ugly girl killed the queen and hid her corpse, so she wouldn't get caught. She put on the queen's bed gown and climbed into the big, wide bed with curtains all around.

It was after dark when the king came home to the castle. The mean woman in the queen's bed said, "Don't light the lamp; it hurts my eyes." So the king couldn't see that it weren't his true queen in her bed. His true queen was always rose-smelly, and this woman weren't. But the king thought maybe they was just times like that with a woman. She weren't gentle with her loving like always before, but the king let that pass. He thought she would be like herself again when he got back from his journey.

He left the next morning before daybreak, and what he took for the queen was asleep. After he left, she stayed in the bed all the time and had things to eat brought to her like a sick person. The true queen never did lay in her bed in the daytime, sick nor lazy. That made the serving woman have her suspicions. She watched; and, in the night, she saw the ghost of the true queen come back and feed the little deer and smooth its pallet. The serving woman was afraid to pry into things any further. She waited till the king came back from his journey. Then she told him what she watched and saw and her worst suspicions.

The king went charging up the stairs and pulled back the curtains to the queen's bed. He saw that ugly old woman laying there and not his true queen. He made her tell where she hid the true queen's corpse, and then he killed her.

He went to look for his true queen's corpse in a little old house down back of the garden. But she weren't a corpse. She had been hid away for a corpse, but she revived and came back to herself. She slipped and tended her little deer at night, waiting till the king came home to set things to rights again. After that she lived happy with the king and her little pet deer.

I would wake up in the night chilly with the cover pulled off and me all scrouged up with so many folks in the bed that I had no room to even stretch out my legs. And I'd lay there and think about the big, wide bed with curtains all around and the little deer sleeping on its soft pallet in a corner of the king's castle. After a time, I would get up out of the bed and put down a quilt pallet on the hearth where it was warm and cover up with Granny's blue yarn coverlid. I'd stretch out my legs and go back to sleep thinking about the true queen and her little pet deer in the king's castle.

SIX | TOLD BY *Sam Caudill*

TALES FOR IDLE TELLING

Sam Caudill

Sam Caudill

Sam Caudill was considerably the youngest of the six narrators whose tales make up this book. He was about forty when he died in the early 1930's; the others were in their sixties and seventies.

Sam worked in a strip mine at least five miles from his home. When the mine was working, we saw little of Sam around the school, for he had to leave for work before daylight, and it was night when he got home on his nag. During slack times at the mine, Sam dug coal from an outcropping coal vein on his own land. He had fitted his own fireplaces with coal grates, since he had a good supply of coal. The surplus from his own needs for coal, he hauled to the school for use in the stoves. His hauling was done in a homemade wooden sled that bumped along the snowless ground. Summer or winter this was the only vehicle of any kind that Sam had.

When he sledded up coal or did other work around the school, Sam liked to talk about his ambitions for his children and their school work. Three of his children—Franklin, Eva,

237

and Ezra—were living at home when the first school was opened in Sam's home community. Before that time, the nearest school was several miles away, but Sam had seen to it that his children had walked "the right smart piece of distance" to school "except in the worst kind of falling weather." So Franklin and Eva could "read and write and figure" when their own school opened, and were eager to learn more. Ezra, the youngest in the family, progressed more slowly and seemed less eager.

"Ezra is a slowpoke by nature," said Sam. "He learns things to stay learned and don't forget nothing, but he don't learn quick and he don't take learning to heart like Evie and Franklin do. Why, that Evie is so took up with reading and other kinds of learning that her Mommy says she's nearly 'bout ruined for helping with the housework and cooking. But Cindy recollects how she pined for a chance to learn when she was a young girl a-raising, and don't give Evie so many jobs about the place, knowing in her heart that Evie ain't turned trifling about work, but has just got her whole mind on learning a heap of things while she's got the chance.

"And that Franklin," Sam repeated many a time, "that Franklin of mine and Cindy's, he'd a heap rather read in a book than eat. But he manages so's he don't have to give up neither one." Sam chuckled. "He just props a book up in front of him at the table and reads all the time he's a-eating. One of the neighbors faulted him for acting like that and not talking and being sociable over a meal's victuals. Cindy stood up for Franklin. She said to the neighbor man, 'Never you mind about the talking Franklin ain't a-doing now. He's got the rest of his lifetime to talk and be sociable after he gets caught up on his learning. I only wished I'd had the chance to read in a book whenever I was a youngun a-raising.' "

To Sam as well as to Cindy their school represented the opportunity they had longed for but never had. They were never happier than when they could do something for the school or the teachers "to show their thanks." Sam and Cindy used to say, "Just stop and set a spell any time it comes handy, and iffen you would stay to a meal's victuals or take a night with us, we'd be right proud."

It did "come handy" to stop at Sam's home, for it sat at the foot of the mountain on the road coming down from the school and just above where the road forked to go down Bull Creek or over the mountain past Uncle Tom Dixon's. Sam's four-room plank house with a porch all across the front was almost hidden in trees, blooming shrubs, rose bushes and other flowers, growing to "suit theirselves."

A stout picket fence surrounded the big yard. "Sam's a plumb fool about his hollies," Cindy explained, "and he put up a stout high fence so's stray dogs and cow-critters can't get in amongst his flower blooms and so's folks coming to meetings can't hitch their nags to his hollies."

Sam's holly trees, the largest anywhere and the fullest of red berries, were his special pride. He would point out their great size, their silvery bark and bright red berries with glossy green leaves against the background of the spruce-pines surrounding the nearby little church at the foot of the mountain. "I wouldn't take a pretty for my hollies," Sam would say. "I raised them a pet, in a manner of speaking. I love to set on my own front porch of an evening time and have all around me my family folks and the things I planted to pretty up my place. Times like that I just bust out a-singing and sing old time song-ballads on into the night—Cindy joining in whenever she's a-mind to."

Many an evening Sam's front porch singing could be heard all the way to school, but Cindy's thin plaintive minor did not carry that far.

At singings, play-parties, and other social gatherings Sam was in demand as a ballad singer. He also sang when we teachers visited at his home. His family liked for him to sing as they sat around the fireplace after supper. At home and elsewhere his special favorite and the ballad always requested was "Little Bessie." It is a tragic ballad of a dying child. Sam's version ran to thirty-six stanzas, though some of the stanzas seem to be borrowed from another ballad of similar theme. As he sang, Sam always became very much affected by the tragic story of the ballad. He never could sing it all the way through without stopping to wipe his eyes and get his breath. He sang so effectively that there was always comment from the audience concerning the sad story, though they had heard "Little Bessie" sung many times. Sam also wept when he sang "The Two Little Orphans" and numerous other tragic ballads. Usually everybody else refused to sing "Little Bessie." They preferred Sam's rendition because he "made it so good and sad."

Sam's method with prose narrative was quite different. Usually he refused to tell a prose tale at all, saying he had "no sleight at tales for idle telling." When he could be coaxed into tale-telling, he told the tale without comment before or after. And he gave none of the "details and particulars" that Uncle Tom Dixon and others of the olden tale-tellers liked to linger on. Sam's tales were hardly more than a synopsis; to quote Uncle Tom Dixon, "He whittled it down to hardly no tale at all." This seemed a deliberate choice of narrative style rather than a matter of forgetting details. Sam could and did comment on omission of details from long stories told by others, and sometimes he supplied the missing details.

Sam said, "I love to hear a good tale-teller tell and let my mind follow along with what he tells. The olden tales have been worth a heap to mountain folks in the generations when they weren't no schools nor no books to read in. But me, I ain't got no good sleight at tale-telling. That's the reason I feel shamed and shy and have to be coaxed to tell."

THE GIRL THAT WEREN'T ASHAMED TO OWN HER KIN

I AIN'T got no sleight with tales for idle telling, but, iffen you would love to hear me tell an olden tale, then I'm a-bound to try what I can do.

A widow woman had a girl that couldn't do any kind of work. The widow woman never tried to train her girl how to spin and weave and sew. She just quarreled at the girl all the time till the girl never had the heart to even try to work.

One day the widow woman was quarreling and fussing at her girl, and the king came passing through. He stopped to find out what was the matter. The widow woman said she was quarreling at her girl to keep her from working herself to death. She said the girl wanted to spin and weave and sew all the time, day in and day out.

The king said that was the kind of girl he'd love to marry his boy to. So he took the girl with him to his castle, aiming to have the wedding the next day. But the queen said they better try out the girl's reputation for working.

The next day the queen put the girl in a room with a spinning wheel and big baskets of wool. She told the girl to spin all that into yarn by sundown. The girl sat there and cried, for she couldn't spin. An old woman with a big, wide thumb came, and said she would spin all the wool into yarn if the girl would ask her to the wedding. The girl said she would, and the old woman spun the yarn before sundown and vanished away.

The next day after that the queen took all the yarn and put it into a room with a loom. She told the girl to weave all the yarn into cloth before sundown. Same as the day before, an old woman came, only this time with a big, wide foot. She made the same kind of bargain and wove all the cloth before sundown and vanished away.

The last day of working, the queen took all the cloth and

told the girl to sew it all into things to wear before sundown.
The old woman that came that day had a big lip that hung
way down. She made a bargain to get asked to the wedding,
and sewed all the cloth before sundown and vanished away.

The queen said she was satisfied, and they had the wedding
the next day. A whole big crowd came to the wedding and
amongst them the three old women that helped the widow
woman's girl.

The girl was proud to see them and made them welcome.
She told the king and queen the old women were her aunts.
The king's son asked them what happened to their thumb and
their foot and their lip. They told him it was from spinning
and weaving and sewing so much. The king's son looked at
his pretty bride and said he wouldn't ever let her spin or weave
or sew another time as long as she lived.

The ugly old women put it in his mind to think that-a-way
and keep the girl from having to work. That way they paid
the girl their thanks for her not being ashamed to own them
for her kin.

THE GIRL THAT COULD DO ANY JOB
OF WORK

A GIRL had a mean stepmother that mistreated her every way
she could think of. One way the stepmother would torment
her was to think up big jobs of work that she figured the girl
couldn't do.

One day she told the girl to sort thirty barrels of feathers
in a day and a night. Thirty different kinds of feathers all
mixed up, and the girl had to sort them out with each kind in
a barrel to itself. She worked hard as she could all day long.
In the dark of night a little old woman came and said to her,
"You done the best you could; now I'll take hold and help you

out." Before morning they had the job done, and the old woman vanished away.

The next day the mean stepmother told the girl she had to dip the pond dry with a spoon. She tried hard as she could all day, but the pond looked full as ever. In the dark of the night the little old woman came and said, "You done the best you could; now I'll take hold and help you out." Before morning they had the job done, and the old woman vanished away.

The mean stepmother thought up the hardest job of all. She told the girl she had to build a high castle in a day and night, and find the rocks to build the castle out of. All day long the girl sledded up rocks, but night came on before she had a pile big enough to build a high castle. In the dark of night the little old woman came and said, "You done the best you could and I'll take hold and help you out." Before morning there was a high castle, but the old woman didn't vanish away.

When the mean stepmother went in the castle to see if it suited her, the little woman pulled the castle down on her and mashed her to death and left her under the pile of rocks that had been a high castle.

A king came passing by and the old woman gave him the girl for his true bride.

THE CHANGEABLE MAN

THE tale about the changeable man I ain't heard told since I was a little boy and then not often. I can't recollect back past where he started to change into different things.

Best I can recollect, he turned into a dog first, and then decided he would rather be a horse. Somehow it came about that a giant bought him for a horse. The giant was too big to ride the horse, so he led it home with a magic bridle. If he took the bridle off of the horse, it would turn back into a man.

The giant told his daughter they would just cook that little old horse and eat it, for it was too little for him to ride. He went to pack water from the spring to boil in the big black wash kettle and butcher the horse. While he was gone to the spring, the horse told the giant's daughter it was a man, but had to stay a horse as long as it had the magic bridle on. The giant's daughter didn't want to cook a man—nor a horse neither, far as that goes. She slipped the bridle off, and the horse turned back into a man—good-looking too.

The giant came back from the spring with a big bucket of water and saw what happened while he was gone. He set down his water bucket and grabbed his sword and started to fight the man. To get out of his reach, the man changed to a bird and flew up in a tree. The giant changed to a bigger bird and flew after. The man-bird flew into the giant's daughter's lap and changed to a golden finger ring. The giant's daughter put it on her finger. The giant changed to a man that made jewels and wanted the giant's daughter to give him the golden finger ring so he could put a diamond set in it. She did.

In the giant's hand the golden finger ring changed to a round worm. The giant changed into a chicken to eat the worm. The round worm got the best of him there. He changed into a red fox and ate the old giant-chicken up. Then he stayed there and married the giant's daughter.

OLD BUSHY BEARD

THEY'S a tale about a rich girl that got big-headed, got above her raising, as the saying is. Her daddy wanted her to marry, but she wouldn't have none of the men that came a-courting her. She made fun of them and said hateful things about their looks and about their clothes, and about their manners. None of them was good enough for her.

Even a king she treated like that. A king with a fine curly beard wanted to marry her, but she wouldn't have him. She made fun and called him "Old Bushy Beard." It hurt his feelings, and he said to himself that he'd get even with her, and he'd learn her a lesson too.

Her daddy got mad at her and all out of patience. He said, "I'll marry you to the next man that comes here whoever he may be."

The next man that came was an old pack peddler. He said he was willing to marry her. The girl didn't want to, but she couldn't help herself. Her daddy married her to the old pack peddler, and told her to go along wherever her husband went and live however he wanted her to.

The pack peddler took her to a little shack of a house and left her there till he tended to some business. When he got back, she was setting there waiting for supper. She was used to being rich and waited on. He made her get up and fix supper.

The next day he made her put on common clothes and he took her fine wedding clothes off with him to sell in his peddler's pack.

Besides keeping house, he made her learn to make baskets and go sell them in town. Them that knowed her when she was rich made fun of her. Same way when he made her weave cloth and sell it in town. All kinds of work he made her do and live poor.

Then, after a time, she learned her lesson and was kind and good. So he told her he was the king she called "Old Bushy Beard," and he took her to his castle to live.

THE FELLOW THAT MARRIED A DOZEN TIMES

THE neighbor's talking about Shibo marrying his third woman puts me in mind of a tale about a fellow that married him an even dozen women, though he done it one at a time, like Shibo. I might say, though, Shibo ain't never been mean to no woman. He just had bad luck with his women.

This here fellow in the olden tale killed each woman in a week's time after her wedding day. He done that to eleven women and piled up their corpses in a room locked up tight.

Whenever he married the last time, he got his match. He lit out for town and gave her a big key to a room she weren't supposed to look into. She went into it anyhow and saw all the gold and other cash money he saved up. Whenever she came out and aimed to lock up the door, the key turned red hot, and it stayed that-a-way.

Her man flew mad whenever he came home, and he aimed to kill her and pile up her corpse with them other women, but she was too shrewd. She caught him peeping into the room with the corpses and shut the door on him sudden-like, pinching his old head right off. And it was pine-blank what she oughta done.

THE DEVIL AND HIS GRANDMOTHER

MAYBE you heard the saying "the devil's grandmother." Well, a Tally that worked in the mines told me a tale about the devil and his grandmother.

A man never got paid for working. It went on that way for a year's time, and he quit his job working in the cornfield. He hid out for a week and was about to starve to death. The devil came up to him—though not in the devil's own shape—

and said he would give him a living for seven years if he would work for him after that.

The devil made him sign some papers to what they agreed on. Then he showed the man how to make gold, so he would have cash money. The devil said they was one way the man could get out of the bargain. In seven years he would ask this man a riddle. If he could answer the riddle, the devil would let him out of his bargain.

When the seven years was about up, the man started to worry. He met a little old woman and told her what a fix he was in. The little old woman was the devil's grandmother, but she had pity on him. She told him the riddle would be three kinds of questions:

What kind of meat?
What kind of spoon?
What kind of glass to drink wine out of?

Then she told him the right answers:

Fish out of the sea for meat.
Cow rib for a spoon.
Hollowed-out horse hoof for a glass.

When the seven years was up, he told the devil the answers to the devil's riddle, and that got him out of his bargain with the devil.

THE GIRL THAT CHANGED TO A
FLOWER BLOOM

A MAN I talked to one time when court set had been in the pen a year—maybe two—down at Frankfort or Atlanta, I don't know which. He said he heard tales a-plenty while he was in the pen, though most of them wouldn't do to tell. I kinda sorted out in my mind the tales he told me, and I picked out two that he said a Tally in the pen told him. They seem to me like right pretty tales.

The Tally tale-teller in the pen said one time they was a king's son that could have all his wishes come true—born that-a-way. But it took a long time for him to find out he had been gifted that-a-way. Being a king's son, he was raised to have whatever he could wish for long before he ever thought about wishing for it.

He got to be an age when the king told him he ought to travel and see the world. The king's son would be the king some day and he couldn't be the best king if he never had traveled away from home and seen the sights.

The king's son was anxious to travel and see the sights of the world, but he hated to go off and leave a pretty girl he was courting. He thought about how everybody said she was pretty as a pink, and he wished she would turn into a pretty flower bloom so he could carry her with him on his journey to see the sights of the world. Soon as he made the wish, there was his pretty girl changed into a flower—if it was a pink or some other I never heard tell—not just a flower bloom, but with roots and growing in some dirt in a flowerpot.

He carried the flowerpot on his journey all over the world. When he wanted it to be a pretty girl, he would pick the flower bloom. Then have his pretty girl with him for company a while. Then he would wish her back into a flower growing in a flowerpot.

One day the girl got tired of living in a flowerpot.

When her lover picked the flower bloom and changed her into a pretty girl, she said to him, "Wish me a fine castle to live in just for today while you rest from your travels. I would dearly love to be in my own castle till you take up your journey again in the morning."

So he wished her a fine castle and they lived in it that day and night. The next morning he got ready to start again. He tried to wish his pretty girl back into a flower growing in a flowerpot. It wouldn't work. He tried and tried, but she stayed a pretty girl.

He thought maybe he made a mistake not wishing her fine castle away first. He tried that and it wouldn't work. What he didn't know was that it broke the charm when he let somebody tell him what to wish for. When he wished for the fine castle his pretty girl told him to get for her, that put a stop to the magic. So he gave up traveling about the world and married the pretty girl and lived in her fine castle.

THE SHINING, BEAUTIFUL LADY

THE other tale from the Tally in the pen was about a girl that went to draw water and dropped the bucket in the well. She was afraid she would be quarreled at for being careless, so she climbed down in the well to get the bucket. At the bottom of the well she found a little door and knocked on it. A shining, beautiful lady opened the door.

The girl said, "Have you seen my well-bucket?"

The lady said, "No, but, if you will give my little boy his supper and sweep my house while I go on a journey, I'll help you find your well-bucket whenever I get back."

The girl fed the little boy his supper and she swept the house, though she couldn't see any dirt.

When the shining, beautiful lady came back home, she helped the girl find her well-bucket, only it looked like new. Then she said, "Would you want a silk dress or calico?" The girl said calico, but the shining, beautiful lady gave her a silk one. Then she touched the girl on the forehead and let her go home.

The girl hurried along, for fear she would get fussed at for being gone from home such a long time. She went to the house with her bucket full of water, and her mother met her at the door and said, "Whatever is that thing on your forehead?"

The girl ran to see herself in the looking glass, and she saw in the place where the shining, beautiful lady touched her a bright silver star. It wouldn't rub off nor wash off. It just shone brighter.

The girl told about how she lost the well-bucket and climbed down the well. She told about the shining, beautiful lady and the little boy that she gave his supper to while the shining, beautiful lady went on a journey.

Her mother said, "That was the Virgin Mary and her little boy Jesus."

NOTES FOR FOLKTALES IN THIS COLLECTION, WITH TYPE NUMBERS

Notes for Folktales in This Collection

THE tales in this book are all of European origin, carried to Kentucky through several generations of oral telling. For folklorists and for others who may be interested, I have listed in this section each tale along with European tales from which it stemmed. The number following the tale is the number assigned to that particular type of European tale as classified by Aarne and Thompson in *The Types of the Folktale* (FFC No. 74). Certain tales which do not appear in the Aarne-Thompson volume are listed in Sean O'Suilleabhain's *A Handbook of Irish Folklore*. For such stories inclusion in the *Irish Handbook* is indicated in the following list. For the stories in this collection from eastern Kentucky, the first title listed is the title given the tale by the narrator from whom it was recorded. The title following the type number is the title by which the tale is designated in Aarne-Thompson *The Types of the Folktale*. Motif numbers are taken from Thompson's *Motif-Index of Folk Literature*.

Since a large proportion of the tale types in this collection are found in the Grimm collection, Grimm numbers have been noted for those tale types, and usually notations from Bolte-Polívka's *Anmerkungen zu den Kinder- und Hausmärchen der Brüder Grimm*. Other citations of parallels are usually from Irish and Scotch Gaelic collections of tales not listed by Aarne-Thompson or Bolte-Polívka. When a title is not given following a Grimm number, the Grimm title is the same as that in Aarne-Thompson. For some tales, citations are made to the discussion of certain tales in Thompson's *The Folktale*. For a number of the tales there are parallels in Leonard Roberts' *South from Hell-fer-Sartin*.

CHAPTER ONE   *Tales With All Manner of Things Golden*

1. THE FLOWER OF DEW   Type 405, Jorinde and Joringel. Grimm 69. Bolte-Polívka II, 69 indicated that this tale has rarely been found outside Germany.

2. THE SPINDLE, THE SHUTTLE, AND THE NEEDLE—ALL GOLDEN   Type 585, Spindle, Shuttle, and Needle. Grimm 188. Bolte-Polívka III, 355, apparently rarely found outside Germany.

3. THE QUEEN WITH GOLDEN HAIR   Type 510B, The Dress of Gold, of Silver, and of Stars (Cap o' Rushes). Grimm 65, "Allerleirauh" (of many different kinds of fur). Bolte-Polívka II, 45, widely collected, especially in Scandinavia. See Cox, *Cinderella*, a world distribution study of Type 510. Also Rooth's study, *The Cinderella Cycle*. L. Roberts, *South from Hell-fer-Sartin*. No. 18.

4. THE GOLDEN RAIN   Type 480, The Spinning-Women by the Spring. Grimm 24. Bolte-Polívka I. World-wide distribution. Detailed study of 440 versions in Warren E. Roberts, *Aarne-Thompson Type 480 in World Tradition, A Comparative Folktale Study*. This version is very close to Grimm, "Frau Holle." L. Roberts, *South from Hell-fer-Sartin*, No. 16c.

5. THREE SHIRTS AND A GOLDEN FINGER RING   Type 451, The Maiden Who Seeks Her Brothers. Grimm 9, "The Twelve Brothers," and 49, "The Six Swans." Bolte-Polívka I, 70, 227, 427. Indicates Scandinavian distribution. This version differs from usual variants of 451 in having only three brothers rather than the usual six, nine, or twelve. Also, they turn into dogs rather than the usual birds.

6. THE GOLDEN CHILDREN   Cf. Type 303, The Twins or Blood-Brothers, and Type 555, The Fisher and His Wife. See also Grimm 60, "The Two Brothers"; 85, "The Gold Children"; 19, "The Fisherman and His Wife." This tale fits none of the entries in Aarne-Thompson, Grimm, or Bolte-Polívka. It is apparently a confusion of two or more tales. Parallel for Type 303, L. Roberts, *South from Hell-fer-Sartin*, No. 3a.

7. THE GOLDEN PRINCESS   Type 516, Faithful John. Grimm 6. Bolte-Polívka I, 46. Varies from Grimm version largely in terms of omissions.

8. THE GOLDEN COMB   Type 316, The Nix of the Mill-pond. Grimm 181.

Bolte-Polívka III, 322. Indicates Scandinavian and Jamaica Negro recording.

9. A SILVER TREE WITH GOLDEN APPLES Type 511, One-Eye, Two-Eyes, Three-Eyes. Grimm 130. Bolte-Polívka III, 60. See M. R. Cox, *Cinderella*, for notes on Type 511. Also Rooth, *The Cinderella Cycle*. L. Roberts, *South from Hell-fer-Sartin*, No. 19b.

10. THE GOLDEN BRACELET Cf. Type 533, an example of "The Substituted Bride," listed in *A Handbook of Irish Folklore*, p. 566, under "International Folktales Told in Ireland." Very little resemblance to variants of Type 533 listed by Bolte-Polívka or of Grimm. Apparently a Gaelic variant.

11. THE GIRL WITH THE GOLDEN FINGER Type 710, Our Lady's Child. Grimm 3. Bolte-Polívka I, 13. See also Beckwith's version from Jamaica, *Memoirs American Folklore Society*, XVII, p. 131. Aunt Lizbeth Field's version follows Grimm rather closely.

12. GOLDEN APPLE Fragment of a tale resembling "Gold Apple, Son of the King of Erin," pp. 64-74, *Irish Folktales*, collected by Jeremiah Curtin, edited by Seamus O'Duilearga. See also No. 22 of "Irish Hero-Tales," p. 605, *A Handbook of Irish Folklore*, in which a stepmother places her stepson under *geasa* to procure Madadh no Seacht glos (Seven-Footed Dog) for her.

13. STOCKINGS OF BUTTERMILK Cf. No. 7, "Irish Hero-Tales," p. 601, *A Handbook of Irish Folklore*. Also "Cahal and the Bloom of Youth," pp. 222-241, Jeremiah Curtin's *Hero Tales of Ireland*.

14. A STEPCHILD THAT WAS TREATED MIGHTY BAD Type 709, Snow-White, ending with Type 480, The Spinning-Women by the Spring. Grimm 53, "Little Snow-White," and 24, "Frau Holle." Of 36 versions of Type 709, from Europe, Asia, Africa, North America, which I read, this version most resembles Grimm 53. According to Dr. Warren E. Roberts, who has made a world-wide study of Type 480, this version used with Type 709 is unlike any of 440 versions included in his study. L. Roberts, *South from Hell-fer-Sartin*, No. 16c.

15. THE LITTLE OLD RUSTY COOK STOVE IN THE WOODS Type 425A, The Search for the Lost Husband. Grimm 127, "The Iron Stove." Differs from Grimm largely by omissions and descriptive touches. The Iron Stove variant of Type 425A. I could find no version of or reference to it except as a Grimm entry. L. Roberts, *South from Hell-fer-Sartin*, No. 15a.

CHAPTER TWO   *A Fine Mort of Olden Tales*

1. THE KING'S GOLDEN APPLE TREE Type 550, The Bird, the Horse, and the Princess. Resembles "The Greek Princess and the Young Gardener" in Jacobs' *More Celtic Fairy Tales*, pp. 110-124, more closely

than it does Grimm 97 or any variants indicated by Aarne-Thompson or Bolte-Polívka. Varies from Curtin's Gaelic version largely by omissions. Parallel in *Arabian Nights*.

2. THE BIRD OF THE GOLDEN LAND Apparently a combination of Type 301 and Type 550, primarily of 301, The Three Stolen Princesses. Cf. Type 329; follows "The Bird of the Golden Land," pp. 14-24, in Curtin's *Irish Folktales* rather closely except for omissions. Varies widely from Types 301 and 550 as given by Grimm and Bolte-Polívka.

3. LITTLE CAT SKIN Type 510B, The Dress of Gold, of Silver, and of Stars (Cap o' Rushes). Grimm 65. Bolte-Polívka II, 45. Cox, *Cinderella*, also Rooth, *The Cinderella Cycle*. L. Roberts, *South from Hellfer-Sartin*, No. 18.

4. ASH CAKES AND WATER Type 480, The Spinning-Women by the Spring. Grimm 24. Details quite unlike Grimm's "Frau Holle." See previous notes on Type 480, Chapter One, No. 4, The Golden Rain.

5. THE WEAVER'S BOY A combination of Type 552A, Three Animals as Brothers-in-law, and Type 302, The Ogre's Heart in the Egg. Very like "The Weaver's Son" and the "Giant of the White Hill," pp. 64-77, in Curtin's *Myths and Folklore of Ireland*. Much variation from Grimm and Bolte-Polívka on Types 552A and 302.

6. THE TERRIBLE VALLEY Cf. Type 301, The Three Stolen Princesses. Closely resembles "Lawn Dyarrig and the Knight," pp. 267-282, in Curtin's *Hero Tales of Ireland*. Varies widely from Grimm and Bolte-Polívka on Type 301. See also "The Three Crowns," pp. 43-53, Kennedy's *Legendary Fictions of the Celts*. L. Roberts, *South from Hell-fer-Sartin*, No. 2.

7. THE FISHERMAN'S SON Type 325, The Magician and His Pupil, Episodes I, II, and part of III. Close parallel in "The Fisherman's Son and the Gruagach of Tricks," pp. 139-156, in Curtin's *Myths and Folklore of Ireland* with omission of Curtin's episodes after sale of race horse and return home. More variation from Grimm and variants from Bolte-Polívka.

8. HEART, LIVER, AND LIGHTS Type 1696, What Should I Have Said (Done)? Grimm 143, "Going a-Traveling." Thompson and Barbeau give American Indian versions. Bolte-Polívka III, 145 deals largely with Scandinavian, Russian, south European variants. Nelt's version is closest to "The Unlucky Messenger" in Kennedy's *The Fireside Stories of Ireland*. Widely variant from Grimm. See also "I'll Be Wiser Next Time," pp. 39-43, Kennedy's *Legendary Fictions of the Irish Celts*.

9. OLD SHAKE-YOUR-HEAD Cf. Types 505-508, The Grateful Dead. Close parallel of "Shaking Head," pp. 186-203, in Curtin's *Myths and Folk-*

lore of Ireland. Grimm, Bolte-Polívka, Aarne-Thompson offer no entries at all like this tale except for the single motif of the grateful dead man.

10. GILLY AND HIS GOAT SKIN CLOTHES Types 571-574, Making the Princess Laugh. Closest parallel, "Adventures of Gilla Na Chreck au Gour" ("The Fellow with the Goat Skin"), pp. 23-31, Kennedy's *Legendary Fictions of the Irish Celts.* Grimm 64, "The Golden Goose." Bolte-Polívka and Aarne-Thompson indicate wide distribution, including American Indians.

11. THE KING OF SPAIN'S MAGIC COW Not listed in Aarne-Thompson, *The Types of the Folktale.* Was in O'Suilleabhain's *A Handbook of Irish Folklore.* Resembles a longer, more complex tale, "Elin Gow, the Swordsmith from Erin and the Cow Glas Gainach," in Jeremiah Curtin's *Hero Tales of Ireland.* Not a Grimm tale, therefore not given by Bolte-Polívka.

12. FOLKS THAT GROWED FUR TO KEEP WARM No entry in Aarne-Thompson, Bolte-Polívka, or Grimm. Apparently a confusion of two tales from Irish folklore: "The Amadan Mor and the Gruagach of the Castle of Gold," pp. 140-162, in Curtin's *Hero Tales of Ireland* for the first part of the tale; "Mon's Sons and the Herder from Under the Sea" from the same Curtin collection for the latter part, including the red, white, and blue cattle and the man-sized green cat.

13. COLD FEET AND THE LONESOME QUEEN Cf. Type 300, The Dragon Slayer and Type 304, The Hunter, Episodes III, IV, and V. Close parallel "Cold Feet and the Queen of Lonesome Island," pp. 242-261, in Curtin's *Hero Tales of Ireland.* Only certain episodes fit Aarne-Thompson, Bolte-Polívka, or Grimm entries for Types 300 and 304.

14. A CURIOUS LAW ABOUT ASKING IN MARRIAGE No listing in Aarne-Thompson or Bolte-Polívka. No Grimm parallel. See No. 9, "Romantic Tales," p. 624, *A Handbook of Irish Folklore.*

15. WHEN FINN WAS A BOY None of the tales from the Finn Cycle have Grimm parallels or entries in Aarne-Thompson or Bolte-Polívka. Contains Motif D1811.1.1, magic wisdom from biting one's own thumb. Episodes from at least three tales from "The Finn Cycle," No. 1, p. 589, *A Handbook of Irish Folklore,* plus the episodes of Finn's encounter with the one-eyed giant and of the speaking ring. See Curtin collections for stories of the birth of Finn. See also *Ancient Irish Tales,* edited by Cross and Slover.

16. FINN'S SEVEN HIRED MEN "The Finn Cycle," No. 26 and part of No. 28, p. 595, *A Handbook of Irish Folklore,* plus other items not listed. See "The Seven Brothers and the King of France," pp. 271-280, in Curtin's *Hero Tales.*

17. OLD WOOLY BACK "The Finn Cycle," in which Finn and his men make war on the country of the cannibals. The end of this tale apparently is a confusion of No. 29, and the latter part of No. 28, p. 595, *A Handbook of Irish Folklore.* Similar to "The Son of Luck" in Volume One of *Popular Tales of the West Highlands,* collected by J. P. Campbell.

18. THREE MEN NAMED THREE DIFFERENT COLORS "The Finn Cycle," No. 35, pp. 596-597, *A Handbook of Irish Folklore.* Ends with Motif D1811.1.1, magic wisdom from biting one's own thumb. See "Black, Brown, and Gray," pp. 281-291, Curtin's *Hero Tales.*

19. CONNIE'S THUMB RING Cf. Motif 731.2 Father-son combat. No. 1 "The Ulster Tale-Cycle," p. 598, *A Handbook of Irish Folklore.* See "The Tragic Death of Conla," pp. 172-175 of "The Ulster Cycle," *Ancient Irish Tales,* by Cross and Slover. Also "The Fight of Cuchulain with His Son Conla," pp. 241-251, *Cuchulain, The Hound of Ulster,* Eleanor Hull.

20. A TALE TOO SAD FOR TELLING The ancient Irish legend of Deirdre told to the point where the King of Ulster takes her from seclusion in which she had been reared because of a prenatal prophecy. A favorite legendary subject for contemporary Irish writers of poetry, drama, or prose narrative. Cf. "Deirdre" in Mary G. O'Sheridan's *Gaelic Folk Tales* or "Deirdre—the Fate of the Sons of Usnach" by Lady Gregory for prose versions. Also "The Exile of the Sons of Usnech," pp. 237-247, *Ancient Irish Tales.*

CHAPTER THREE *Tales Where Things Go in Threes*

1. THE JAY BIRD THAT FOUGHT A RATTLE SNAKE This tale begins with Motif B261, War of Birds and Quadrupeds. The body of the tale is a combination of several tales: Type 553, The Raven Helper (A jay bird in this variant); Type 300, The Dragon Slayer; Types 313c, 314, The Magic Flight. There is no tale in the Grimm collection or in Bolte-Polívka that is such a combination as this tale made by combining or confusing those types listed above. All three types are widely distributed tales, frequently combined or confused with other tales. L. Roberts, *South from Hell-fer-Sartin,* No. 8 (Type 313).

2. THREE GIRLS WITH JOURNEY-CAKES Cf. Types 510, 550, 554 for Grateful-Animals beginning. "The Corpse Watchers," pp. 54-57, Kennedy's *Legendary Fictions of the Irish Celts* has the vigil with the unquiet dead man, which belongs to none of the types listed above. Somewhat resembles Type 480—could be a special Celtic offspring of "The Spinning Women by the Spring" except that here there are *three* girls, one kind, two unkind. See *Handbook of Irish Folklore.*

About 50 versions of Type 480 have three girls, two unkind, one kind. See Roberts' study of Type 480.

3. THE THREE BOYS WITH JOURNEY-CAKES Type 513B, The Land and Water Ship. Only the beginning similar to "The Three Girls with Journey-Cakes." Grimm 71, "How Six Men Got on in the World," and 134, "The Six Servants" are closer to 513A, which, according to Aarne-Thompson and Bolte-Polívka, has been more widely collected than 513B.

4. THE GIRL THAT MARRIED A FLOP-EARED HOUND-DOG Type 425A, The Monster (animal) as Bridegroom (Cupid and Psyche). Aarne-Thompson and Bolte-Polívka indicate widespread collection of 425A; 425B and C much rarer. Grimm 127, "The Iron Stove," a variant of 425A, of Type 425, The Search for the Lost Husband. Roberts' *South from Hell-fer-Sartin*, No. 15a. See J. O'Swahn, *The Tale of Cupid and Psyche*, Lund, 1955. Study of French-American and Spanish-American versions.

5. THE SNAKE PRINCESS Apparently a confusion of several tales, mainly Type 400, II, III, IV, and V, The Man on a Quest for His Lost Wife. Of Grimm variants of Type 400, only 92, "The King of the Golden Mountain," at all resembles this tale, according to Aarne-Thompson and Bolte-Polívka. Type 400 has been widely collected and much discussed in writing.

6. THE CABBAGE HEADS THAT WORKED MAGIC Type 567, The Magic Bird-Heart. Grimm 122, "Donkey Cabbages." Widespread distribution of Type 567. The cabbages in this variant replace the usual apple which turns whosoever eats it into an ass. In that respect, this variant seems closely akin to the Grimm version.

7. THE DONKEY THAT WAS A BOY Type 430, The Ass Plays the Lyre. Grimm 144, "The Donkey." Rarely collected, according to Bolte-Polívka II, 234; III, 152.

8. THE PRINCESS THAT WORE A RABBIT-SKIN DRESS Type 510B, The Dress of Gold, of Silver, and of Stars (Cap o' Rushes). Cf. variants and notes "The Queen with Golden Hair" Chapter One and "Little Cat Skin," Chapter Two in this collection. The variant listed above in No. 8 is a close parallel to "The Princess in Cat Skin," Kennedy's *The Fireside Stories of Ireland*. L. Roberts' *South from Hell-fer-Sartin*, No. 181, Type 510.

9. THE GIRL WITHOUT ANY HANDS Type 706, The Maiden Without Hands. Grimm 31, "The Girl Without Hands." Closest parallel found for No. 9 above is "The Bad Step Mother," Kennedy's *Legendary Fictions of the Irish Celts*, pp. 17-22.

10. THE BOY THAT WAS FOOLISH WISE Type 1561, The Lazy Boy Eats Breakfast, Dinner, and Supper One After the Other Without Work-

ing. Apparently not widely collected. Of six entries in Aarne-Thompson, five are European. Close parallel is "Shan and His Master," Kennedy's *The Fireside Stories of Ireland*. I found no Grimm variant.

11. THE FARMER'S BOY THAT GOT EDUCATED No listing in Aarne-Thompson, Bolte-Polívka, or Grimm. Close parallel "The Farmer's Boy," Campbell's *Popular Tales of the West Highlands*, Vol. I.

12. THE BOY THAT WAS TRAINED TO BE A THIEF Type 1525D, The Master Thief. Grimm 68, "The Thief and His Master," has little resemblance to No. 12 above. Close parallel "The Shifty Lad," Campbell, *West Highland Tales*, Vol. I. Bolte-Polívka III, 390.

13. THE DEVIL FOR A HUSBAND Cf. J. Balys, *Lietuviu Liaudies Sakmes* I. nos. 367-369, mt. 3253: "The Girl Married to a Devil." Only the devil-husband motif fits this tale, otherwise unlike the Lithuanian tale. Not listed in Aarne-Thompson, Bolte-Polívka, or Grimm. Perhaps the tale is Spanish.

14. THE GOLDEN ARM Cf. motif 235.4.1, return from dead to punish theft of golden arm from grave. Cf. Type 366, The Man from the Gallows. The beginning and the tale as a whole do not fit any type. Only the ending appears to belong to Type 366. L. Roberts, *South from Hell-fer-Sartin*, No. 12a.

CHAPTER FOUR *Tales Picked Up Along with Doctoring*

1. THE WATER OF LIFE Type 551, The Sons on a Quest for a Wonderful Remedy for Their Father. Grimm 97, "The Water of Life." Shorter than Grimm version, otherwise quite similar. Bolte-Polívka II, 394. Somewhat resembles Type 550.

2. THE DOCTOR THAT ACTED A PARTNER WITH DEATH Type 332, Godfather Death. Grimm 44. Bolte-Polívka I, 377, listings largely Scandinavian.

3. DOCTORS AIN'T SMART AS THEY THINK THEY BE Type 660, The Three Doctors. Grimm 118, "The Three Army-Surgeons." Bolte-Polívka indicates oral collecting only from North European countries. In translating a Latin edition of the *Gesta Romanorum*, I found a version of this tale, indicating something of its literary history.

4. THE SNAKE-DOCTOR Type 612, The Three Snake Leaves. Grimm 16. Somewhat resembles Type 610, the Healing Fruits.

5. THE BOY THAT HAD A BEAR FOR A DADDY Type 650, Strong John. Grimm 90, "The Young Giant." The Grimm version is quite unlike the version given above. No close parallel indicated in Bolte-Polívka for "The Boy That Had a Bear for a Daddy." No parallel in the *Irish Handbook*.

6. THE BLACKSMITH THAT TRIED DOCTORING Type 753, Christ and the Smithy. Grimm 147, "The Old Made Young Again." Bolte-Polívka

lists collecting in Scandinavia. Thompson in his *The Folktale* says this is essentially a saint's legend. Close parallel "The Share-Smith and the Stranger," pp. 59-63, Curtin's *Folktales*.

7. THE MAN THAT NEVER WASHED FOR SEVEN YEARS Type 361, Bear-Skin. Grimm 101. Thompson in his *The Folktale* says Type 361 known over all parts of Europe, not reported from Asia. Bolte-Polívka indicates popularity in Germany and the Baltic States.

8. THE BIRD LIVER Type 567, The Magic Bird Heart. See notes on No. 6, Chapter Three, "The Cabbage Heads That Worked Magic."

9. THE GOLDEN FILLY CHEST Type 510B, The Dress of Gold, of Silver, and of Stars (Cap o' Rushes). See notes No. 3, Chapter One, No. 3, Chapter Two, and No. 8, Chapter Three. This version is close to "The Three Dresses," Campbell's *Popular Tales of the West Highlands*, Vol. I. L. Roberts, *South from Hell-fer-Sartin*, No. 18 (Type 510).

10. THE FARMER'S DAUGHTER Type 875, The Clever Peasant Girl. Grimm 94, "The Peasant's Wise Daughter." Thompson discusses the history of this tale and its similarity to the Emperor and the Abbot, Type 922 (*The Folktale*, pp. 168, 266, 270, 444). See Jan de Vries' study of "The Clever Peasant Daughter." The version given above as No. 10 is close to "The Innkeeper's Clever Daughter," pp. 95-97, Ausubel's *A Treasury of Jewish Folklore*.

11. THE BEGGAR WITH THE BASKETS Type 311, Rescue by Their Sister (The Bluebeard Story). Grimm 46, "Fitcher's Bird," which above version resembles, especially in the method of rescuing the sisters and in the bird disguise of the heroine. The skull in the window is omitted. L. Roberts, *South from Hell-fer-Sartin*, No. 6.

12. THE CONTRARIOUS PIG Type 2030, The Old Woman and Her Pig. Example of a cumulative tale. Wide distribution; details vary greatly. This version is very like one I heard as a child in Southern Illinois, also like variants, pp. 28-32, in Fauset's *Folklore from Nova Scotia*.

CHAPTER FIVE   *Tales Old Men Followed Telling*

1. THE JUNE APPLE TREE Type 720, The Juniper Tree; My Mother Killed Me, My Father Ate Me. Grimm 47, "The Juniper Tree," which this version resembles more than other variants. Bolte-Polívka I, 412, indicates north European collecting of this tale. Thompson in *The Folktale* says it is known in all parts of Europe, and is found in Africa, Australia, and among Louisiana Negroes. L. Roberts, *South from Hell-fer-Sartin*, No. 27a.

2. THE WITCH FROM THE OCEAN WATERS Beginning Type 316, I. Remainder of tale, Type 300, The Dragon Slayer. None of sources consulted gave a combination like this, though the Dragon Slayer is

rather frequently found in combination with other tales or parts of tales. Thompson in *The Folktale* discusses this borrowing.

3. A GIRL THAT WOULDN'T DO A HAND'S TURN Type 901, The Taming of the Shrew, ending with the beginning of Type 956B, The Clever Maiden Alone at Home Kills the Robbers. Boas' collection of Zuni Indian tales contains a version of Type 901. Grimm's collection has no Type 901, though Grimm 52, Type 900 somewhat resembles the plot of Type 901. Parallel "The Lazy Daughter," Campbell's *More West Highland Tales.*

4. A QUEEN THAT GOT HER JUST DESERTS Cf. Type 465A, Quest for the Unknown; Type 403B, Search for Berries in Midwinter. Could find no parallel for this combination of parts of two tales except a tale my grandfather used to tell called "A Crock of Butter," though the title had nothing to do with the story details.

5. TWO WOMEN THAT TURNED INTO NIGGERS Type 403, The Black and White Bride. Grimm 135, "The White Bride and the Black Bride." Of several variants this tale most resembles Grimm, though here the kind girl gets only two wishes; the Grimm tale allows her three. Some likeness to Grimm 13, in the kind and unkind motifs. Tales of the substituted bride widely scattered over the world, several hundred versions in Europe alone. L. Roberts, *South from Hell-fer-Sartin,* No. 13a.

6. THE JEW THAT DANCED AMONG THE THORNS Type 592, The Jew Among Thorns. Grimm 110. In *The Folktale,* Thompson indicates wide distribution over every part of Europe and in America. Mentions frequent treatment in literature since the fifteenth century. Frequently combined with other motifs mentioned in Aarne-Thompson.

7. THE CAT THAT WENT A-TRAVELING Type 130, The Animals in Night Quarters. Grimm 27, "The Bremen Town-Musicians." Close parallel "The White Cat," Campbell's *West Highland Tales,* Vol. I. A variant in Crane's *Italian Popular Tales.* Related to Type 210 in which animals and objects travel together. L. Roberts, *South from Hell-fer-Sartin,* No. 1.

8. A BUNCH OF LAUREL BLOOMS FOR A PRESENT Type 425c, The Girl as the Bear's Wife, with a man-sized frog instead of the bear as husband. Episodes III, IV, and V omitted. Close resemblance to a version of 425c in Gardner's *Folklore from the Schoharie Hills;* 425A much more widely collected than 425c. Grimm parallel for 425c, No. 88, "The Singing, Soaring Lark "

9. MY FAVORITEST OLDEN TALE Type 450, Little Brother and Little Sister. Grimm 11, "Brother and Sister." Bolte-Polívka I, 79. Thompson *The Folktale,* pp. 118-119, for discussion of this tale, especially in its relation to other tales with the substituted bride motif.

CHAPTER SIX *Tales for Idle Telling*

1. THE GIRL THAT WEREN'T ASHAMED TO OWN HER KIN Type 501, The Three Old Women Helpers. Grimm 14, "The Three Spinners." Close parallel "The Lazy Beauty and Her Aunts," Kennedy, *The Fireside Stories of Ireland.*

2. THE GIRL THAT COULD DO ANY JOB OF WORK Cf. Motifs H1091, task of sorting a large amount of grain, etc. in one night; H1113, task of bailing out a pond; H1104, task of building castle in one night. Not a complete tale; simply three motifs, one or more of which are found in a variety of tales where impossible tasks are set.

3. THE CHANGEABLE MAN Cf. Episode IV, Type 325, The Magician and His Pupil. See Thompson, *The Folktale,* pp. 69-70, for discussion of the type for which we have here only a fragment.

4. OLD BUSHY BEARD Type 900, King Thrush Beard. Grimm 52. Related to Type 901, The Taming of the Shrew. See notes on No. 3, Chapter Five.

5. THE FELLOW THAT MARRIED A DOZEN TIMES Forbidden chamber motif of Type 311, Rescue by Their Sister. See previous notes on "The Beggar with the Baskets," No. 13, Chapter Four. L. Roberts, *South from Hell-fer-Sartin,* No. 6a.

6. THE DEVIL AND HIS GRANDMOTHER Type 812, The Devil's Riddle. Grimm 125, "The Devil and His Grandmother." Bolte-Polívka, III, 12. The questions and answers for the riddling part of this tale vary greatly. This version close to Grimm 125, the chief difference being minor omissions and slight changes in the riddling.

7. THE GIRL THAT CHANGED TO A FLOWER BLOOM Cf. Type 652, The Prince Whose Wishes Always Came True, and Type 407, The Girl as Flower. Apparently a confusion or combination of these two types. See Thompson, *The Folktale,* pp. 95-96, for discussion of these two types.

8. THE SHINING, BEAUTIFUL LADY Type 480, The Spinning-Women by the Spring. Parallels the first half of "The Bucket" in Crane's *Italian Popular Tales.* Only the half of the story about the kind sister is given in Sam's "The Shining, Beautiful Lady." According to Dr. Warren E. Roberts' world-wide study of Type 480, the bucket in the well is typically German, and The Virgin Mary and the star, Italian and Spanish.

BIBLIOGRAPHY

Bibliography

Andrews, Elizabeth. *Ulster Folklore*. New York: E. P. Dutton & Co., 1919.

Ausubel, Nathan, ed. *A Treasury of Jewish Folklore*. New York: Crown Publishers, 1948.

Balys, Jonas, ed. *Lietuviu Liaudies Sakmes (Lithuanian Folk Legends)*. Publications of the Lithuanian Folklore Archives. Kaunas, 1940.

Baughman, Ernest Warren. *A Comparative Study of the Folktales of England and North America*. (Indiana University dissertation, 1953.) Microfilm Service. Ann Arbor, Michigan, 1954.

Beckwith, Martha Warren. *Jamaica Anansi Stories*. Memoirs of the American Folklore Society, vol. 17. New York, 1924.

Bolte, Johannes, and Polívka, Georg. *Anmerkungen zu den Kinder- und Hausmärchen der Brüder Grimm*. 5 vols. Leipzig: Dieterich, 1913–1931.

Campbell, John Francis. *Popular Tales of the West Highlands*. Orally collected and translated from the Gaelic by J. F. Campbell. 4 vols. Paiseley: A. Gardner, 1890–1893.

——. *More West Highland Tales*. See McKay, John G.

Chase, Richard. *Grandfather Tales*. Boston: Houghton Mifflin Co., 1948.

Cox, Marian Roalfe. *Cinderella*. Publications of the Folklore Society, no. 31. London, 1893.

Crane, Thomas Frederick. *Italian Popular Tales*. London: Macmillan Co., 1885.

Cross, Tom Peete, and Slover, Clark Harris, eds. *Ancient Irish Tales*. New York: Henry Holt and Co., 1936.

———. *Motif-Index of Early Irish Literature*. Indiana University Publications, Folklore Series No. 7. Bloomington: Indiana University Press, 1952.

Curtin, Jeremiah. *Hero Tales of Ireland*. Boston: Little, Brown, and Co., 1921.

———, *Irish Folk-Tales*. Edited with introduction and notes by Seamus O'Duilearga (James Delargy). Published for the Folklore of Ireland Society. Dublin, 1943.

———. *Myths and Folklore of Ireland*. Boston: Little, Brown, and Co., 1890.

Delargy, James A. *The Gaelic Story-Teller*. With some notes on Gaelic folktales. London: G. Cumberlege, 1947.

Fauset, Arthur Huff. *Folklore from Nova Scotia*. Memoirs American Folklore Society Series, vol. XXIV. New York, 1931.

Gardner, Emelyn Elizabeth. *Folklore from the Schoharie Hills, New York*. Ann Arbor: University of Michigan Press, 1937.

Gesta Romanorum. Edited by H. Oesterley. Berlin: Weidmann, 1872.

Grimm, J. and W. *Household Tales*. Translated into English by Margaret Hunt, London, 1884. New edition without M. Hunt's notes, with an introduction by Padraic Colum. New York: Pantheon, 1944.

Guterman, Norbert, tr. *Russian Fairy Tales*. With folkloristic comment by Roman Jakobson. New York: Pantheon, 1945.

Halpert, Herbert Norman. *Folktales and Legends from the New Jersey Pines*. (Indiana University dissertation, 1947.) Indiana University Library.

Hull, Eleanor. *Cuchulain, the Hound of Ulster*. London: Geo. G. Harap and Co., 1909.

Hyde, Douglas. *Beside the Fire*. A collection of Irish-Gaelic Folk

Stories. English and Irish on opposite pages. London: D. Nutt, 1910.

Jacobs, Joseph. *Celtic Fairy Tales*. London and New York, 1892.

———. *More Celtic Fairy Tales*. London: D. Nutt, and New York: G. P. Putnam's Sons, 1895.

Kennedy, Patrick. *The Fireside Stories of Ireland*. Dublin: M'Glashan and Gill, 1870.

———. *Legendary Fictions of the Irish Celts*. London: Macmillan and Co., 1866.

Larminie, William. *West Irish Folk-Tales and Romances*. Coll., ed., and tr., by W. Larminie. London: E. Stock, 1893.

MacDougall, James, and Calder, George. *Folk Tales and Fairy Lore in Gaelic and English*. Edinburgh: J. Grant, 1910.

McKay, John G. *More West Highland Tales*. Transcribed and translated from the original Gaelic by J. G. McKay. J. F. Campbell, comp. Published for the Scottish Anthropological and Folklore Society. Edinburgh: Oliver and Boyd, 1940.

O'Sheridan, Mary Grant. *Gaelic Folk Tales*. Boston: Richard Badger, 1926.

O'Suilleabhain, Sean. *A Handbook of Irish Folklore*. Introductory note by Seamus O'Duilearga. Published by the Educational Company of Ireland for the Folklore of Ireland Society. Dublin, 1942.

Randolph, Vance. *Who Blowed up the Church House? and Other Ozark Folk Tales*. New York: Columbia University Press, 1952.

Roberts, Leonard W. *South from Hell-fer-Sartin*. Lexington: University of Kentucky Press, 1955.

Roberts, Warren E. *Aarne-Thompson Type 480 in World Tradition, A Comparative Folktale Study*. (Indiana University dissertation, 1953.) Microfilm Service. Ann Arbor, Michigan, 1954.

Rooth, Anna Birgitte. *The Cinderella Cycle*. Lund: C. W. K. Gleerup, 1951.

Thompson, Stith, *European Tales Among the North American Indians*. Colorado College Publications, vol. 11, no. 34. Colorado Springs, 1919.

———. *The Folktale*. New York: The Dryden Press, 1946.

———. *Motif-Index of Folk-Literature*. 6 vols. Helsinki and Bloomington: Indiana University Press, 1932–1936.

———. *The Types of the Folk-Tale*. (FF Communications No. 74) A Classification and Bibliography. A translation and enlargement of Antti Aarne's *Verzeichnis der Märchentypen* (FF Communications No. 3). Helsinki, 1928.

White, Newman I., and others. *The Frank C. Brown Collection of North Carolina Folklore*. Vol. 1, Folk Tales and Legends, edited by Stith Thompson. Durham, N. C.: Duke University Press, 1952.

Wood-Martin, William Gregory. *Traces of the Elder Faiths of Ireland, A Folklore Sketch, A Handbook of Irish Pre-Christian Traditions*. 2 vols. London, New York, Bombay: Longmans, Green, and Co., 1902.

Yeats, William Butler, ed. *Irish Fairy and Folk Tales*. New York: Boni and Liveright, 1918.